Robin Jenkins was born i[...]
spent his childhood in La[...]
at Hamilton Academy an[...]
duating in 1935 with an [...]
He married in 1937 and [...]
in Glasgow and Dunoon for a number of years. He
has three children. His first novel, *So Gaily Sings the
Lark* was published in 1950 and twenty-three other
books of fiction have followed, including a collection of
short stories, *A Far Cry from Bowmore* (1973). *The Cone-
Gatherers* (1955) received the Frederick Niven Award
in 1956, and *Guests of War* (1956) and *The Changeling*
(1958), were highly praised by many critics.

Robin Jenkins left Scotland for Afghanistan in 1957,
teaching for three years in Kabul. From then until his
retirement in 1968 he lived abroad, working for the
British Institute in Barcelona and teaching in Sabah
(North Borneo) in what was once part of colonial
Malaysia. Afghanistan and then Malaysia became the
settings for six further novels, most notably *Dust on the
Paw* (1961), and *The Holly Tree* (1969). Robin Jenkins
now lives in Dunoon and recent novels, such as the
Arts Council Award-winning *Fergus Lamont* (1979) and
the much praised *Willie Hogg* (1993), have returned to
Scottish settings.

ROBIN JENKINS

Just Duffy

Introduced by
MARGERY PALMER
McCULLOCH

CANONGATE
CLASSICS
62

First published in 1988 by Canongate Publishing
Ltd. This edition first published as a Canongate
Classic in 1995 by Canongate Books Ltd, 14 High
Street, Edinburgh EHI ITE. Copyright © Robin
Jenkins 1988. Introduction copyright © Margery
Palmer McCulloch 1995.

The publishers gratefully acknowledge general sub-
sidy from the Scottish Arts Council towards the
Canongate Classics series and a specific grant
towards the publication of this title.

Set in 10pt Plantin by Palimpsest Book Production
Limited, Polmont, Stirlingshire. Printed and bound
in Finland by WSOY.

Canongate Classics
Series Editor: Roderick Watson
Editorial Board: Tom Crawford, John Pick,
Cairns Craig

British Library Cataloguing in Publication Data
A catalogue record for this volume
is available on request from the
British Library.

ISBN 086241 551 9

Introduction

I first came across Robin Jenkins' *Just Duffy* in 1989, having picked it up by chance in my local library, and was immediately captured by this suspenseful modern morality drama. For me, one of the most interesting aspects of the book – and, indeed, of much of Jenkins' work – is the way in which it gives form to the concerns and voices of contemporary life while maintaining a continuity with earlier traditions in Scottish writing, and most especially with the fiction of the nineteenth century and its preoccupation with the forces of good and evil.

In *The Cone-Gatherers*, for example, one of his best-known early novels, this metaphysical theme is played out on a country estate during the Second World War where two forestry workers, the hunchbacked Calum and his brother Neil who protects him, have been sent to gather cones for reseeding purposes. Their previous happiness in their 'Garden of Eden' forest life is disrupted and in the end tragically destroyed by the enforced change of occupation and by the malevolence of an obsessive, frustrated game-keeper. The impact of *The Cone-Gatherers* with its rural setting and symbolic theme has tended to obscure Jenkins' equally powerful capacity to capture the idioms of the West of Scotland urban scene. What is so striking about *Just Duffy*, therefore, is the way in which this traditional philosophical struggle between good and evil is translated into the contemporary secular world of run-down inner cities and soulless housing schemes, of an alienated teenage culture and shifting or ambivalent moral and social values.

Like George Friel's *Mr Alfred M.A.* and James Kelman's

recent *How Late it Was, How Late*, *Just Duffy* is especially relevant to a Britain which is becoming increasingly preoccupied with the disintegration of what used to be called 'society', with the widening of the gap between the well-off and those who live on the margins, and with a rebellious lawlessness on the part of those who feel they have no say in the running of their communities. Like Neil Gunn's dystopian fable *The Green Isle of the Great Deep*, the book is also a frightening demonstration of idealism taken to extremes and of the narrow dividing line between idealism and totalitarianism, between the intention to wage war on evil to bring about good, and a subsequent 'justified' descent into the employment of evil as a means to achieve the original objective. In this respect, *Just Duffy* would appear to be a twentieth-century descendant of James Hogg's *Confessions of a Justified Sinner* and its main character, Duffy, a relation of the self-deluded or evil Robert Wringhim. And as in Hogg's novel, ambiguity of characterisation and moral ambivalence prevail throughout the text. There are no certainties to reassure us here.

Just Duffy is set in the fictional Lightburn, a town within easy reach of Glasgow but old enough and large enough to have its own town hall, abbey ruins and ancient kirkyard, with the modern additions of working-class housing schemes and private housing estates; a town similar to Cambuslang, perhaps, where Jenkins was born, or a neighbour like Rutherglen or Hamilton, and a former mining area with Covenanting and Disruption associations. Its eponymous hero is an apparently harmless teenager, finished with school but jobless, not over-bright but polite and helpful to neighbours, the kind of youth one doesn't need to think too much about or be wary of. He's 'just Duffy', as he tells the policemen who question him from their patrol car. Initially, then, Duffy would appear to be one of a succession of 'innocent' characters in Jenkins' novels, characters such as Calum in *The Cone-Gatherers* or Tom in *The Changeling*. He believes that 'truth, at its core,

was simple' and that 'the greatest favour you can do people
is to force them to face the truth about themselves'. His
single parent mother and his history teacher Flockhart try
to instil some everyday common sense into him, the teacher
telling him that truth 'looks different according to the angle
you view it from' and his mother with her 'You're looking
for perfection, Duffy, and it doesn't exist . . . You've got
to make allowances. We're only human'. Yet, for Duffy,
this last excuse is the most inexcusable of all: 'they were
only human. Yet they took for granted that they were so
favoured by God that He had made the whole universe for
their benefit'. Remembering his mother's complaint that
'he preferred animals to people', he tells himself that 'if
he did their lack of presumption was one of the reasons'.

As the story unfolds we come to suspect that there
may be more to Duffy than appears on the surface and
in consequence the title of the novel begins to take on
deeper resonances. 'Just Duffy' is also *just* Duffy, who
has his own code of morality and a judgemental attitude
towards his fellow – and fallen – human beings which
accepts no excuses. 'What gave nations the right to declare
war and thereafter claim that the killing of the enemies was
permissible and legal', he had asked the history teacher.
And when Flockhart had replied in his usual somewhat
cynical manner, 'Most of them would say God', Duffy was
certain that if he 'ever declared war he too would give God
as his excuse, but with more right, for his purpose would
be to save not to destroy'.

And so *just* Duffy with his perception of human in-
adequacy becomes translated into *justified* Duffy, who
determines wage war on 'the defilers of truth and abusers
of authority' in order to bring them to a realisation of their
sins. He paints his Declaration of War on the wall of the
town hall one dark, wet night, then, like the warring nations
about which he had questioned Mr Flockhart, and as in the
Old Testament stories about the God who made the rivers
of Egypt run with blood, he feels justified in making use of
evil to bring about ultimate good.

There is a relationship here between Duffy's self-election as destroyer of evil and the behaviour of a Calvinist such as Robert Wringhim in Hogg's novel. Yet, although Duffy's campaign makes occasional symbolical references to God and Christ, it is a sublunary rather than a religious or other-worldly campaign. His mother might find that his censuring eyes remind her of a priest, 'except that a priest would want to save my soul. You don't give a damn whether I go to hell or not'. But neither heaven nor hell features in Duffy's scenario. His interest is in the here and now and his aim is to force people to live the good life on earth. When his barmaid mother conveniently departs for a Spanish holiday with a well-off admirer – 'a trial honeymoon' as she optimistically miscalls it – the stage is cleared for Duffy to embark on his evangelistic crusade, assisted by three not altogether reliable accomplices, who join him for their own ends.

Just Duffy is a taut novel, with a suspenseful storyline and an acute sense of place and ear for the speaking voice. Although the focus is on the deprived areas of the town where Duffy lives, there is a wider community created here, even if a community which has fragmented into layers of social distinctions from the St Stephen's churchgoers who hold the power and who thus become the principal targets of Duffy's campaign, through the gradations of private estates and better-class council housing to the older, but still reasonably respectable tenements where Duffy lives and, below him, to the schemes which house what the Victorians would have called the *un*deserving poor. Urbanised teenage working-class culture is a phenomenon much in evidence in everyday life and on the media, but one not so often given attention in 'serious' fiction. Jenkins' teenagers are completely convincing in talk and activity, and the shifting narrative perspectives in the book give us changing insights into their behaviour and into the behaviour and motivations of characters from other milieus and occupations.

Indeed, for me one of the most disturbing aspects of

this novel is the way in which it unsettles our moral and social judgements, our sense of what we call right and wrong. In this regard it is quite different from the earlier *Fergus Lamont*, where there is also a playing out of the theme of hypocrisy and self-delusion and where Calvin's *religious* Elect have been replaced by Fergus with a belief in an aristocratic election which provides the justification for his actions. In this earlier novel, however, we *know* Fergus to be on the wrong road and that his beliefs are mistaken. And although his actions can be uncaring, or even callous, one could hardly describe them as evil, and in the end Fergus himself is the chief sufferer as a result of them. In *Just Duffy*, on the other hand, one cannot be certain. Is Duffy a genuine 'innocent', corrupted by a corrupt world? Is he a simple, backward youth who 'wanted to be clever but hadn't the brains for it', as his accomplice Helen Cooley suggests, or is he a hypocrite, as his mother believes? Has he finally become insane?

Alongside the ambiguity in the characterisation of Duffy, there is also depicted the moral ambivalence and shifting values of the late twentieth century. Duffy's simple-minded perceptions point us towards the immorality in our society, both in the everyday world of personal and social relations, and in the larger world of international relations with its duplicity and sanctioned killings in time of war. Is Duffy 'mad' because he cannot or will not accept what most of us have conditioned ourselves to categorise as 'inevitable', 'beyond our personal control', 'the way the world goes round'? Is Duffy mad because he has 'expected too much'? Yet, despite his reputation for helpfulness and courtesy, Duffy is deficient in human warmth. His gods are cleanliness, order and efficiency. He cannot show or accept affection. Can such 'goodness' be true goodness? Is there not the arrogance of evil in his self-election as the scourge of evil?

There is moral ambivalence in the details of the novel's subplots also: in the characterisation of Helen Cooley, for example, the reform school girl who, despite her irregular life-style, has more clarity of judgement and human understanding than the children's panel who condemn and sentence her; in the delight in giving sexual pleasure of the fat and educationally backward Molly, which is set against the sexual exploitation practised by her boyfriend and against the sexual abstinence of the righteous but cold Duffy. There is also the inference that today's young people are being betrayed by their society, by its exploitative sexual mores and class segregation, by poor education and unemployment. Duffy's mates are unattractive misfits, but we notice how those in authority automatically assume their wrongdoing, while the anti-social 'high spirits' of their middle-class counterparts are overlooked. Even the teacher Flockhart can be seen ultimately as irresponsible in that he gives the kind of 'honest' or worldly-wise answers to his low-grade class which they have not the intelligence or experience to understand fully.

Just Duffy is an absorbing novel, which leaves us with the problem of how to create a socially just society where truth and authority are not abused and where human frailty is acknowledged and taken account of; which leaves us, too, with the philosophical problem of good and evil in human life, familiar in a previous religious context, but here re-examined in a secular world. Described by one critic as a 'bleak masterpiece', Robin Jenkins has written to me that he finds it 'one of my most hopeful books' in that 'Duffy in the end sees the quiet everyday friendliness towards one another of the churchgoers as beautiful. You have to be an outcast like him to see it'.

The novel has had a frustrating publication history. Written about 1984 or 1985, according to its author, it was put away in a drawer for a number of years, a practice Jenkins says he pursued in order to be able to look at his works 'whole' with the distance of time, something he felt unable to do in the process of creation in daily instalments over a period of weeks or months. Published ultimately by Canongate in 1988, it then went out of print, so disappearing from critical view and thus from accounts of Scottish fiction in the late 1980s and early 1990s. I'm delighted, therefore, to be able to introduce this new edition. I find it one of the most important of recent Scottish novels, significant in relation to the course of Jenkins' own work but also in the context of contemporary and historical Scottish fiction writing. It speaks powerfully to us in the voices of our own time of an ancient and continuing human dilemma.

Margery Palmer McCulloch

CHAPTER ONE

'When I come back,' she said, 'there could be big changes.'

Her dressing-gown fell open, revealing her plump white breasts. She knew he hated her to expose herself to him, so she did it often. She had never forgiven him for being born sixteen years ago.

'There would be no place for you, Duffy. That's what I mean.'

She pretended to speak sadly, but her lips, mauve with lipstick, were pleased. Like everybody else she thought her selfishness was a secret known only to herself.

She nibbled Slimcea bread and had put a tiny pellet of Sweetex in her coffee. She was terrified of becoming fat but could not stop being greedy. Before the day was out she would guzzle chocolates and drink gin.

'You've only yourself to blame,' she whined. 'If you'd done better at school you'd have got a job and been able to support yourself.'

He knew boys who had got several certificates but were still without work. He said nothing. He never contradicted anyone. He let them think their lies succeeded.

'If you're backward, Duffy, God knows you didn't get it from me. When I was your age I was fending for myself.'

She had been nineteen when she had had Duffy, in circumstances that she had always refused to speak about. Though she called herself Mrs Duffy he suspected that she had never been married to his father, who had disappeared before Duffy was born. That had been in Glasgow. They had come to Lightburn when Duffy was three. She seemed to have no relatives. At any rate Duffy had met none.

His own Christian name was Thomas but he was always

called Duffy. When he had been an infant learning to speak if asked his name he had replied Duffy. Besides he had never been close enough to others for them to call him by his first name.

She sighed. 'Don't think I don't love you.'

It was a word he had learned to distrust. He had seen people who loved their own dogs throwing stones at other people's dogs. He had heard mothers screaming abuse at other mother's children. He knew women whose loving husbands beat them.

Ash from her cigarette dribbled on to the tablecloth.

'You make it hard for me,' she whined. 'You never try to enjoy yourself like other boys your age. You're not natural. All your teachers said so. That history teacher – what's his name? – Flockhart, told me you were a mystery.'

Mr Flockhart was the kind of teacher who not only asked questions, he answered them too, as honestly as he could. Once, during a lesson on the Second World War – Duffy had a great interest in war – Duffy had asked what gave nations the right to declare war and thereafter claim that the killing of their enemies was permissible and legal. Many teachers would have rebuked him for being stupid and impertinent, but Mr Flockhart, showing his bad teeth in a bearded ironical grin, had replied: 'Most of them would say God.'

If Duffy himself ever declared war he too would give God as his excuse, but with more right, for his purpose would be to save not to destroy.

His mother was staring sullenly at him. Inside her dressing-gown she was pinching her left nipple.

'I disgust you, don't I? We all disgust you.'

It was despair he felt but there was disgust in it too. He could not help it. Often a feeling of revulsion and futility seized him unawares. At times it was so intolerable that he could not bear human company. He would crouch for hours in the shed on the rubbish dump half a mile out of town while hundreds of gulls screamed like demons overhead.

'You think we're all hypocrites, don't you? But you're the worst hypocrite yourself. Duffy, that wouldn't hurt a fly. Duffy, that all the little kids like and the old women. Always a helping hand. Always a nice smile. The wee girls are safe with Duffy, though he is a bit simple. They don't know, do they, that you despise them all?'

She had never been able to understand him. He despised nobody though he had learned to be wary of everyone. He had seen those wee girls, whose laughter was so delightful, indulge in instant resentful rages, and those old women who fed stray cats harbour implacable hatreds, if they thought their pride had been hurt or they had been cheated out of what they considered their rights. That reluctance or indeed the inability to forgive on the part of people he saw daily in the street had terrified him as a child.

Here was his mother, bathed, perfumed, and powdered, hair dyed blonde and permed, nails painted red, legs and oxters shaved. In an hour a taxi was coming to take her to Glasgow Airport where she was to meet Mr Harrison and fly with him to the Costa del Sol for what she called a trial honeymoon. Mr Harrison was a whisky salesman she had met at the hotel where she was a barmaid. A childless widower with a bungalow in Bearsden he was more than twenty years older than she. In Spain she intended to debase herself in order to entice him into marriage. She had shown Duffy the transparent black nightdress she was taking. If, after all that self-abasement, Harrison cast her off she would hate him and despise herself for the rest of her life.

Love easily turned to hate. The bitterest enmities were within families. Civil wars were the most savage.

Dressed in green costume and musquash coat, with her bag of crocodile leather at her feet, she sat waiting for the taxi. A cigarette hung from her lips. Now and then hope went out of her face, leaving it dull and clownish. She knew that disappointment and humiliation might await her in Torremolinos, but no one in the world could have persuaded her not to go.

'Don't look at me like that, for God's sake,' she muttered. 'You remind me of a priest.'

She must have been born a Catholic. In her jewellery box was a silver crucifix. He had seen her kissing it. Perhaps she had it in her bag now, to bring her luck.

'Except that a priest would want to save my soul. You don't give a damn whether I go to hell or not.'

Both of them knew that it was his constant priest-like regard she resented.

'I've got a right to better myself,' she whimpered.

She did not mean becoming kinder and wiser, she meant improving her position in society, having more money, and living among a better class of people.

Her voice hardened. 'I don't want you bringing in any dogs or cats while I'm away. I think you're fonder of animals than you are of people. As for that awful young bitch Helen Cooley, I don't want her in my house, do you hear? I heard she's been attending the VD clinic. Some girlfriend, I must say, for somebody that washes his hands twenty times a day.'

Cooley was not his girlfriend. He just liked her, though according to his principles he should not. It was true that she had had gonorrhoea. She took nothing seriously, herself least of all. She lied, swore, smoked, shoplifted, and took no pride in her appearance.

'I hope you understand, Duffy, that if I marry Mr Harrison he'll want me to go and live with him in Bearsden. It would be a new beginning for me. There wouldn't be a place for you. You wouldn't fit in. It's your own fault. You've got everybody body thinking you're simple. He thinks it. He asked me if it was hereditary. Not on my side, I told him. He wants a family of his own. I'm not too old.'

She had once brought Mr Harrison to the house and slept with him. He had asked Duffy sly questions and offered him money. Duffy had seen that he was just making use of her: he would never want to introduce her to his middle-class Bearsden friends, far less marry her.

'You frighten me, Duffy. I can never tell what you're thinking.'

A car horn sounded down in the street.

She rose. 'That'll be the taxi. Carry my case, will you?' She stubbed out the cigarette in an ash-tray. Hope made her face bright again. 'Aren't you going to wish me luck?'

'Yes.' He picked up the suitcase and led the way downstairs.

Wrapped in overcoats three neighbours were waiting at the close-mouth.

His mother despised them all.

Duffy himself admired Mrs Ralston. A few days ago her husband Jack had been brought home from hospital, dying of cancer. Her eighteen-year-old daughter Cissie was married to a man who was cruel to her. Cissie's child had been born with spina bifida and was expected to die soon. Yet Mrs Ralston remained undaunted, always seeing compensations, in a way typical of Glaswegians. Also for a woman nearly forty she was beautiful, with a tawny complexion like Cleopatra's (his mother said jealously it was caused by a kidney disease), brown eyes, shining black hair, soft delicate neck, and a slim well-shaped figure. She always gave Duffy encouraging smiles. 'That wee darkie Ralston fancies you, Duffy,' Cooley had once joked. 'Do you know something else? I think you fancy her.'

Mrs Stuart was twenty, newly married, hugely pregnant, and unhealthily pale. She often borrowed romantic paper-backs from his mother.

Mrs Munro was stout and suffered from bunions. She was wearing carpet slippers. She liked telling dirty stories.

His mother had been unable to resist boasting about her trip to Spain with her gentleman friend. Therefore Mrs Munro had a handful of rice ready.

'That's for good luck, Bella,' she cried.

His mother smiled, haughtily. 'Thank you, Mrs Munro. My name is Isabel.'

'Under the bedclothes what's the difference?'

Mrs Stuart fingered the fur coat. 'I hope you have a nice holiday, Mrs Duffy.'

'Thank you.'

'Send us a postcard with a bullfighter on it,' said Mrs Ralston.

'Send us a bullfighter,' cried Mrs Munro, with a shriek of bawdy laughter. Her husband Alec, small and quiet, was a champion domino player, an accomplishment that gave her no pleasure.

'Common as dirt,' murmured his mother. 'The sooner I get away from them the better.'

The taxi-driver put her case in the boot.

She arranged a scarf over her hair. On this cold wet morning in March the street was at its dreichest.

'I can't wait to see sunshine and blue skies,' she said. 'You'll be all right. I've left you plenty of money. You don't need me. If I thought you did I wouldn't go. I swear to God I wouldn't. We've got nothing to say to each other. What will I bring you?'

He shook his head.

It angered her that he seldom asked for anything. Other mothers could buy their sons' affection, why couldn't she?

'Good luck,' he said.

'Goodbye,' she snapped, as she got into the taxi.

As it drove away she was rearranging her scarf.

Duffy was very polite as he slipped past the three women on his way back up to his house. 'Excuse me, please.'

He paused inside the close, where he could hear without being seen. He had to know what they were saying about him.

'She's got a damned cheek leaving a boy like that on his own for a week,' said Mrs Munro. 'She should be reported.'

'Duffy can look after himself,' said Mrs Ralston.

'You'd never think, would you,' said Mrs Stuart, 'that he was backward? He's got such beautiful manners.'

'Better not let Phemie hear you say he's backward,' said Mrs Munro. 'She thinks he's just sensitive.'

Phemie, short for Euphemia, was Mrs Ralston.

'But, Mrs Ralston, they all say he was a dunce at school.'

'Maybe, Agnes, he wasn't very interested in what they taught him. I never was myself.'

'She bought him a whole set of the Children's Encyclopaedia,' said Mrs Munro. 'Twelve big books with thousands of pages and pictures. He sits for hours looking at them, taking nothing in.'

'How do you know he takes nothing in, Maggie?'

'Because, Phemie, he never has anything to say.'

'Fools often have a lot to say.'

'Is that personal, Phemie?' But Mrs Munro laughed, to show her feelings weren't hurt.

'Maybe he's just shy,' said Mrs Stuart. 'He's so good-looking. If he wanted he could have all the girls running after him.'

'That's the last thing he wants, Agnes. His mother's not pleased that he's so interested in war – he's got a whole history of war in twenty-four parts. I told her *that* was natural for a boy his age. What isn't natural is that he's got no interest in girls. My Billie tells me that these days with so many girls on the pill any boy that wants it can get it for the asking, and at Duffy's age it's all they think of, with that thing in their breeks stiff half the day and all night. But Duffy's different, if you see what I mean.'

Mrs Stuart lowered her voice. 'You're not saying – ?'

'That's what I'm saying. He'd rather hoover a carpet than kiss a girl.'

'But he doesn't walk funny, in the way they do. What do you think, Mrs Ralston?'

'Duffy's waiting for the right girl. He's got plenty of time. Whoever she is she'll be lucky.'

'Well, Phemie, she'll get plenty of help with the housework.'

'She'll be treated with kindness and courtesy.'

'I've seen him with that terrible Helen Cooley,' said Mrs Stuart. 'She's the kind that could ruin him for life.'

'It's just like Duffy to stand by her when everybody else is against her,' said Mrs Ralston.

'Everybody else has sense, Phemie.'

'I wonder who his father was,' said Mrs Stuart. 'I asked her once and she nearly snapped my head off.'

'We've all had our heads snapped off for asking that, Agnes,' said Mrs Munro.

Mrs Stuart giggled. 'I said to Bruce it must have been some lord's son. I mean, to account for him being so refined-looking and well-mannered.'

'Not to mention weak-minded. You've been reading too many romantic stories, Agnes. Take my word for it Duffy's simple. He believes everything you tell him, like a ten-year-old child.'

Duffy went on up the stairs, smiling. He knew why Mrs Munro was convinced he was a simpleton. Shortly after the New Year, returning from one of his nocturnal patrols of the town, he had come upon her in the recess at the back of the close, with Mr Logan, a local house-painter. Her arms were round his neck and her white knickers were at her feet. Mr Logan had been grunting and thrusting. Over his shoulder she had seen Duffy. There had been a silly smile of contentment on her face. Next day she had come to Duffy's door with a chocolate biscuit for him. She had explained that she and Mr Logan had been discussing the repapering of her living-room: it was to be a surprise for Mr Munro. It was a wee secret therefore between her and Duffy. He had nodded and thanked her for the biscuit. She had gone away satisfied that he had swallowed her story. A few days later he had asked her if Mr Munro liked the new paper in the living-room. At first she hadn't known what he was talking about. Then, remembering, she had said that she had changed her mind: redecoration was too expensive these days. She had delved into her shopping-bag and brought out a sugared doughnut for him.

CHAPTER TWO

According to his mother Duffy had been pernickety even in his cot. Other babies had slavered their bibs, he had kept his dry. He had learned to use a chamber-pot before he was a year old, earlier than any other baby she had heard of: it should be in the *Guinness Book of Records*. He had insisted too on being alone when seated on it or at least on having his back turned. She had wondered if his revulsion at dirt was a disease, the kind royalty might suffer from, like blood that wouldn't thicken.

As he got older she ceased to find his obsession with cleanliness amusing. She saw it as a showing up of her own sluttishness.

That morning as usual he had to clean up after her. Her cup was smeared with lipstick, her saucer soiled with cigarette ash. The ash-tray was full of cigarette stubs. In the bathroom wet towels lay on the floor, the top was off the toothpaste, hairs steaked the wash-hand basin. In her bedroom the bed wasn't made, used underclothes were scattered over the carpet, and tissues used to wipe off face cream littered the dressing-table.

Behind the bar in the hotel she was always smart and attractive. It was in private that she gave way to her natural slovenliness. Mr Harrison was fastidious. He had congratulated her on her house being so well-kept. She hadn't told him it was Duffy's doing. In the hotel room in Spain she would be terrified that she would give herself away.

Like most people she did not have the courage and resolution to scrape away the many layers of self-deception. She was too afraid of what she might find underneath.

On the dressing-table was the latest paperback romance she had been reading. In gaudy colours a woman with long fair hair and an angelic smile and a dark-haired handsome man in riding breeches were standing hand-in-hand in front of a vast house with purple mountains in the background.

As a child Duffy had read many of these stories. They had left him with a distrust of books. In them goodness always had too easy a triumph, and only villains were dishonest and unkind. There were no women like Mrs Ralston and Mrs Munro.

In his apparently ingenuous way Duffy had asked Mr Flockhart if history books told the truth.

The teacher had found it difficult to answer. 'Truth, Duffy, isn't simple. It looks different according to the angle you view it from. Some historians think the Covenanters were irresponsible fanatics, others that they were godly men fighting for their rights. Russian historians don't take the same view of the Second World War that British historians do. We all believe what we want to believe, whether we're professional historians or school janitors.'

Duffy understood all that but he still believed that truth, at its core, was simple. It was like a jewel hidden under many wrappings. To look upon it meant having to throw away lifelong prejudices. Few people could bear to do that.

Duffy read his encyclopaedia and *History of War* with an understanding that would have amazed Mrs Munro, but his main field of study was Kenilworth Court, the housing scheme in which he lived. Mrs Munro herself had been the source of many discoveries.

He was compiling a book of his own. In a jotter bought in Woolworth's he wrote down every outstanding instance of human depravity he came across. His sources were mostly newspapers. 'If it's just facts, with dates and places given, they can be trusted, more or less,' Mr Flockhart had said. 'Not if it's opinions.'

The last entry was about a young Harijan in India whose

eyeballs had been gouged out and his hands chopped off.

Other entries concerned a two-year-old child thrown into scalding water by its mother, a cat soaked in paraffin and set alight by two seven-year-old boys, and a sick old woman raped and robbed by three youths.

Duffy was well aware that though most human beings were capable of atrocities very few committed them and the great majority condemned them utterly: except of course if they were done to win a war. No one cared how many babies or cats were burnt to death in Hiroshima or Dresden.

His mother had come upon the jotter. She had been horrified. 'What sort of boy are you that you get pleasure copying out such things? No wonder you get bad dreams. Are you trying to drive yourself mad? Maybe you are mad already. If I don't wash a pot carefully enough you're disgusted, yet your mind's full of terrible things like these.'

A few days later, coming home from work tipsy and self-piteous, she had tried to explain to him.

'You're looking for perfection, Duffy, and it doesn't exist. You've got to take into account that people have troubles nobody else knows about or cares about. Money troubles. Family troubles. Health troubles. Love troubles. You're too young to understand. How can people be at their best if they can't pay the rent or think they have cancer or the person they fancy fancies someone else? You've got to make allowances. We're only human.'

That was the excuse they fell back on: they were only human. Yet they took for granted that they were so favoured by God that He had made the whole universe for their benefit.

His mother had said that he preferred animals to people. If he did their lack of presumption was one of the reasons.

CHAPTER THREE

In the afternoon he went to the electricity company's office to pay a bill. His mother did not mind being in debt but it worried him, like a kind of uncleanness.

On the other side of the main street two girls yelled and came running across.

He got his idiot's smile ready.

They were big Molly McGowan and wee Cathie Barr. His mother called them and their like the lowest of the low. It astonished her that he who was so particular would have anything to do with such scum. Even Mrs Munro regarded them as far beneath her socially.

Molly was big all over, especially in the bosom and bottom, but small in intelligence. The doctor had agreed to put her on the pill over a year ago because her mother already had eight others besides Molly, most of them mentally dim like Molly herself, and Molly was likely to be equally prolific. She was passed on from one young lecher to another. Her blue duffel coat was covered with badges. One proclaimed: DON'T KICK AGAINST THE PRICKS. She had pale skin with many freckles, white eyelashes, and long thin pinkish hair. Her hands were always damp. She seldom stopped chewing gum.

In Duffy's presence she was shy, showing it by slower movements of her jaws and an infantile desire to touch his face.

'Hello, Duffy,' she said.

'Hello, Molly.'

'I heard your mother's going to Spain for a holiday. Would you like me to come and keep you company? We could watch telly and listen to records.'

Cathie was small, skinny, and sharp. 'If Mick lets you,' she said.

Mick Dykes, a brawny curly-haired youth, was Molly's present possessor.

Molly did not dispute his ownership. 'Mick likes Duffy. If you wanted me, Duffy, it would be all right with him. He said so.' She stopped chewing: she had something serious to say. 'You and me, Duffy, they all think we're dumb, and maybe so we are, but together we could show them, couldn't we? When's your mother going?'

'She left this morning.'

Why was he encouraging her? Not because of Cooley's advice: what you need, Duffy, to make you like everybody else, is ten minutes in bed with big Molly.

'That's great, Duffy. How long is she going to be away?'

'A week.'

'I could come and stay with you. It would be like a holiday for me. At home I never get any sleep. I've to share a bed with two of my sisters, and wee Effie's got a cough that goes on all night. Do you know what my wardrobe is, Duffy? It's two coathangers on the back of a door.'

He pitied her. In spite of her promiscuity she was innocent, like an animal.

'I'm not a bad cook. Ask Cathie.'

'She's good at buying fish suppers if she's got the money,' said Cathie. 'I've got a message for you, Duffy. From Cooley.'

'Duffy doesn't want to hear about Cooley,' said Molly, jealously.

'Maybe you've heard, Duffy. She's been sent to a reform school in Aberdeen, so she's done a bunk. The Children's Panel did it. That Mrs Porteous. Cooley says she hopes Porteous gets raped by a big nigger with pox.'

'Cooley's got pox herself,' said Molly.

'She's cured. Not everybody's got your luck, Molly.'

'She's plukey.'

Cathie had a spot or two herself. 'And you're freckly.'

'Freckles are a sign of delicate skin. She's got no boobs either.'

Cathie's were very small. 'Not everybody likes having bags of haggis on her chest.'

'Men like big boobs. Mick said so.' Molly was careful not to ask Duffy if he liked them. What she felt for Duffy was different from her usual sexual slavishness. She wanted him to respect her.

'She had an airbag with Singapore Airlines on it,' said Cathie. 'She said she was going to Singapore to marry a rich Chink. She wants to see you before she leaves town. She said you'd know where to find her.'

Molly had no irony in her. She sneered. 'Some rich Chink! Mick said Cooley wouldn't even make a good whore.'

'He wouldn't know it,' said Cathie, 'for all his brains are in that big dick of his, but he was paying her a compliment.'

'She wouldn't make a good wife either.'

'Well, that's the message, Duffy. I said I'd tell you if I saw you.'

'Thanks, Cathie.'

'When I see Mick will I ask him if I can come and stay with you?' asked Molly.

'Isn't it Johnny Crosbie you should ask?' asked Cathie. Didn't Mick promise you to him? Isn't he going to give Mick six packets of fags for you?'

'I don't have to go with Johnny if I don't want to.' But fear had come into Molly's eyes.

Johnny Crosbie was in Duffy's book because of his stoning a swan to death. Duffy himself had not seen the incident but he had had it described to him by boys who had. There had been blood on the white feathers. Crosbie had exulted. 'Like Tarzan.' No one had tried to stop him. He had a knife of which everyone was afraid. He had used it to subdue a girl called Sally Cooper. She had charged him with rape and then withdrawn it. Her brother Archie, a soldier in Northern Ireland, was going to settle with Crosbie next time he was home on leave. Mrs Crosbie told everybody that Johnny's was a medical condition: he took terrible headaches. The doctors had said he would grow out of it. She had said that when he was five, she was still saying it now that he was sixteen. Nobody believed her but not many blamed her either. It was not easy for any mother to have to admit that her only child was evil.

'I don't like Johnny,' said Molly.

'Tell me who does,' said Cathie.

Molly had no older brother to fight for her. Her father was a useless drunk. She thought of the police as persecutors, not protectors.

'If you wanted me, Duffy,' she said shyly, 'Mick would let you have me instead of Johnny.'

'It's for you to say, not Mick,' said Cathie.

'You know I can't.'

Cathie nodded, grimly. Molly was her friend but she was a big lump of helplessness. There were women in Lightburn who ran away from their men who beat them up, but they always went creeping back for more. It was no good telling them that they were weak-minded fools: they knew it better than anybody else but they could do nothing about it. They didn't go back either just because of the children, they went back to be beaten up again. Molly was like them, only she hadn't the excuse that she was married to the brute. All that wee Cathie's grim nod conveyed.

'You might be lucky,' she said. 'Archie Cooper's coming home this weekend. Sally says he's bringing a buddy, a big fellow like a gorilla. Crosbie's goolies are going to be sore for months.'

'He told Mick he was going to stay in the house till Archie went back.'

'He'll come creeping out in the dark, like a rat. Everybody will tell Archie where he is.'

She spoke on behalf of the tribe. Crosbie must be protected from the police but not from the Coopers who were entitled to their revenge.

At last Molly found the courage to touch Duffy's face.

He had learned not to shrink back or shudder. All his life he had hated being touched. His mother thought it was because of his excessive modesty but it was more than that. When he was small, bigger girls, noticing his peculiar reluctance, had hugged and kissed him. They had meant to be affectionate but they had also enjoyed his shudders. It had been his first lesson on how kindness could have in it elements of malice.

Molly though was never malicious. She patted his cheek again. 'If somebody comes chapping at your door one of these nights, Duffy, it could be me.'

'Better not,' said Cathie. 'You'd just get Duffy into trouble with his mother. If you see Cooley, Duffy, wish her luck for me. Come on, Molly.'

Molly let herself be led away. She looked back and waved.

She needed to be with people even if they were mocking her and making use of her. For him it was just as necessary to be alone.

All the same what if the great gesture he intended to make was to take the form of becoming Molly McGowan's boyfriend and later her husband? If he saved her from being made use of and gave her happiness, whatever the cost to himself, he would have, in a way, redeemed and benefited all humanity.

CHAPTER FOUR

Many years ago Lightburn had been surrounded by coal mines. They were now defunct and with one exception had been reclaimed, with houses built and playing fields laid out. The Brandy still had relics of the surface workings and its bings of dross, but to these had been added heaps of garbage for it was now used as the town's rubbish dump. Situated about half a mile out of town, it was inhabited by thousands of gulls and many rats. In winter, especially, it was an eerie, forsaken, maladorous place. A small shed of corrugated iron had been let fall into disrepair, for the men who brought the garbage here preferred to drink their tea in pleasanter surroundings.

This was the sanctuary where Duffy sometimes went and where he was sure he would find Cooley hiding.

The way to it was an earth track through fields. There were many muddy puddles. Duffy wore Wellingtons and a raincoat, for it was raining. A gate shut off the side-track leading to the dump. There was a notice saying Private. The gate should have been padlocked but wasn't. People were not supposed to bring their own garbage here but some did.

Not far from the shed, in the midst of the mounds of rubbish, Duffy trod on something soft. A stink, worse than all the others, sickened him. He shone his torch. It was a dead dog, showing its teeth as if in pain. Parts of it had been gnawed away. Perhaps, poisoned or ill, it had crawled here to die, or more likely its owner, to avoid the labour of burying it or the expense of having its remains disposed of by a vet, had dumped it here.

Duffy patted its head.

Parts of the shed were loose and rattled in the wind. He imagined Cooley inside, waiting for him.

He pushed open the door and shone his torch. 'Cooley, it's me, Duffy.'

She was there all right, sitting in an armchair that had two petrol cans for its front legs. She put up her hand to protect her eyes from the torchlight but it could have been to keep him from seeing her tears. She had once boasted that she would let no one, not even him, 'especially not you, Duffy,' see her crying.

'What kept you?' she asked, hoarsely.

She took her hand away. Her eyes were dry enough now and as bold as ever. 'Don't waste your battery,' she said.

He switched off the torch. 'I had to wait till it was dark.'

'Didn't you want the gulls to see you?'

'Cathie Barr said the police were looking for you.'

'So they are, the pigs. Did you bring me a fish supper and a bottle of coke? I've been sitting here telling myself Duffy would come and bring me a fish supper and a bottle of coke.'

'Come and have a meal in my house, Cooley. You could stay the night if you wanted.'

'Has your mother gone then?'

'This morning.'

'She wouldn't want me in her house, especially after I've spent a night in this stinking hole.'

'You could have a bath.'

'I'd like that. Thanks. All right, I'll come, but I'll not stay the night. If you could lend me a few quid I'd go to Glasgow. I'm heading for London.'

'Do you know anybody there?'

'What difference does that make? I prefer strangers. They leave you alone. But I do know somebody. Sadie Turnbull. She went there about three years ago and is doing very well.'

It was said that Sadie Turnbull had become a prostitute. She had the body for it, like Molly McGowan.

'What does she do?'

'She's manageress of a hotel for Cypriots. She said I could get a job there any time.'

'What kind of job?'

'Well, it won't be in a knocking-shop anyway, if that's what you're thinking. Who'd pay good money to fuck me? Blacks wanting cut rates maybe. Christ, I'm stiff as a board. Let's go.'

'I'll carry your bag.'

He started to laugh.

'What's funny? I haven't got Porteous's head in it.'

'Singapore Airlines.'

'Oh, that. I found it. No, that's a lie. I nicked it. I've always wanted to go to Singapore. It's hot and there are lots of rich Chinks.'

There were pictures of Singapore, the Lion City, in his encyclopaedia.

They set off towards the lights of the town. It was still raining. The wind was chilly.

'I expect Cathie told you they want to send me to a reformatory in Aberdeen? Tight-pussy Porteous suggested it.' In spite of her chittering teeth she mimicked Mrs Porteous's deep, stern voice. '"It's for your own good, Helen. You are out of your parents' control, you know. This is a very nice place. It has its own tennis court." Christ, Duffy, can you see me in wee white shorts playing tennis? If it's such a nice place why doesn't she send her own daughter Margaret there? Wasn't it her and her smart friends painted Burns's statue red-white-and-blue?'

'That was never proved, Cooley.'

'They took fucking good care not to prove it. The sons and daughters of the most respectable citizens in the town mustn't have their careers ruined. What about my career?' She laughed. 'But I forgot, you used to fancy Margaret Porteous, didn't you, when you were at school?'

'I've never spoken to her in my life.'

'What difference does that make? I fancy John Travolta and I've never spoken to him.'

She had to stop walking to cough.

'You're taking a cold, Cooley.'

'It feels like double pleurisy.'

They went on again.

'What about you, Duffy? If your mother hooks this guy she's gone to Spain with and goes to live in Bearsden among the toffs, why shouldn't she take you with her? You look the part. All you'd have to do would be to stop acting as if you were simple. I know it's just an act but why do you do it? Whatever you are it's not simple. You worry me, Duffy. I don't know what the hell's going to happen to you.'

'What's going to happen to you, Cooley?'

'Oh, that's easy. I'm going to marry Prince Edward and live in Buckingham Palace.'

'Seriously, Cooley.'

'Oh, seriously? I'm going to become a junkie and get my throat cut. Are you sure you didn't bring any fags?'

'You shouldn't smoke, Cooley.'

'And you shouldn't call me Cooley.'

He was astonished. She must be joking. Usually she dared people to call her Helen, too many sarcastic teachers had called her that. Nor did diminutives like Nell and Nellie please her.

'What do you want me to call you?'

'I shouldn't have to tell you that, should I? In some ways you really are simple. You should be able to think of something. Like honey.'

'Honey?' How could he call this bitter, humorous girl honey?

'Skip it.'

She stopped. They were not far from Kenilworth Court. Rain stotted on the pavement. Her head was soaked.

'Before I go another step I want to know why you're doing this for me.'

'You're my friend.'

'Some friend. If I was to kiss you or just take your hand you'd grue. What sort of friend am I then? I can stand all those bastards trying to kick me around for they hate my guts and I hate theirs, but I can't stand somebody being kind to me that would grue if I kissed him or took his hand. Do you know something Duffy, with everybody else I've got no pride, I'd steal from a blind man's tinny, I'd even take a job from Porteous if she offered me one, but with you it's different. You make me ashamed of myself.'

He had known that she had deeper feelings than she was given credit for, but he had not realised how fond she was of him. She really did want him to call her honey.

'Let's talk about it in the house,' he said, 'or you will take double pleurisy.'

She couldn't stop shivering. 'I don't want to get you into trouble with your mother. I'll take a few quid if you can spare them and catch a bus to Glasgow.'

'My mother won't know.'

'What about that nosy fat cow across the landing that's always spying?'

'It doesn't matter.'

'I wouldn't want to make the wee darkie upstairs jealous.'

'Mr Ralston's been brought home from hospital. He's dying of cancer.'

'Isn't he lucky? All right, then, just for an hour or two till I get dried.'

The close-mouth was in darkness because the street lamp there had been smashed. No one was about. Everybody was indoors watching television. Duffy hurried on ahead to open the door.

He had always imagined himself as waging his war alone, but if Cooley really wanted to be his comrade and if she took him seriously he might ask her to join him.

CHAPTER FIVE

Cooley did not take him seriously.

To begin with his deft household movements and dutiful face reminded her of a butler she had seen in a comic film. She told him so. He smiled, looking more than ever like that butler.

She decided there was less heartbreak in laughing at him than in loving him.

He ran her bath and laid out fresh towels. He pretended not to hear when she saucily invited him to stay and scrub her back.

A few minutes later he was knocking at the door and handing in some clothes of his mother's. Cooley's own, he said, were in the washing machine.

The pink crêpe-de-chine knickers, white blouse, multi-coloured dirndl skirt, and fluffy red jumper were all several sizes too big for her. She would look a freak in them but Duffy, the butler, wouldn't laugh. She had never heard him laughing.

In the kitchen he had a high tea prepared: sausage, bacon and eggs with HP sauce, fresh bread, cream cookies, and a big pot of tea under a tartan cosy. He was not only an efficient housewife, he was also a good cook. He would make a marvellous husband for some girl with no sense of humour. Like Molly McGowan.

Maybe, she thought, as she tucked in, he was mad and dangerous and afterwards intended to chop her into pieces with his usual neatness. She might find herself back at the dump, a bloody package, hidden under mattresses soiled by shitty old men. Still, she was hungry, the kitchen was warm, the food was tasty, she wasn't itching any more, and there were no rats running over her feet, so what the hell. She ate with enjoyment and boldly met Duffy's solemn brown eyes with her own winking blue ones. She could wink with either. She doubted if Duffy could wink at all.

She offered to help clear the table and wash the dishes. He said no, she was a guest. Really he thought she would be too slapdash. He took her through to the living-room and saw her settled in an armchair in front of the gas-fire. She liked being pampered like this, even if, she thought with an inward chuckle, she was going to be butchered as soon as he had done the dishes. It was as well she couldn't stop yawning. It kept her from laughing.

'Could I have the telly on?' she asked.

'Of course.' He switched it on. It was a programme she usually enjoyed, with people doing and saying daft things.

'Could I have another one of your mother's fags, please?'

He went away and brought a packet with three in it. They were scented but would have to do. She lit one and then curled up in the chair. Maybe later she would ask for a vodka and lemonade. She had looked in the sideboard and seen that it was well-stocked.

He murmured that he wouldn't be long and returned to his domestic duties.

She found she didn't want to watch television but couldn't be bothered getting up to turn it off. Her own situation, in a house alone with a nutcase, was more interesting.

She warned herself, with more chuckles, not to fall asleep, or she might wake up in a dozen pieces.

He came in. He had removed his apron but not his butler's look.

'Is it a good programme?' he asked. 'I heard you laughing.'

She added 'honeys' in her mind but managed to keep her face straight. 'Do you want to watch something else?'

'I would like to talk to you. Seriously.'

'Is it about who'll win the Cup?'

He frowned. 'I said seriously.'

'What could be more serious than who'll win the Cup? Go into any pub and ask.'

'Do you mind if I turn off the television?'

She gave up adding 'honey'. 'It's your house.'

He turned it off and then sat on the sofa and stared at her.

Was he going to propose that they elope to Gretna Green? He was certainly solemn enough.

'I have never discussed these things with anyone before.'

'Well, thanks, Duffy.' Inwardly she quaked. Was he going to tell her about his sexual hang-ups? Like others she had often wondered what Duffy thought or did about sex. There was an opinion, openly expressed in Dirty Chuck's, the café that the youth of the east end frequented, that Duffy had been born either without balls or with tiny ones. Though he was over sixteen his cheeks and chin were still smooth. He had never been known to make a pass at any girl, though quite a few, including Cooley herself, had encouraged him to do so. He walked away when dirty jokes were being told. At school in the gymnasium or swimming baths he had always turned his back when undressing, so as not to let anyone see his dick, though all round him others, like Mick Dykes, had swaggered about swinging theirs proudly. Maybe, being from outer space, Duffy had some other arrangement.

One girl never joined in this fun at Duffy's expense. She was big Molly McGowan. She said that Duffy was just shy, like her. She had once confided to Cooley that even when she was a wee girl in primary school she had fancied Duffy, who had been in the same class. Cathie Barr had warned her that when she grew up she mustn't marry someone as dumb as herself, otherwise her kids would be born idiots. Brains weren't everything though, were they? She and Duffy could have beautiful kids who might not be all that stupid either, for her sister Morag was very bright, all her teachers praised her, and Duffy's mother was a smart woman, wasn't she?

Was Duffy in his turn about to confess that all his life he had loved big Molly but was too shy to tell her so?

They would make a comic pair all right, he so shut-in, she so wide-open.

'Two kinds of people deserve to be shown up,' he said.

A hell of a lot more than two, she thought, before bewilderment hit her. What the hell was he on about now? He was a dunce trying to talk like a university professor. He got ideas and big words out of his encyclopaedia, but he didn't understand them any more than she did. That was the sad thing about him, he wanted to be clever but hadn't the brains for it. There was that mysterious tract which had come through his letter-box about a year ago. He had looked out of the window and seen that it had been delivered by an old man with a beard and a bowler hat. He had spoken as if he thought the old bugger had been sent by God or was God Himself.

She humoured him. 'What two kinds?'

'Defilers of truth and abusers of authority.'

As she'd feared, straight out of the tract. He had shown her his book of horrors once. She had noticed that the worst ones had been committed by religious maniacs.

'Who are they, when they're at home?' she asked.

'Defilers of truth are those who tell lies for their own advantage.'

The world was full of them. She was one herself.

'If everybody respected the truth the world would be a better place.'

He must have heard that on television on 'Late Call' or perhaps it was in the tract. She doubted if it was true. She herself lied not just to gain an advantage but also to avoid trouble. Prime Ministers did it to keep out of wars.

'There are defilers of truth in Lightburn.'

Liars were everywhere. Come to think of it, perhaps it was by lying or at any rate by not telling the truth about one another, that people were able to live in peace together.

'And abusers of authority.'

Yes, and she knew better than he did who they were. Sergeant Milne, who had called her a disgrace to her sex. Porteous who had got her sent to a reform school. Purvis who had ordered her out of the public library. Teachers who had been sarcastic to her. Others she could have named given time.

She would have blown that lot up, never mind shown them up.

If this was his idea of a game she might as well play it. 'What are you going to do about them? How are you going to show them up?'

'I intend to declare war on them.'

Trust Duffy to put it like that. He fancied himself as an expert on wars, from those of ancient Greece to those of today. He studied his *History of War* as often as he did his encyclopaedia. It was full of pictures of battlefields, bombed cities, and successful generals.

Come to think of it, she herself was already at war with abusers like Milne and Porteous. The trouble was they had all the weapons.

Duffy on the other hand had never so much as thumbed his nose at a policeman. Purvis welcomed him into her library.

'How are you going to do that?' she asked.

'You see, if I declare war on them they can't call what I do afterwards a crime. That is their own rule.'

Was he joking? It was hard to tell, for it would have been the first time, and there wasn't the glimmer of a smile on his face.

At the same time she could see what he was getting at. In war killing wasn't called murder, nor was destroying a whole city called vandalism. But only countries could declare war on one another. She didn't know much but she knew that. Countries had armies, navies and air forces. Duffy didn't even have a knuckleduster.

She couldn't resist teasing him. 'What are you going to do? Burn down the police station?'

'You know I don't believe in violence.'

'How can you have a war without violence?'

'Instead of weapons I would use symbols.'

At first she thought foolishly he meant the things the

Salvation Army banged together. She pictured Porteous's well-cared-for snobbish face between them getting well and truly banged.

'What are they?' she asked, feebly.

'Signs. For example, I intend to break into the public library.'

Some violence would be needed, if only the breaking of a snib. But the very idea was ridiculous. What would breaking into the library be a sign of?

She had to hold on to her own commonsense. 'What's there to steal in the library?'

'I would be a soldier, not a thief.'

'I thought soldiers lifted everything they could lay their hands on. It's called loot.'

'All I will do is tear a page out of as many books as I can in two hours.'

He must mean it as a kind of game, but a very silly one, in her opinion. It would infuriate Purvis who thought the library was her own personal property, but there were better and easier ways of doing that. 'Why not just burn the whole fucking place down? Sorry.' The apology was for the swear-word, not for the suggestion of arson. She had once or twice thought of burning the library down herself, not to mention the police station and the school and Porteous's Ceramics Factory.

'You see, Cooley, the greatest favour you can do people is to force them to face the truth about themselves.'

That was baloney. It was the last thing people she knew wanted to do.

Suddenly she saw what was the matter with him. Being simple himself, in his own peculiar way, he couldn't help seeing everybody else as similarly simple. Show Porteous and Milne that they were arrogant bastards and off they would go and become meek and fair-minded. Prove to liars that they were liars and in shame they would vow to tell only the truth in future. What a hope! Of course they could all stop being arrogant bastards and liars, if they wanted to, for they already knew what they were, but they didn't want to, they enjoyed being arrogant bastards and liars.

'You see, Cooley, there would be no hope for human beings if there wasn't more good than bad in most of them.'

'Wait a minute.' She had to think about that. In fact she would need a whole lifetime to think about it. To begin with, how did you measure goodness and badness? And what one person would call good another person might call bad. It was a lot more complicated than Duffy seemed to realise or was willing to admit.

'Books give people false ideas about themselves,' he said.

That was the strange thing: he spoke more intelligently than she ever could, and yet she understood the ways of the world so much better. He lacked a necessary cunning. Even a clown like Mick Dykes had it.

She seldom read books herself but they had always seemed to her harmless. Come to think of it though, the people that looked down on her most were the kind that read books: like the white-haired ladies who had approved when Purvis had ordered her out of the library. Still, what good would tearing out pages do?

'It would be a gesture, a symbolic act.'

Jesus, she thought, we're back at symbolic again. She wondered if she should ask for that vodka and lemon-ade now.

'Who are the abusers of authority in Lightburn?' he asked suddenly, like a teacher to a pupil not paying sufficient attention.

She yawned. It was a genuine yawn but it was also a hint that she had had enough of this nonsense.

He waited for an answer.

'The cops, I suppose.'

'All of them?'

'Sure, all of them. Some worse than others. Big Milne the worst.'

'Who else?'

'Tight-pussy.'

He frowned.

'That's what I call Porteous. She hates sex. You should have heard her asking me how I got the clap.'

'Who else?'

'Blue-nose.' That was Miss Purvis. Everybody said it was because of her secret tippling, but it was probably indigestion.

'All these people have something in common, Cooley.'

'They're all arrogant bastards.'

'They're all members of St Stephen's church.'

It was in the west end among the leafy avenues and villas. It was the biggest in the town, with the highest spire. Everybody that thought himself or herself important was a member.

'A famous writer once said that every judge should have a toilet roll in front of him.'

'Who told you that? Flockhart?' Another nutcase.

'To make him remember that he was human like the person he was about to sentence.'

She grinned. 'Are you going to put a roll on top of the minister's big Bible?' It would be a good laugh. Wee white-haired Cargill, with the medals on his chest, like a good Christian would want to flog whoever had done it.

'What I am going to do is put a spot of excrement on their hymn-books.'

It was the daftest thing she had ever heard.

'Excrement?' She knew what it meant, but maybe he didn't. 'You mean shit?'

He frowned: the word was too vulgar for him. 'Yes.'

'Human?'

'There would be no point if it wasn't human.'

She began to lose patience. 'It would be a lot less smelly if it was horses'.' She pictured him putting a dab on all the hymn-books, like a minister giving communion. She did not smile, though. If he was caught he wouldn't be sent to a reform school but to a hospital for lunatics. She had to try and make him see sense. 'It's a good

joke, Duffy, as long as you just think it and don't try
to do it.'

'Was it just a good joke when God turned all the rivers
of Egypt into blood?'

She blinked. She knew about the plagues of Egypt but
could see no connection. Nobody right in the head could.

'It was to achieve a good purpose. It was to make the
Egyptians let the Children of Israel go.'

A religious nutcase: the worst kind. 'So that's what the
Children of Israel got out of it. What would you get
out of it?'

So far as she knew all those arrogant bastards in St
Stephen's had done Duffy no harm and disgusting them
with shit on their hymn-books would do him no good.

'If a country's at war, Duffy, it's out for something, isn't
it? Maybe it's some other country's land, maybe it's to be
top dog. What are you out for? Is it just a game, like killing
cats is a game for Johnny Crosbie?'

'If you could make people more truthful and less arrogant, if you had that power, Cooley, would you use it?'

'Nobody's got that power, Duffy. No, I wouldn't use
it. Why the hell should I help them if they refuse to help
themselves? That's what they say to me. Look, Duffy, I
can hardly keep my eyes open. I'll have to go to bed.'

'In a minute. I've told you all this, Cooley, because I
would like you to join me.'

She was horrified. 'To tear out pages and mess up
hymn-books?'

'To fight falsehood and hypocrisy.'

'Count me out, Duffy. I'm going to London.' Where
there were any number of weirdos, but none like Duffy.

'Before you go.'

She shook her head. 'Sorry.' An imp of mischief caused
her to add: 'If you want recruits what about Mick Dykes
and Johnny Crosbie?'

She was astonished to see him nodding.

'It would be symbolical,' he said, 'using evil to bring
about good.'

She had had enough. A night spent at the dump wasn't the best preparation for wrestling with Duffy's loony ideas. She stood up. 'Can I go to bed now?'

'You can use my mother's room.' He led the way.

She was entranced by the plush pink wall-to-wall carpet, the big bed with the crimson quilt, the array of cosmetics on the dressing-table, and inside a wardrobe the selection of nightdresses.

'Take any one you want,' he said.

'Thanks, Duffy.'

It was mean of her to think it but his hospitality was another sign of his lack of everyday gumption. Certainly his mother would have thought so.

'If you need anything just ask,' he said.

She was about to propose that they should sleep together in the bed just for company's sake like the Babes in the Wood but decided against it, not because he might have been offended but because he might have accepted. She didn't want to hear any more about tearing out pages or anointing hymn-books.

When he was gone she stripped and walked naked about the room, loving the feel of the silky carpet on her feet. She dabbed perfume under her oxters and behind her ears. She chose a white nightgown trimmed with pink. It was too wide and long but it delighted her. Looking in the mirror she found the sight of herself almost bearable.

She could not resist opening drawers. She did not want to steal or even to covet but simply to enjoy seeing and touching so many knickers, slips, bras, and tights. She had few clothes herself and what she wore was usually grubby but she loved finery.

In one drawer she came upon a bank-book. At first she let it lie. She was a guest in the house, being treated with kindness. Duffy was a nut but that didn't mean his trust should be betrayed. She shut that drawer therefore and went on opening others, but soon found herself returning to it. This time she picked up the bank-book. It was Duffy's mother's. To her surprise there was £385 in it. In it too was a slip for withdrawing money, already signed Isabel Duffy, though the amount to be withdrawn had been left blank.

It would be easy to write in £50 and add the date. The bank clerk would be familiar with Mrs Duffy's signature. Unfortunately he or she would be suspicious if Cooley herself came in with the slip. It would have to be done by Duffy whom they probably knew.

With £50 she would be off to a great start in London.

It shouldn't be difficult to talk a gomeril like Duffy into cashing this slip. She could say it was to provide funds for his war. In spite of the big words and weird ideas he was just a dunce who had never passed an examination in his life.

She stared at herself in the mirror. To defilers of truth and abusers of authority should be added betrayers of trust.

She could volunteer to take part in his war. Soldiers after all had to be paid for taking risks.

A few minutes later she was snuggled under the bedclothes, reeking of scent and pretending she was a high-class whore in London. Was her next customer to be Prince Andrew or Mick Jagger? Tut, she had forgotten.

Reassured by her own daftness, which she much preferred to Duffy's, she soon fell asleep, but not before thinking again of that bank-book.

CHAPTER SIX

There was a picture in *The History of War* of the British ambassador arriving at the Chancellery in Berlin to deliver the declaration of war in 1939. He was wearing a cocked hat and gold-striped trousers. Duffy too dressed for the occasion, in his Sunday suit and raincoat. He would have to be careful not to get white paint on them from the aerosol can with which he was going to spray his declaration on the wall of the town hall. There was no town council now and the building was used mainly for dances and Bingo but it had once been the administrative centre of the town and so corresponded to the German Chancellery.

At half-past twelve he set out, leaving Cooley fast asleep. He met no one on the stairs. The streets too were empty because of the lateness of the hour and the heaviness of the rain. There would be little danger of his being spotted by police, who, as Cooley had said, sought cosy corners on cold wet nights, like cats.

Rain poured down loudly from broken rhones and rushed along gutters, glittering in the lamplight. He was reminded of rivers turned to blood.

In most of the houses the windows were dark. He was surrounded by hundreds of people and yet felt utterly alone. This was how it would be after an attack by neutron bombs that killed living creatures but did not destroy property. The people would have died in bed or watching television or making tea. They would be like those in the fairy tale who had all fallen asleep wherever they happened to be or whatever they happened to be doing, because at that very moment the princess had fallen under a spell, owing to the wickedness of a witch: except that in the real world no prince would come and break the spell.

If there was someone like Duffy in every town in every country determined to show up the defilers of truth and the abusers of authority the great catastrophe might be prevented.

In the distance a dog howled. It was hungry and homeless but it was alive. Tears came into his eyes.

His route took him through an old part of the town where people still lived in crumbling tenements with outside lavatories. He knew an old woman who lived here, in a single-end, one room in which she lived, cooked, and slept. She suffered badly from arthritis. Every Tuesday he went errands for her.

Politicians said there was no money to clear away slums like these and build good houses, yet thousands of millions of pounds were spent every year on armaments.

'I'm afraid it's not as simple as that, Duffy,' Mr Flockhart had said. 'You're forgetting national pride. Given the choice between better houses and bigger bombs most people would choose the bombs, even those living in slums, if they were told often enough that their enemy is just waiting to attack them, and of course they're told that almost every day. As individuals we seem able to get on well enough without a deadly enemy, but not as nations. With us it was France for hundreds of years, then it was Germany, now it's Russia, and afterwards, if there is an afterwards, it could be America. No, Duffy, it's not so simple.'

But it *was* simple. All that was necessary was for the good in people to be encouraged instead of the bad, here in Lightburn and all over the world.

The people of Lightburn were proud of their main street, one of the widest in the country. Plane trees grew out of the pavements and in summer baskets of geraniums were hung from lamp-posts. The town hall was an old building of grey stone, with a square turret and four clocks. Next to it were the ruins of a fourteenth-century abbey, and an ancient kirkyard, enclosed behind a high stone wall, with a small iron gate kept locked to keep out drunks who would have used it as a lavatory. There was frequent agitation to have these relics of the past replaced by shops which would have paid high rates for so advantageous a site, but so far those proud of the town's history had prevailed. One of them was Mrs Porteous. Another was Mr Flockhart.

The history teacher had once brought 4X here and told them that the abbey had been founded in Robert the Bruce's time. He had shown them the corner where six Covenanters had been buried. Fleeing from the rout at Bothwell Brig they had been caught up by Claverhouse's dragoons and slaughtered.

Johnny Crosbie had enacted the episode, comically, pretending that his head had been slashed off by a sword. Mick Dykes had rebuked him, muttering that it wasn't lucky to mock the dead.

Crosbie had no conscience. He would have made fun of Jews going into the gas chambers. For some twisted reason of his own he admired Duffy and wanted to be friends with him.

Tonight the main street was rainswept and desolate. No cars passed, no dogs foraged in garbage bins outside shops, no policemen tried the doors of banks.

There was an arcade in front of the town hall door. In the past it had given shelter to dignitaries and their wives as they had walked from their carriages. Among them once had been a member of royalty. In those days it must have been splendid, with its ironwork painted gold and red and its glass roof sparkling. Now it was dingy and decrepit.

Taking his time, for it had to be neatly done and correctly spelled, Duffy sprayed his challenge on a part of the wall kept dry by the arcade:

WAR IS DECLARED
ON DEFILERS OF TRUTH
AND ABUSERS OF AUTHORITY.

He had just finished when he heard people approaching. They were a man and a woman. She tottered on high heels.

Duffy stood back in the shadows.

They stopped under the arcade. They reeked of alcohol.
The man had no raincoat, the woman no umbrella. Duffy
recognised her. She was Mrs Moncrieff whose husband had
decamped years ago, leaving her with four young children.
Her companion looked at least twenty years older than she.
He had a weak sad face and grey hair, as Duffy saw when he
took off his cap and beat it against one of the iron pillars.

They must have been at a party and stayed longer than
they had intended. She was worried about her children.
The oldest was only nine.

'I hope to Christ they haven't turned on the gas,' she
whimpered. 'That's what I'm feart of, Jimmy. Wee Archie's
always turning it on.'

'They'll all be sound asleep, Chrissie.'

'I promised to be back by eleven. What time is it now?'

'It's not one o'clock yet.'

'For God's sake, Jimmy, stop a taxi, will you?'

'There are no taxis at this time, hen.'

'The cruelty men will come for me. Neighbours have
complained. It was your fault, Jimmy. If I begged you
once to come away I begged you a dozen times.'

'We were enjoying ourselves, Chrissie. We've got a right
to enjoy ourselves. I love you, hen.'

'You've got no weans to worry about.'

'Bella and me never had any.'

'I know that, Jimmy. I'm ashamed of myself for casting
it up. No, Jimmy, cut that out. Not here, for God's sake.
To tell you the truth I'm bursting for a pee. Wait till we
get home, lover. I'll make you happy then. Say, can you
smell paint?'

'Paint?' Jimmy sniffed.

She turned her head and saw Duffy. She let out a scream
and fled. Jimmy ran after her, asking tenderly what was the
matter. He hadn't seen Duffy.

They were the kind of people Duffy's mother and no
doubt Mrs Porteous despised. They wasted on drink what
little money they had. They neglected their children. They

depended on others to keep them. They took the dignity out of love-making.

Duffy pitied them. They were victims. They were like that dog howling in the distance. There were millions of them.

When he was safely home he took off his wet clothes and had a bath. He did not hurry though he was very tired. He stood by Cooley's bedside, looking down at her for almost half an hour. Once or twice she mumbled but he could not make out what it was. He was tempted to lie beside her, for company. It might save him from dreaming. He had never been able to understand why he who loved cleanliness and hated violence should have so many dreams of filth, sex, and blood.

CHAPTER SEVEN

Next morning he was up long before Cooley, ironing her clothes and preparing breakfast. He had not slept well. He had had one of his most disquieting dreams.

Naked, he had run through a landscape of endless desolation, screaming that it was too late. In a place like the dump, on a mattress soiled with blood and excrement, he had made love to Mrs Ralston; she had been naked too. When, weeping, he had told her it was too late, she had smiled and turned into his mother. Afterwards he had come upon other couples having sex: Mick Dykes and Mrs Porteous; Mrs Munro and Sergeant Milne; Crosbie and Cooley; and Mrs Veitch and Mr Flockhart. They had all paused to listen to him telling them that it was too late.

For a minute or two that morning, after he was awake, the feeling of being too late was still overwhelming and terrifying; but he could not think what it was he had not done and now never would be able to do in time.

Cooley was in an edgy mood. All she wanted for breakfast was a cigarette and a cup of coffee.

'I've been thinking, Duffy. Those things you were saying last night. They're mad. Forget them. Here's a sensible idea. Come to London with me. Nobody knows us there. We could get jobs. We could help each other. But we'd need money to give us a start. I saw your mother's bank book in a drawer. I looked in it. Do you know how much she's got in the bank? Over £300. She won't need all that, when she marries this guy she's gone to Spain with. There's a slip all ready signed. You could draw out as much as you liked. When you make your fortune you could pay her back. Didn't you say that after we'd declared war nothing we did would be a crime? Right, we've declared war. So what's stopping us? They know you at the bank, don't they? It would be dead easy. Think about it, Duffy. There's no future for you here. Your mother would be glad to get you out of her way. If you stay here, do you know what will happen? Big Molly will get you.'

He was disappointed but not angry. 'I don't think you understood what I said last night, Cooley.'

'Maybe I understood better than you did yourself. The first rule is: look after yourself. Christ, Duffy, even dogs and cats know that.'

'You're asking me to steal from my mother.'

'I'm asking you to borrow from her. I'm asking you to oblige her. I don't want to hurt your feelings, Duffy, but she'd think it cheap at the price to get rid of you. Fifty pounds wouldn't be too greedy, and it would still leave her plenty, if this guy from Bearsden doesn't marry her. Think about it, Duffy.'

He felt sad. Last night he had offered her an opportunity to take part in an idealistic mission and this was her reply, urging him to become a liar, cheat, and thief.

Later, after his housework was done, he said he had to go out to keep an appointment with Mrs Veitch, the Careers Officer.

Cooley sneered. 'Do you still think she'll find you a job? How many interviews has she sent you for?'

'Four.'

'If it had been forty it would still have been the same: no job for somebody that's got no certificates. Christ, you need a certificate to get a job as shelfboy in the supermarket. In London it'd be different. If you see Mick Dykes will you ask him to come and see me?'

'Here?'

'If you don't mind. His uncle's a lorry driver. He knows other lorry drivers. Maybe he could get me a lift to London. I'd have to give him something. Five quid, say. All I've got is 80p. So I'm counting on you, Duffy. You'll find Mick in Dirty Chuck's or the amusement centre or just mooching around. Just Mick himself, mind. Not Crosbie. I can't stand him. He gives me the grue. I want to tear out those queer eyes of his. Oh, and bring me some decent fags. These stink. Will it be all right if I play records?'

'Yes, but not too loudly. Mr Ralston upstairs is dying.'

'Of cancer. So you've told me, at least three times. He'll be doped and hear nothing. Give Veitch my regards. I don't know why I left her out of my list of arrogant bastards last night. I forgot, though. She's another one you've got your eye on. Are you sure when you go out on your midnight strolls you don't pay her a visit? That love-bite on her neck, was it you who did it?' She laughed at his puritanic frown. 'It's too easy to kid you, Duffy. You're simple, all right. If you don't watch out big Molly will get you.'

He had let Cooley into his secret and found he could not trust her. If he did not give her money she might betray him. She would look after herself, even at his expense, though she claimed to be his friend. She had sneered at Molly McGowan, but Molly, he felt sure, would never let him down, at any rate not wittingly. She had the fidelity of a dog: even if abused she would still be faithful. He ought to make some effort to rescue her from Dykes and Crosbie. Unfortunately like a dog shown kindness she would attach herself to him and neither harsh words nor even stones would drive her away.

After the rain and dull skies of the past few days the sunshine and pleasant air that morning caused the people in the main street to be cheerful and friendly. He received his share of neighbourly smiles. All the same, as he smiled back, he reflected that if nuclear war broke out and millions were killed it would not be governments and generals who were most to blame but ordinary, good-hearted, well-disposed people like these, who had let themselves be deceived by official lies and instinctive fears. It was as if deep down they did not really believe that the human race deserved to survive. Otherwise why did they look on with approval and complacency when scientists on their behalf made weapons more and more destructive and governments by their dishonesty and arrogance made the use of such weapons more and more likely? And why did they condemn as misguided fools or even traitors those who did protest?

A small group was staring at his declaration of war on the town hall wall.

'It must have been one of them religious sects, Bessie,' said an old woman.

'Like Jehovah's Witnesses, do you mean?'

'Aye. It's a bit out of the Bible, isn't it?'

'I think so, but they shouldn't have made a mess of the wall. Think what it'll cost to rub it off.'

'I hope it's not the Irish coming here with their bombs,' said another woman.

Two old men were indignant. 'What were the police doing when this was done?' asked one. 'They're always getting big rises in pay and yet they're never where they should be.'

'It's not fair to blame the police, Willie,' said his companion.

'Their hands are tied. The rope and the birch should be brought back.'

Mr Flockhart had once pointed out to 4X that one of society's most difficult problems in a few years' time would be the care of the old, especially those physically or mentally incapable of looking after themselves. There would be so many that looking after them would be an impossible burden. Crosbie had promptly offered a solution: gas chambers. Most of 4X had agreed.

Duffy had asked the teacher if he really believed that wholesale extermination of the old and disabled would have to be resorted to in the future. 'I don't see how it can be avoided, Duffy. It would be a matter of self-preservation. The necessary callousness would be found.'

That last remark had remained echoing in Duffy's mind.

Mrs Veitch was having her morning coffee in a mug made by Lightburn Ceramics. There was a picture of the town hall on it.

'Good morning, Duffy,' she said, cheerfully. 'Take a seat. I think I've got some good news for you for a change.'

He sat down, smiling. He liked and trusted her, though her desk was always a muddle of papers and she smoked incessantly so that she reeked of tobacco and her fingers were stained. She was about thirty-five and divorced. She dressed gaudily, this morning in a polo neck purple jumper and a long red skirt. She wore long earrings and four rings.

What Cooley had called a love-bite on her neck was really a scar. According to Duffy's mother she had once appeared in the lounge bar of the Caledonian Hotel with Mr Flockhart who had spent most of the time whining about how his wife was making his life a misery. Mrs Veitch had not listened very attentively.

'You've heard of Mrs Porteous,' she said. 'She owns Lightburn Ceramics that made this mug. She's one of the biggest employers of labour in the town.'

He nodded. Everybody in Lightburn knew of Mrs Porteous. Her name was in the local newspaper every week, in some connection or other. She was a district councillor as well as chairman of the Children's Panel. She was a widow. Her husband had been a lawyer.

'Well, I got a telephone call from her yesterday, asking if I could nominate some deserving young person who would like to make a career in pottery, someone diligent and artistic. I was surprised because I'd been told there were no vacancies and in fact people were being laid off, but one doesn't contradict Lady Bountiful, so I said yes I could nominate such a person, who was very well-spoken, had beautiful manners, was always neat and clean in appearance, had the face and hands of an artist, and was most conscientious. She replied that he sounded the very person she had in mind. Would I please send him to see her as soon as possible?'

Mrs Veitch laughed at Duffy's puzzled expression. 'Didn't you recognise yourself in my description? It was all true. You would notice I left out any mention of your scholastic record. She made it appear that it was artistic temperament she was looking for, not academic ability. It could depend on the impression you make at the interview. By the way, do you go to

church? She particularly wanted to know. I said I thought
you did.'

He nodded. He went at night, when the churches were
empty. He had been in St Stephen's twice.

'Good. Shall I give her a ring and find out when she
would like to see you?' She picked up the telephone and
dialled. Then she waited, with her fingers crossed.

Here was a blow of good luck that he had never expected
and therefore was not on guard against. His resolution to
wage war faltered. Capitulation might after all be more
advantageous.

There was another Duffy besides the idealist and revo-
lutionary. This Duffy did not want much but what he did
want had to be the best. His mother had first become aware
of it when he was five and she was buying clothes for him
to go to school. 'He's forgetting,' she had said to the shop
assistant, 'that his mother's a poor widow.' She had been
rather proud of his good taste, inherited, she thought,
from her, but as he had grown older she had not been
so indulgent. Did he think she owned a factory like Mrs
Porteous? He would have to learn to make do with a great
deal less than the best, until he was able to support himself,
and God knew when that would be. He was going to find
it very hard, having expensive tastes without the means to
satisfy them, but if it was anybody's fault it was his own: he
should have done better at school so that one day he could
get a well-paid job. Only by taking great care of his clothes
had he managed to appear as well-dressed as boys whose
fathers were comfortably off.

He had always been fascinated by Margaret Porteous,
from the first day he had seen her, at the High School,
where she had been in the highest classes and he in the
lowest. He had never spoken to her nor she to him but
he had often gone out of his way just to look at her, even
from a distance. He had watched her playing hockey and
had attended school debates to hear her speaking. He had
discovered, with delight and surprise, that her views on
many things were like his own. She expressed them in

an angry, scornful way that puzzled him. He of course never expressed them at all. She understood politics better than he did and once, at a mock election, she had stood as the Communist candidate because no one else would. Teachers had been scandalised, her mother had been appealed to, and the headmaster had had a friendly chat with her. Forced to withdraw, she had afterwards attended the meetings of all the other candidates and heckled them from the Communist point of view.

One of the favourite topics of 4X had been the fuck-worthiness of girls. Margaret Porteous had been low on the list because she was always haughty and unapproachable. At the top had been Molly McGowan. Almost every boy in the class had had the use of her body, whereas none had got as much as a glance from Margaret Porteous.

One summer evening Duffy had sneaked up the drive of 'The Poplars', Mrs Porteous's villa. Hidden behind rose bushes, far enough from the house not to be smelled by the fawn-coloured Labrador, he had watched Margaret and her friends playing badminton on the lawn. He had envied them. Their fathers were doctors, lawyers, accountants, and shopkeepers. They were all doing well at school and would go on to University. They drove cars. They took part in escapades like the painting of Burns's statue. From what he had overheard of their conversation it was not all that intellectual. Given the chance, he could easily have taken his place among them.

Perhaps that chance had now come.

Mrs Veitch was speaking to Mrs Porteous. 'This afternoon at three? Yes, I'm sure that would be suitable. Thank you very much, Mrs Porteous.'

She put the telephone down. 'She didn't sound quite as enthusiastic this time. I hope she hasn't changed her mind. As you probably noticed I had to do a wee bit of evading. She showed signs of being interested in your scholastic attainments. You may not be successful, Duffy, but I'm sure you won't let me down. I wouldn't mention it to anyone in the meantime, except of course your mother.'

'She's gone to Spain for a holiday.'

'Oh yes, I heard she was going. So you're on your own?'

'Yes.'

'I'm sure you'll manage.' She hesitated. 'You're a friend of Helen Cooley's, aren't you?'

'I know her.'

'Did you know she's been sent to a reform school in Aberdeen? Or she will be when they catch her. She's run away.'

'She said she was going to London.'

'That's just the reckless thing she would do. What on earth does she think she can do there? Do you know, Duffy, she sat in that chair and was very uncomplimentary about the size of my bottom because I'd had the impudence to advise her to take a job as scullery maid in the hotel where your mother works. Did I think she was going to spend her life washing dishes for effing toffs? She'll be lucky to get such a job in London.' Again she hesitated. 'If you want to get on in the world, Duffy, she's the kind best avoided.'

'That's what my mother says.' He rose. 'Thank you, Mrs Veitch.'

'Remember, it's just a possibility. Don't bank on it too much. Come in and tell me how you get on.'

'Yes, I will. Good morning.'

No Etonian could have taken his leave more graciously. As Harry Flockhart had said Duffy was a mystery. She herself had never been able to make up her mind whether the boy was a bit simple, as most people believed, or was very astute, in his own peculiar way. Perhaps he was a late developer. Many famous men had not done well at school.

Waiting for him outside the careers office were Mick Dykes and Johnny Crosbie. They had seen him go in.

They too were the kind best avoided if he wanted to get on in the world. Scum, his mother called them. No doubt Mrs Porteous thought so too but as a politician she would be too prudent to say so.

In spite of his pride in his curly hair and physical bigness Dykes was unsure of himself. His jeans were worn out and dirty, his anorak had holes at the elbows. He grumbled that his mother and sisters would not wash or mend for him, but it never occurred to him to do it for himself. He had been warned by Sergeant Milne and others not to take up a career of crime because, being so stupid, he would be sure to spend most of his life in jail.

Crosbie was smaller and much more knowing. His eyes, as Cooley had said, were queer, not only because of their different shades of blue but also because they had a habit of going suddenly skelly, when one of his headaches afflicted him. His fair hair stuck up in sharp tufts, like a Mohican's. Round his waist was a belt made up of imitation bullets. Stuck in it was an imitation tomahawk, made of rubber. His jeans and jerkin were black. Inside one of his high-heeled cowboy boots was a compartment where he kept his knife. This wasn't imitation, being sharp enough to cut a cat's throat with one slice. He boasted he had killed eight. He leered like an imbecile but was really alert and cunning. Disconcertingly, he had a quiet soft voice, and seldom swore.

They were pleased to see Duffy. Dykes often cadged money from him.

'Got a job, Duffy?' he asked.

'No.'

'Didn't need to ask, did I? You and me, Duffy, and Johnny, no cunt wants us. Well, we don't want them, do we?' He laughed but his big fat babyish face was sullen and unhappy. He wanted very much to be liked and to have lots of money.

'Big Molly and wee Cathie were telling us your mother's gone to Spain,' said Crosbie.

'Yes, so she has.' He always played the simpleton with them. Sometimes he wondered if Crosbie was taken in.

'Molly was saying you wanted her to go and stay with you,' said Dykes, grinning lewdly. 'It's all right with me,

Duffy, except that I promised her to Johnny. He said he'd give me three packets of fags.'

'If you want her, Duffy, she's yours,' said Crosbie, 'as long as I get a wee shot whenever I want.'

'If you'd like to give me a couple of quid, Duffy, that'd be fine. She's a great ride.'

'Mick hires her out at 50p a go.'

'Just to pals,' said Dykes. 'She doesn't keep on asking what you're going to give her, like lots of other birds. Christ, as if I ever had anything to give anybody.'

He then proceeded to give a self-piteous account of his life.

His mother allowed him only 40p per week pocket money and expected him to buy clothes out of it at jumble sales. She wouldn't let him into the house even if it was pouring rain but ordered him to go and find a job. He didn't have a proper bed and had to sleep on the floor in the living-room, which meant he had to wait till they'd all stopped watching television. His two older brothers had a room to themselves and wouldn't let him share it. They said his feet smelled. So they did but it wasn't his fault. He had only two pairs of socks and they were often soaked because his shoes let in water. His married sisters made fun of him. They kept asking if it was true he had the biggest dick in Lightburn. Women were more dirty-minded than men. Did Duffy know that? It was true he had a big dick but he was big all over and still growing. His mother laughed at him and said he'd be able to join the Scots Guards, but maybe he would one day, just to show her.

All that was uttered in a whine of great seriousness.

'Mick fancies your mother, Duffy,' said Crosbie, with a wink of his light-blue eye.

Dykes grinned. 'He's a liar, Duffy.'

'He fancies Veitch too. But do you know who he's got? Mrs Burnet, Fat Annie they call her. She's over forty and she's got four kids. Her man's in England working, or so she says.'

Duffy could hear his mother's shocked voice: 'Are these the kind of friends you have?'

Dykes wasn't sure whether to regard his possession of Mrs Burnet as something to brag about or be ashamed of. 'She's not so fat, and she gives me cans of beer.'

Duffy had seen Mrs Burnet in the street, pushing a pram. She was like what Molly McGowan would become in twenty years or so, if no one saved her.

He remembered Cooley's message. He had to get rid of Cooley. She was the only one in a position to guess that it was he who had painted the challenge on the town hall.

'Cooley wants to see you, Mick. She wants you to ask your uncle to get her a lift to London.'

'Where is she? We heard she had done a bunk.'

'She's hiding in my house.'

Dykes grinned. 'Me and Johnny can't see why you fancy Cooley. She's got no tits and she's so bloody quarrelsome. Isn't that right, Johnny?'

'Sure is. She's had the clap, too.'

'She wouldn't say who gave it to her. She can keep a secret all right. Have I to come to your house to see her?'

'Yes, Mick. Tonight, at seven.'

'Can I come too?' asked Crosbie.

'Yes, Johnny.'

Crosbie's presence would make her all the more impatient to leave.

They were now walking along the main street towards the town hall.

People were staring at the words painted on the wall.

'What's up?' asked Dykes. 'What are they all looking at?' He pushed forward and tried to read the words. 'What the fuck does it mean, Johnny?' he asked.

Crosbie read it out.

'Fucking nonsense,' muttered Dykes.

'Watch your language, you,' said a woman with a wart on her nose.

'What do you think it means, Johnny?'

'Ask Duffy. He did it.'

'Don't be fucking stupid, Johnny. Duffy doesn't know words like that.'

'Maybe he got them out of a book.'

'Tell him he's a silly cunt, Duffy.'

'I'm not putting up with this,' cried the woman with the wart as she marched off to complain to Sergeant Milne and Constable Hastie in a police car parked not far away.

'She's shopping you, Mick,' said Crosbie, gleefully.

How had he known, thought Duffy, that I wrote those words? Was it a lucky guess or does he have some insight into my mind?

Duffy shivered.

'Don't worry,' muttered Dykes. 'I can handle these cunts.'

The policemen had come out of the car and were approaching. The other onlookers drifted away. They wanted nothing to do with either foul-mouthed youths or officious police.

Sergeant Milne was a big dour man who made no attempt to disguise his contempt. 'I've just had a complaint about you, Dykes. Using filthy language.'

'Was it that whure with the warty nose? I wasn't speaking to her.'

'Maybe not, but she heard you. It's an offence to use that kind of language in public.'

'Everybody uses it. I've heard cops use it. Why pick on me?'

Milne nodded towards the writing on the wall. 'Is that your handiwork?'

'I don't even know what the fuck it means.'

'Likely enough you didn't do it yourself, for you can't write, but maybe you know who did do it.'

'I don't know anybody that uses words like that. Do we, Johnny?'

Milne glowered at Crosbie whom he especially dis-liked.

'You see, sergeant, we're not religious,' said Crosbie.

Constable Hastie tried not to grin. Detective Sergeant McLeod in charge of the investigation had suggested that it was the work of religious cranks: he was religious himself. Sergeant Milne thought political subversives were to blame. Constable Hastie himself was inclined to think the culprits were the same High School show-offs who had painted the statue red-white-and-blue.

Sergeant Milne turned to Duffy. 'What's your name? Where d'you live?'

'Duffy, sir. 86 Kenilworth Court.'

That artful 'sir' caused the sergeant's attitude to soften. He had time for young people who respected authority.

'Don't tell me this pair are pals of yours.'

'They were in my class at school.'

Well, said Milne's expression then, you couldn't have been bright, but being backward's not a crime and good manners and neat sensible clothes go a long way to make up for it.

'What does your father do, Duffy?'

'He's dead, sir. My mother works in the Caledonian Hotel.'

Constable Hastie whispered in the sergeant's ear. Some of the younger policemen frequented the lounge bar and knew his mother.

'If you want to keep out of trouble, Duffy, stay away from this pair. I'm sure your mother would agree with me.'

'Yes, sir.'

'Get along then.'

As Duffy walked away he heard the sergeant say: 'Leave that lad alone, do you hear? He's just the sort you two would corrupt.'

'What's corrupt?' asked Dykes, suspiciously.

Suppose, thought Duffy, I don't get the job and decide to carry on with my war. Dykes and Crosbie would make suitable recruits. In no war in history had soldiers been asked to pass a test of moral fitness. According to Mr

Flockhart among the Crusaders there had been adven-
turers, villains, and cut-throats. All that was required of
participators in wars was instant and complete obedience,
whether the order was to tear pages out of books or drop
bombs on cities.

Cooley wanted to know where he was going all dressed up.

'For an interview.'

'About a job?'

'Yes.'

'What job?'

'At the pottery factory.'

'Porteous's place?'

'Yes.'

'You mean to tell me you'd be willing to work for that stuck-up bastard, after what she's done to me? Talk about defilers and abusers! She's the worst.'

He said nothing.

'What kind of job? Sweeping the floors? That's all she'd think you good for. Anyway they're on slack time at the factory. Was it Veitch that arranged it?'

'Yes.'

'She's a dizzy bitch. She gets things wrong. Because she's in love, maybe. Her boyfriend's in Aberdeen. He's got a good job in oil. He visits her whenever he can and they spend most of the time in bed. She's knackered for days afterwards. She's worried he'll not marry her. So she gets things wrong.'

'Who told you all this?'

'Wee Cathie. Her mother knows Mrs Calderwood who does Veitch's cleaning. I expect it'll be wee Johnson the manager you'll see.'

'My appointment is with Mrs Porteous.'

'You really have a high opinion of yourself, Duffy. Why would her ladyship want to interview a floor-sweeper?'

'I have to see her at three o'clock.'

'You're early then.'

'I'm going to the bank first.'

'Now you're talking. How much are you going to take out?'

'Enough.'

'How much is enough? Depends on what you want to do, doesn't it? Remember what I said about coming to London with me. If you don't get this job, and you won't, come with me. Mick's uncle could get both of us lifts. It'd be safer if there were two of us. You want excitement, well here's your chance.'

'Why are you so sure I won't get the job?'

'For Christ's sake, Duffy, why should Porteous give you a job when she's turned down dozens with certificates? Out of pity? She's got a heart of stone. Because you fancy her daughter? She doesn't know that, but if she did she'd be more likely to warn the cops. I don't care what Veitch said, it'll not be Porteous you'll see but the manager and he'll tell you nothing doing, no floor-sweepers required, thank you very much, goodbye.'

'It's not a floor-sweeping job. Mrs Porteous wants an apprentice to learn the whole business of pottery.'

'Did she tell Veitch that?'

'Yes.'

'I don't believe it, but if it was true, why the hell would Veitch send you?'

'Why shouldn't she send me?'

'Because, Duffy, she may have a soft spot for you but like everybody else she thinks you're daft, or half-daft anyway. You've put on too good an act, Duffy. Sometimes I'm not sure myself that it is an act. Like last night when you were havering about defilers and abusers. Now here you are imagining you'll get this job and work your way up to the top and become manager and marry Margaret and live in a villa in Ballochmyle and have kids that you'll send to private school so as not to be contaminated by the scruff at the High School. Like in one of your mother's story-books.

You really are simple, Duffy, if you believe that's going to happen.'

Perhaps he did not believe it was going to happen but he let himself hope that it would. So much so that on his way to the bank he saw people differently from the way he had seen them that morning. Then he had blamed them for their complacency which he had thought would bring about the destruction of the world. Now he approved of their refusing to embitter their lives with useless protests. Besides it could be that they were right after all and war could be averted only by the possession of bigger bombs than the enemy's. If he was to join the human race, as Mr Flockhart had ironically suggested he should, it would be people like these, sensibly dressed, clean, respectable, and hard-working that he would want to associate with, not unwashed long-haired hippies that went on protest marches, nor foul-mouthed louts like Mick Dykes, nor punks without conscience like Crosbie.

Cooley had jeered about him making his fortune, as if it had never been done before. Andrew Carnegie had gone to America a poor unknown boy and had become one of the richest men in the world, and a famous philanthropist. Mrs Porteous had once said, when addressing the Lightburn Women's Business Club – it had been reported in the local newspaper – that the best way of helping the poor was not through hand-outs from the State but through the efforts of successful men and women in creating businesses that gave employment and brought prosperity to the whole country.

In the bank the clerkess without hesitation handed him five five-pound notes, the amount he had entered on the slip. 'How's your mother?' she asked, cheerfully. He replied that his mother was in Spain on holiday, the money was to pay bills. 'I'm green with envy,' she replied, with a wink.

The other people in the bank accepted him as one of them. They approved of the careful way he placed the notes in his wallet and then put the wallet into his inside pocket.

By showing respect for money he was also showing respect
for those who valued it properly.

A workman was scrubbing the declaration of war off
the wall.

Duffy saw it as symbolic: his war was off. He was another
person.

At the back of his mind sounded faintly a warning not to
be too confident. He did not heed it. He was convinced he
would be able to win over Mrs Porteous.

The girl in the reception office was only a year or two
older than himself.

'I've to see Mrs Porteous at three,' he said, shyly.

She consulted a diary. 'Is your name Thomas Duffy?'

'Yes.'

'You're in good time.'

The clock on the wall said five minutes to three.

'Sit down,' she said. 'Mrs P. has someone in with
her.'

She wanted to be inquisitive but was afraid he might be
a friend of her employer. 'Do you live in Lightburn?'

'Yes.'

'I can't say I've seen you around.'

He hadn't seen her either. It wasn't strange. The town
had only twelve thousand inhabitants but they lived in
cliques.

'Have you come to see through the factory?' she asked.

He had, in a way. So he nodded. He wondered if Mrs
Porteous herself would conduct him.

The telephone on the desk rang. She picked it up. 'Yes,
Mrs Porteous, he's arrived. Very good.' She put it down.
'She'll see you now. It's the first on the left. Her name's
on the door.'

'Thank you.'

'You're welcome.' She was charmed by his good manners.

He knocked, a woman's deep voice called: 'Come in.'
He opened the door and went in, very respectfully.

At the large desk, behind a vaseful of flowers, sat the

worst abuser of authority in Lightburn. She had used her influence to have Cooley sent to a reform school, she did not allow her employees to belong to a union, and she had taken the lead in having tinkers removed from Crochan Wood, though they had encamped there for years.

Because it suited him he saw her as the woman who was going to give him an opportunity to make his fortune. She could not help looking high-and-mighty, being so tall and handsome with her fair hair massed in coils, held in place by two silver combs. She wore a green tweed costume and a necklace of green stones, emeralds perhaps.

What struck him most about her face, however, wasn't its arrogance and handsomeness but the traces of weeping on it. He had seen these on his mother's face too often to be mistaken. Recently, perhaps that very day, she had wept. Powder, eye-shadow, lipstick, and even rouge had been used to cover up the physical effects, and haughtiness, more suited to her face than the humility of tears, had been restored to it by an effort of will. Most people would have thought her as sure of herself as a successful business woman should be, but Duffy saw more deeply. He had seen before those winces of the lips and that hurt in the eyes. He had known what had caused them in his mother's case, but what disappointment in love could so proud and self-satisfied a woman have suffered? Had someone close to her died or become seriously ill? Had she quarrelled with her daughter Margaret, known to be stubborn and headstrong? Was she worried about the state of her business? Duffy did not think any of those was the reason.

She stared impatiently at him, as if he was to blame for her trouble, whatever this was. 'Thomas Duffy?' Her voice was cold and a little hoarse.

'Yes, ma'am.'

She did not return his smile. 'Sit down.'

However she tried, and she did not seem to be trying all that hard, she could not stop looking haughty. To think highly of herself was a lifelong habit.

He sat down, looking modest and alert, but showing no sign that he was aware of her stress.

'I'm afraid Mrs Veitch must have misunderstood me.' She paused. 'I thought I had made it clear that the young person I had in mind was one who had done very well at school but was unable to continue with his or her studies owing to parental circumstances. I'm afraid you do not come into that category. Far from it.'

He had let himself be caught off guard. He had given someone an opportunity to humiliate him. He smiled, meekly.

'Naturally I made enquiries as to your scholastic record. I was informed you had left school without a single O-level certificate. Is that the case?'

'Yes.'

'Really. I am surprised at Mrs Veitch. How on earth did you do so badly?'

Because, he could have said, I never wanted to compete: the questions asked did not interest me. She would not have understood any more than his mother had.

In primary school his teachers had been sorry for him, he looked so thoughtful and yet was evidently not all there. An attempt had been made to have him transferred to a school for the mentally retarded. His mother had resisted it. The psychologist sent to examine him had declared, to the astonishment of the teachers, that he was as smart as any other seven-year-old and knew a great deal more than most. One or two more percipient teachers, like Mr Flockhart, had wondered if he might not be playing some impudent game, but they had not been able to believe that a child of seven, say, or a boy of fifteen could be so deep and deceitful, nor could they see what, if it was deliberate, his purpose could possibly be.

To Mrs Porteous now he was simply one of the numerous poor on whom years of expensive education had been wasted.

'I am very sorry, Thomas, but really you are not suitable for the position I have in mind.'

Showing neither hurt nor anger he played the simpleton. 'Mrs Veitch said I was to get a chance to learn all about pottery.'

There were moments when she seemed to have forgotten him altogether.

'Mrs Veitch should have made it clear that you were coming for an interview only.'

'She said I had artistic hands.' He held them up. 'I used to make things out of plasticine. I like drawing and painting.'

She glanced at her gold wrist-watch. 'I'm sure you will find some more suitable employment. Perhaps I might be able to help. Please give your address to the girl when you go out.'

'Am I not to get the job?' he asked, his mouth wide open, as if in incredulity.

'I'm afraid not.'

'But Mrs Veitch said –'

'I'm sure Mrs Veitch did not intend to misinform you, but it would appear that she must have done.'

He saw that there were moments when her mind wasn't on him at all but on the trouble that had caused her to weep.

'She said you wanted to know if I went to church.'

She was disconcerted by that irrelevancy.

'I sometimes go but I don't like going by myself.'

She felt obliged to show interest. 'Doesn't your mother take you?'

He shook his head solemnly. 'She used to be a Catholic, you see.'

She saw all right. Her attitude to Catholics, though more discreetly expressed, was the same as Mick Dykes'. Her father, from whom she had inherited the factory, had been a high official in the Masonic Lodge.

'I like St Stephen's church best,' said Duffy. 'It's got the highest spire in Lightburn. The higher the spire the nearer to God. Someone said that.'

As a Christian she had to show compassion. As a business

woman whose time was being wasted by a fool, however
innocent, she felt embarrassed and annoyed.

'There must be other churches nearer your home. St
Cuthbert's, for instance.'

'I went to St Stephen's one Sunday and there were
men at the door asking people their names. I didn't like
to go in.'

'They were elders. They weren't asking people their
names. They were welcoming them.'

'I was told the seats in Stephen's belong to people. Not
everybody can sit in them.'

'Some pews are named but that's because some families
have been members since the church was built over a
hundred years ago. There are other pews where anyone
can sit.'

'If I went on Sunday would I get in?'

'Of course, but I really think you should try some church
nearer your home.'

'Mr Cargill's the minister, isn't he? He's the High School
chaplain. I've heard him preach. He's got white hair.'

Duffy had overheard Mr Flockhart saying to another
teacher that old Cargill made no attempt to reach the minds
of the children. He used words few of them understood. It
was as if he wanted to anaesthetise them with boredom.

'If I went on Sunday would you ask them to let me in?'

'I don't think there would be any need for that.'

He saw that she would have liked to point out how
impertinent his request was, but he was obviously very
childish for his age and in the Bible Christ had said that
little children should be allowed to come to Him. So she
nodded, with a frown. 'Very well. If I can be of assistance
I shall be glad to.'

She pushed a button at the side of her desk. In a few
moments the girl came.

'Mary, Thomas is leaving now. Would you please take
a note of his address? And perhaps you could find one of
our pens for him.'

'Yes, Mrs Porteous.'

Duffy did not move. He smiled trustingly, as if he had no idea he was being dismissed.

'Go with Mary, Thomas.'

He rose, looking bewildered. 'Have I to leave now?'

Mary took him by the sleeve and led him out.

She was puzzled. Mrs Porteous could be severe and had had more than one female employee in tears, but she had never had an effect quite like this.

In the reception office she said, suspiciously: 'What was that all about? Why were you acting daft?'

'I don't know what you mean.'

'Don't try it on with me. What's your address?' She sneered as she wrote down Kenilworth Court. 'That's a council housing scheme, isn't it?'

'My mother's going to buy one of the new bungalows near the public park.'

'Is she indeed? Are you sure she can afford it? They cost over fifty thousand pounds.'

She took a ballpoint pen from a drawer. It was white with LIGHTBURN CERAMIC on it in red. 'Here's your pen.'

He was as pleased as a child of five. 'Can I try it, please?'

Still suspicious, but contemptuous too, she put a sheet of paper in front of him.

In childish block letters he wrote her name Mary.

She couldn't help laughing. 'Either you're very crafty or you're daft.'

He laughed too as he carefully put the pen in his breast pocket.

Now that he was at war, against forces so much stronger than his own, deceit was necessary and permissible.

CHAPTER TEN

Cooley had not given a promise to stay out of his room, but if she had she would not have kept it. In an important matter, like not betraying him to the police, she would take trust seriously but not in a small matter like having a scout round his room while he wasn't there. For all his peculiar ways he wasn't likely to have any terrible secrets. If you were sixteen and lived in Kenilworth Court and had a barmaid for your mother and were, to be truthful, half-cracked, what secrets could you have? Suppose she found a bundle of magazines with pictures of scuddy women with huge boobs fingering their twats it wouldn't really be a secret for most boys had at least one or two. Everybody was dirty-minded, but in Duffy's case it would be a surprise. Besides if there was anything he did not want her to see he should have locked the door: he knew how nosy she was. She could honestly say too that it was anxiety about him that made her curious.

In her favour she could say she put it off as long as she could. She listened to records. She watched television. She tried on Mrs Duffy's clothes. She even read a page or two of one of Mrs Duffy's paperback romances, about a girl who worked in a milliner's but was really a lord's daughter and heiress to a large estate. It was interesting but a load of crap. In any case Cooley had never been able to read more than five minutes at a time.

She was in the living-room trying to write a letter to her married sister in Glenrothes, explaining why she had decided to escape to London, when there was a loud knock on the outside door. She thought it might be Mick Dykes come early, but just in case waited behind the door, saying

62

nothing. Duffy had said Mick would be bringing Crosbie with him. There was only one person out there, and she soon jaloused who it was, for she heard grunts and the shuffle of sore feet. It was Munro, Duffy's neighbour across the landing. She must suspect that Duffy had someone living with him.

Cooley put her fingers to her nose.

She did not return to her letter-writing but went straight into Duffy's room.

At a first glance there was nothing extraordinary about it, except its tidiness. There were no muddy football boots, no pieces of model tanks or aeroplanes, no comics. A hospital nurse could not have made the bed more neatly. In a small bookcase were his encyclopaedias, arranged in alphabetical order. She had not expected to see posters of famous footballers or naked women, as she would have in any ordinary boy's room, and there was none. The pictures that were there, two of them, about the size of posters, were startling, especially when looked at closely. They were paintings by Duffy himself. These were the first specimens of his work that she had seen, and they were weird. They were very alike, so that she wondered if they were meant to be a puzzle, the kind where you had to pick out the eight or so differences, everything else being identical. They consisted of swirls of red, black, and yellow, with, at the centre, what she decided was a face, white as death. Yes, that was the mouth, open, as if to scream: there were the eyes, with blobs of red under them like tears of blood. They were not only weird, they were scary. Though it was still daylight, and she was wearing an ankle-length dress of silver and crimson, and she could hear women laughing down in the street, she felt more scared looking at that face than she had done among the rats at the coup. She was sure it was meant to be Duffy's own. She had been joking last night when she had imagined him murdering her and chopping her body into pieces, but she hadn't seen those faces then. She knew that creatures of violence and menace did not come from outer space but from the darkness of the human mind. Duffy must find it harder to contain his than other people did because his were more horrible.

Christ, Duffy, she thought, pitying him.

On a shelf were the twenty-four issues of his illustrated *History of War*. The first one told about ancient wars and the last about wars of today.

Could it be possible that Duffy wasn't really human? She had seen a film once in which a woman mysteriously became pregnant. One night while she was asleep the devil came and fucked her. The child conceived was Satan's son. Knowing that she was being daft, Cooley let herself wonder if something like that hadn't happened to Duffy's mother sixteen years ago. After all, she had never told him who his father was. Perhaps, like the woman in the film, she didn't know.

There was a drawer in the small table he used as a desk. It was unlocked. Inside she found his jotter with its tales of atrocities and also some blue folders marked Private and Confidential. With only a momentary hesitation and with her heart beating faster she took one out and opened it. To her astonishment it contained pictures cut out of the local newspaper and the High School magazine: they were of Margaret Porteous. Here she was receiving a cup for winning a tennis tournament, here making a speech during the school debate, here with an armful of book prizes, and here in a bikini sunbathing in a garden. God knew how he had got hold of that one. Cooley did not know whether to be amused or indignant or alarmed. When she had accused him of fancying Margaret Porteous she had been teasing. Now she saw that either he did fancy the black-haired snobbish bitch or had picked her out to be done in. Jesus, I don't really believe that, do I? thought Cooley, and had to admit that though she didn't quite believe it she didn't altogether disbelieve it either. Cooley herself had nothing against Margaret Porteous except that she was a snobbish bitch, but if she was in any danger of being done in by crazy Duffy then she ought to be warned, though Cooley herself

wouldn't be able to do it, being far away in London, thank
Christ.

In another folder was a jotter in which was written what
appeared to be an account of Duffy's nightmares.

Christ, Duffy, she thought, you really ought to be
locked up.

On the cover of one folder were drawn, very neatly, the
signs of the Zodiac. There was her own: Cancer the Crab.
The last time she had read her horoscope in the newspaper
about a week ago it had said: Your friends have not been
appreciating you as they should. This will soon change.

Inside this folder was the yellow tract, Duffy's message
from God.

It was full of quotations from the Bible. In brackets were
the names Ezra, Jeremiah, and Isaiah. As far as she could
make out it announced that the world was full of sinners
who if they didn't repent soon would be destroyed, not by
a flood this time but by the fires of a nuclear holocaust.
Apparently God was going to borrow bombs from the
Americans or Russians, or maybe from them both. In
blacker letters than the rest she saw the bit about defilers
of truth and abusers of authority.

She was amazed that Duffy had let himself be taken in
by such guff. She didn't know much but she could have
told him that tracts like these were produced in millions by
religious loonies all over the world. Another thing she knew
was that sex or rather the desire for it, if not appeased, could
cause wild dreams. Perhaps she hadn't been far wrong
when she had said that what he needed was ten minutes
in bed with big Molly McGowan.

There was also a picture of a man with a shaven head
burning like a torch.

She put everything back where she had found it.

She wished she hadn't looked into those folders. She felt
now that she ought to do something about Duffy but had no
idea what. Molly was a cure that would have to be carefully
administered if it wasn't to make the patient worse instead
of better.

There was herself, quite cured the clinic said; but she would as soon make love with a baboon. Unlike Molly she had a mind and an imagination; also she had seen those faces in the paintings. You could, if you shut your eyes and clenched your teeth, cuddle a baboon, for you'd know what the poor bugger was looking for. Not with Duffy, though.

She thought of going upstairs and consulting the wee darkie, who liked Duffy. If she had been still at school she might have asked Flockhart's advice.

No one could help. One thing she could do was stop asking him to steal his mother's money. Some cure that for bad dreams.

She had herself to look after. If Duffy was doomed and was going to end up in a loony-bin it wouldn't matter very much then that he had stolen fifty pounds or so from his mother.

I'm a selfish bastard, she thought. But then who isn't? Isn't that Duffy's trouble? We all accept it. He can't.

CHAPTER ELEVEN

When he returned she was still wearing the crimson and silver dress and had put on a blonde wig of his mother's. It made her look more ridiculous than alluring but it would be useful as a disguise. She was going to find it hard to look him straight in the face, not just because she'd sneaked into his room without permission, but also because she'd be reminded of the two ghastly faces in the paintings. Sure as God, she might burst out laughing, hysterically.

The safest plan would be to try and act as if everything was the same as before. She was convinced he hadn't got the job so that didn't come into it.

'You're late, husband,' she said, pertly. 'What kept you? Have you been seeing another woman?'

He didn't even smile. 'I promised Mrs Veitch I would tell her how I got on.'

'Well, how *did* you get on?'

She had to wait until he went into his room and changed his clothes. She prayed he wouldn't notice she had been prying.

When he came back into the living-room she was relieved. He couldn't have noticed for he wasn't angry. He was now wearing his jeans and pullover, his working garb evidently, for he began to tidy up the room.

She watched as he swept up potato crisp crumbs off the carpet, took a glass she had used – whisky and lemonade – to the kitchen and washed it, and put some magazines she had been looking at back in their rack. She said nothing. This obsession with order could be his way of keeping his monsters under control. She certainly didn't want them on the loose.

'You were going to tell me how you got on,' she said. 'Though you don't have to. You didn't get it, did you?'

'No, I didn't get it.' He smiled.

She remembered the faces. Her blood turned cold. 'I said you wouldn't. Was it the manager you saw?'

'I saw Mrs Porteous.'

'You're kidding. Her ladyship leaves that kind of thing to the manager. What was she wearing?'

'A green costume, with a necklace of green stones. Two silver combs in her hair.'

'All right, you saw her; but she could just have been passing by. What did she say?'

'She said I was too stupid to work for her.' Again he smiled.

Cooley found that hard to believe. Stupid was the kind of word Porteous would think but never say, being too much of a lady. 'Did she actually call you stupid?'

'That's what she meant.'

Why did Cooley have then a vision of Porteous with her proud throat cut and the emeralds all sticky with blood? It must be because of those paintings and that tract. Christ, Duffy, she thought, you'll have me as batty as yourself.

'She's the kind of person who makes other people pay if she's in trouble.'

Though startled by the remark, Cooley thought there were any number of people like that, who got their own back wherever they could. But what had happened to make Duffy think Porteous was one of them?

'How do you know she's in trouble? She didn't tell you.'

'No, but I could tell.'

Cooley glanced up at herself in the mirror above the fireplace. She looked as comic as hell. They should both be roaring with laughter at her appearance and making jokes at Porteous's expense. Instead here was Duffy, as likely to laugh as Dracula about to sink his teeth into a victim's neck, and here she was herself, feeling her own neck stiffen with fear.

'How could you tell?' she asked, 'She wouldn't **give** herself away to anyone.'

'She had been crying.'

Cooley had lit a cigarette. It almost dropped from her shaking hand. 'She hasn't cried in a hundred years, but if she did she'd never let you or anybody see it.'

'Not many people would have seen it.'

'But you did?'

'Yes, I did.'

And they think you're simple, she thought, with a shudder. What you are, Duffy, is mad and mysterious. Christ knows what you're thinking. You'll end up murdering somebody. I'll have to make sure it isn't me.

She tried to be jocular. 'What could make her cry? What trouble could she have? She's got pearls as well as emeralds. She's got two cars. Has Margaret got herself bairned? By Stephen Telfer? That'd be a laugh.'

He wasn't laughing, though. She was a bloody fool. She'd warned herself not to mention Margaret Porteous and yet she'd done it, in the very way to provoke him; and she went on doing it. 'Well, what goes on after the badminton? Those wee white shorts would make it convenient. I expect though she'd get an abortion: his father being a doctor.'

'Mrs Porteous's trouble is personal.'

'Personal? Do you mean she's in love and he's jilted her? Duffy, you're a scream. Why do you think I call her Tight-pussy? She thinks sex is filthy. I've heard her saying it, well almost saying it. Maybe it's because her man died young, or maybe it's religion. You should have seen the look she gave me when she asked if it was true that I had "a disgusting disease". She wanted to know who I had got it from. I told her it was none of her business. *You've* never asked who I got it from, Duffy.'

And he still wasn't going to ask. So she told him.

'I expect like all the rest of them you think I've been fucked by everybody in Lightburn with a cock, except yourself of course. Well, it's not true. I'd rather eat a

Mars bar any day. Three times only, Duffy. The first time
out of curiosity. I was just thirteen at the time. So was
he. Jackie McBeth. You know him. Ears like handles, wee
serious eyes. It was in a stairhead lavatory in Crimea Street,
before the buildings there were condemned. He lived there.
It was his first time too. There was so little room I had to
hold on to his ears. The cistern kept running. The seat was
soaked. There was a stink. Somebody kept coming and
hammering on the door. The french letter he'd borrowed
was like this dress, ten sizes too big: it kept falling off. It was
near Christmas too and freezing. So it wasn't what you'd
call a great success. That was the first time. The second
time I did it for money. This was about a year later. I'm
not going to tell you who he was. He was a married man
with two kids. I was hard up. He offered me three quid. It
was summer so we did it in a flower-bed in the public park,
about midnight. I remember hearing the town hall clocks
striking twelve just when we'd finished. He wasn't pleased.
I hadn't co-operated. He wanted his money back. So I said
if he didn't give me another three quid I'd tell the cops. I
wasn't sixteen so what he'd done or what he'd tried to do
was illegal. He cursed but he paid up. That was the second
time. The third time it was for love. I fancied him. I think I
still fancy him, the bastard. He said he fancied me. We'd go
steady and get married. So when he invited me to his house
I went like a shot. We did it on his bed, with all our clothes
off, in the dark. I wanted to see what was going on but he
said it was more romantic in the dark. I tried to enjoy it
but I kept wanting to laugh at how busy he was. It's not
just Mick Dykes thinks he's got a champion. They all do.
Well, a day or two later I found I'd got the clap. So I went
to him and asked what about it. Do you know what the liar
said? That he'd got it from me. You'll not believe me when
I tell you who he is. This was just two months ago, mind.
David Martin. His family owns that big furniture shop in
the main street. Boy Scout, Bible class, Scripture Union.
I used to have to mind my language when talking to him.
I heard afterwards from wee Cathie that he'd screwed half

the girls in town, and I thought he loved me, and me alone. You're not laughing, Duffy.'

He had listened like a priest. True enough it had been a kind of confession on her part. She waited for him to rebuke her, and then, as priests did, tell her she was forgiven.

Instead he said, 'I'll make the tea. Do you like scrambled eggs?'

He really was a scream. Certainly she felt like screaming. Yet it was a sensible enough question.

'I like everything except liver.'

'I usually put melted cheese in it.'

'That should make it a lot tastier.'

Screaming, but in silence, she followed him into the kitchen and watched him put on his apron.

'Would you like chips?'

'I'd love chips.'

She watched him washing the potatoes. 'While you were out Munro came to the door.'

'How do you know it was Mrs Munro?'

'She grunted.'

He didn't smile. Even Mick Dykes had more humour, and *he* had to have jokes explained to him, especially if they were about himself. Poor Mick. All the same, forced to choose, with a gun at her head, between Mick and Duffy as a boyfriend, she'd have to take Mick. A knee in the right place at the right time would knock most of the bounce and brag out of him. With Duffy it would have to be a stake through his heart.

She watched him cutting the potatoes into chips with a wickedly sharp knife. She imagined it slicing open her stomach.

'Do you think Mick will bring big Molly?' Here she was at it again, poking through the bars at his monsters. If she did get her stomach sliced open it would be her own fault.

'Why should he bring her?'

'Because she'll want to come. She fancies you, Duffy. She says you and she are going to get married one day.

She thinks you and she could have beautiful kids: a bit soft in the head maybe but beautiful. You know, Duffy, she's maybe what you need. All these weird ideas, all the bad dreams, they could be caused by sex gathering in your mind like a big boil. It's got to be lanced and all the pus let out. Molly would lance it for you.'

Should she run and get the silver crucifix out of his mother's jewellery box, just in case? She should certainly keep her mouth shut. But no, here she was poking again. 'She'd make you human. You'd hate it at first but you'd get used to it. She'd get rid of your monsters.'

He was beating up eggs. Fat for the chips sizzled on the cooker. If she wasn't careful she'd be getting it poured over her wig.

'What monsters?' he asked, quietly.

'Everybody's got monsters. You should see mine.'

'Why did you go into my room?'

Had she put the tract back in the folder upside-down? 'Who said I went into your room?'

'There was a smell of perfume.'

No wonder. She had stank of it.

'I just had a peep in. I didn't think you'd mind. The door wasn't locked. You'd do well in the Army, Duffy, everything exactly in the right place.'

'I thought I could trust you, Cooley.'

'I thought you weren't supposed to call me Cooley any more. Call me Helen. You've got a lot to learn, Duffy. I've told you the first rule: look after yourself. The second rule is: people can be trusted only if there's something in it for them. Will I set the table? I know, fork to the left, knife to the right.'

'I think you should wash your hands first, and remove that silly wig.'

'Jesus!' She ran to the bathroom where she washed her hands and shed an angry tear or two. 'Fuck you, Duffy,' she said to herself in the mirror. She did not remove the wig.

She went back to the kitchen. He had set the table himself.

They were eating when he said: 'We're breaking into the library tonight.'

'Who's we?'

'Mick Dykes, Johnny Crosbie, you, and me.'

'Me? I don't remember saying I would go. I thought you'd given up that crazy idea.'

'Tomorrow night St Stephen's church. I would like you to come with us, Helen.'

She wished she hadn't asked him not to call her Cooley. She wasn't sure who this Helen was. 'All right, it's daft but I'll go. How much do I get?'

'Ten pounds.'

'Couldn't you make it twenty? All right. I'd be a lot happier if Crosbie wasn't in on it. In the church you might have a mad idea about showing up a shower of hypocrites but he'll just see it as a chance to do something rotten and filthy.'

'He will obey orders.'

'What if we're caught? It would be the comicalest reason in the world for getting sent to the nick. You'd be all right, you've got no record, you could say the rest of us led you into it, and they'd believe you for you've got them all thinking you're simple. They'd go on thinking it for the rest of your life, Duffy. They'd laugh at you in the streets. Wee kids would bawl 'Loony'. It'd make some sense if there was anything worth stealing.'

'I told you we would not be thieves.'

'Crosbie would steal the eyes out of your head and come back for the holes.' She grinned at her own effrontery. The remark had been applied to her, years ago, by an elderly neighbour, whose dog's collar she had pinched.

'Not while he is under my command.'

All she could say to that, with her eyes blinking, was: 'Yes, general,' and salute.

CHAPTER TWELVE

When the three conspiratorial knocks were heard Cooley hurried to open the door. She was still wearing the long dress and the wig.

Gaping with enchantment, Mick thought he must have come to the wrong door. He gave her the shy version of his possessor-of-the-biggest-dick-in-Lightburn smile. He was dressed for visiting. He had on his usual mucky jeans and torn anorak but his white shirt with red stripes was clean though its collar was frayed. He had subdued his curls with some foul-smelling cream.

Beside him, a midget by comparison, Crosbie had on a long black leatherette coat useful for slinking undetected in the dark but also an Australian hat conspicuous in any Lightburn street a hundred yards away. That was Crosbie, a mixture of conceit and caution, with more than a dash of viciousness. Some said he couldn't help being vicious, it was the way he was born, with a kink in his brain, but Cooley was convinced he just liked being treacherous and cruel.

'Is Duffy in?' asked Mick, politely. His nose twitched between his pudgy cheeks, like a bull-dog's smelling a bitch in heat.

'General Duffy is studying his plans,' she said, in a voice that was a parody of Mrs Porteous's.

No matter how thick Mick looked he could always look thicker. 'Duffy said we'd to come at seven.'

'It's me, you silly bugger. Cooley. Come in.'

'You smell wonderful, Cooley.'

'I smell like a cheap whorehouse.'

She was tempted to push Crosbie out and slam the door on him.

'Did you speak to your uncle, Mick?'

'Sure, Cooley.'

'Good. Johnny, you go into the living-room. Duffy's there. I want to ask Mick about what his uncle said.'

She showed Crosbie where the living-room was and then took Mick into the bedroom.

He was awed by the big bed with its red quilt. 'Is it Mrs Duffy's?'

'It's mine in the meantime.'

'I wouldn't mind being in it with her,' he confessed, wistfully. 'I bet she'd like it too. Older women are better in bed.'

'Well, they've had more practice.'

'It's not just that. It's because they're more grateful.'

'Grateful for what?'

'For being made feel young. But it's got to be done right.'

'All the same, Mick, I don't think you've got much chance with Mrs Duffy. She'd rather have a man with a big bank-book. What did your uncle Fred say?'

He took a piece of notepaper out of his pocket. 'He said if you're at the depot in Glasgow on Monday morning at seven and show this to a driver called Dougie he'll take you as far as Rugby: that's not far from London. Uncle Fred said I'd to warn you that thousands of young people from all over the country run away to London and end up as whores and junkies. Some even get murdered.'

'Right, you've warned me. Thank your uncle. Listen, Mick, Duffy's going to ask you to do something for him.'

'I'd do anything for Duffy.'

'I want you to tell him you want to be paid for it.'

'When you oblige a pal you shouldn't want to be paid.'

Jesus, give me patience, she thought. This was the clown who thought he owned Molly McGowan and could sell her for packets of fags; who boasted he could make middle-aged women grateful for the services of his over-sized cock; and who had excused the killing of a swan, not to mention of at least eight cats, as Crosbie's idea of fun. Yet here he was preaching at her like somebody who'd won prizes at Sunday school. Such as David Martin.

Crosbie came in. He had taken off his coat and hat. Cooley imagined she could see badness rising off him like red steam.

'Duffy says you've to come,' he said. 'Is that Mrs Duffy's bed, Mick?'

Mick was lying on it, with his size-ten shoes on. Holes could be seen in his soles.

'He fancies her, Cooley. He says he could make her happy.'

The conceit of males, thought Cooley. Here was this penniless lout with the pea-sized brain thinking that a woman like Mrs Duffy would give up everything for the privilege of being fucked by him.

'Do you know who he visits, Cooley?' asked Crosbie, eager to tell tales.

Mick grinned. If being betrayed meant also having his prowess as a lover praised he was prepared to put up with it.

'Mrs Burnet that lives in Kilchattan Street.'

'Her they call Fat Annie?'

'That's her. Her man's down in England working.'

'But she's got three kids.'

'Mick says its better if they've had kids.'

'So it is,' said Mick, earnestly.

Cooley didn't know whether to laugh or scream. 'Are you big, Mick, or do you just brag?'

He sat up. 'Would you like me to show you?'

She wasn't sure that she did. 'Seeing's believing,' she said, recklessly.

He got to his feet, unbelted his jeans and pulled them down, as proud and delighted as a young mother drawing aside a shawl to reveal the face of her first-born. He gazed down at the enormous white slug with the same adoration.

She might have snatched off one of her stiletto-heeled shoes and attacked that symbol of male arrogance if she hadn't again been reminded of the young mother and her baby. Somehow Mick's joy was as innocent as hers.

He laughed. 'Annie says it's the most beautiful thing she's ever seen.'

Cooley had heard that Fat Annie, who deserved her nickname, entertained a variety of men friends. No doubt they paid her, if only in cans of beer. Mick would be a kind of pet.

'If you like, Cooley,' he said, grinning, 'I'll give you a demonstration.'

'Thanks, Mick. But I'm not completely cured yet. Another week the clinic said.'

Hastily but reverently, like a jeweller putting diamonds in a safe, he pulled up his jeans and stuffed the precious thing away.

'Duffy's waiting,' said Crosbie.

CHAPTER THIRTEEN

In the living-room Duffy had set up a child's black-board on an easel. He had drawn a kind of map on it.

'Sit down,' he said, as if he really thought he was a general about to brief his officers.

It's true though, thought Cooley, that we all live more in our imaginations than we do in the real world. There's Mick dreaming of making well-off juicy widows happy in big soft beds. There's Crosbie wondering if he should rape me first and then cut my throat, or do it the other way round. Here's me thinking about them.

'What about a drink?' she asked. 'There's whisky, gin, and vodka.'

'I could do with a beer,' said Mick.

'No drinking,' said Duffy, sharply. 'We must have clear heads.'

'Is it all right if we smoke?' she asked. 'It'll help to steady our nerves.'

He nodded. 'Give them ash-trays.'

'Give them ash-trays yourself.'

'Where are the ash-trays, Duffy?' asked Crosbie. 'I'll get them.'

Cooley did not trust his meekness.

He fetched ash-trays from the sideboard. They had the name Caledonian Hotel on them.

'Your mother smokes, doesn't she, Duffy?' asked Mick.

Duffy nodded.

Mick puffed happily. If Mrs Duffy liked smoking why shouldn't she also like lying in bed with him?

'Ready now, general,' said Cooley.

'Duffy doesn't like you to call him general,' said Crosbie, with one of his evil leers.

'Then he shouldn't act like one.'

'You're just being sarcastic.'

'Take it easy, Cooley,' said Mick. 'We're in Duffy's house, remember. What do you want us to do, Duffy?'

'That declaration of war on the town hall wall,' said Duffy. 'I did it.'

'Johnny said it was you,' said Mick. 'I didn't believe him.'

'What declaration of war?' asked Cooley. 'When did you do it, Duffy?'

'Last night, when you were asleep.'

'I must have been sound. My God, you could have raped me and I wouldn't have known. Maybe you did. What does it say, this declaration of war?'

'It's been scrubbed off,' said Mick. 'Tell her, Johnny.'
Crosbie told her.

'Jesus!' was all she could say.

'Those taking part in a war should know what they are fighting for,' said Duffy.

'You've said it,' said Mick, nodding wisely. He scowled at Cooley. Just like a woman, he meant, giggling when men were talking seriously.

'What are we fighting for, Duffy?' she asked. 'Free fags and free beer? Up the revolution.'

'For truth and justice.'

Again all she could say was 'Jesus!' Words like those, she knew, were heard with suspicion and distrust even if it was the Prime Minister saying them in Parliament. Here was Duffy, a dunce, saying them to a refugee from reform school recently cured of clap, a swan-killer, and a curly-haired penis. No wonder she was speechless, especially when the penis said, solemnly: 'Me and Johnny are with you all the way, Duffy.'

Duffy was staring at her with hate. She had never seen such a look on his face before. There was a change in him all right. Was it because Porteous had hurt his pride? Cooley's own pride had been hurt a hundred times and she didn't really hate anyone, not even Mrs Porteous, but then she had never had a message from God.

'We know,' Duffy was now saying, 'that if the Russians and Americans stopped telling lies about each other and co-operated in peaceful activities instead of making nuclear bombs the world would be safer and happier. Forty million people die of hunger every year, while every day tons of food are wasted.'

'I saw that on television,' said Mick.

Everybody had seen it on television, thought Cooley, but it had made no difference. 'Are we going to fight the Russians and Americans?' she asked.

'Our war has to be fought here in Lightburn.'

Mrs Porteous, thought Cooley, probably made donations to Save the Children.

Suddenly she felt angry with Duffy. He didn't give a damn for anybody, not even his mother. He did good deeds out of principle, not kindness. He had said he liked the man upstairs but that was because Ralston was dying. Hadn't he once told her that the whole human race would destroy itself and deserved to?

'What do you want us to do, Duffy?' asked Mick.

'Tonight we are going to break into the public library and tear a page out of as many books as we can in two hours.'

Even Mick was aware of some incredibility and irrelevancy in such a proposal. 'Is it a kind of competition, Duffy?'

'Books contain lies,' said Duffy, with a vehemence that surprised Cooley.

He was wrong, too. Books contained imaginations or fantasies, which weren't the same as lies. Everybody that read the silly story about the girl in the milliner's who was really the daughter of a wealthy lord knew it was silly. They enjoyed it, especially if they were women, because their own lives were so dreary. Didn't most people dream of winning the football pools? It did no harm.

'Flockhart told us not to believe everything just because it was in print,' said Mick.

So even Mick had benefited from his education. Wonders would never cease.

Cooley waited for Duffy to do the really difficult part of the trick, which was to explain how it was all symbolical.

He shirked it, and began to talk about the plan drawn on the blackboard. 'This is the window where we'll get in. It's a lavatory window.'

'Is that symbolical?' asked Cooley.

'Won't it be snibbed?' That was Crosbie.

'I took the snib off this afternoon.'

'Smart work, Duffy,' said Mick.

'We'll need a ladder,' said Cooley.

'If we stand on Mick's shoulders we can reach it.'

Mick hunched his shoulders to show how big and strong they were.

'What about Mick?' she asked. 'Is he to stand on his own shoulders?'

'Mick will stay outside, to help us down.'

'Fuck it, Duffy, it'll be freezing cold,' said Mick.

'I want you to go to Chuck's and wait there.'

'I've only got about 30p.'

'I'll give you a pound.'

'You're not frightened, Duffy,' said Cooley. 'After three cokes Mick will blab out everything.'

'Don't listen to her, Duffy. I can keep my mouth shut.' He winked at Crosbie.

Duffy didn't notice but Cooley did. Mick wouldn't go to Chuck's but to Fat Annie's.

'We'll gather the loose pages in black plastic bags,' said Duffy.

Crosbie took out a lighter and flicked it into flame. 'They'll make a good bonfire.'

'No, Johnny. There must be no other damage, and nothing must be stolen.'

Mick grinned. 'It's a funny war, Duffy, nothing to be damaged and nothing to be stolen.'

'Why don't we burn the place down?' asked Crosbie. 'Then the school. Then a shop or two.'

Cooley couldn't resist saying: 'And Porteous's factory.'

'No,' said Duffy. 'Not yet.'

'Whatever you say, Duffy,' said Crosbie.

'You're the chief, Duffy,' said Mick.

Again they exchanged winks, and again Duffy did not notice.

That he thought he could get this pair of freaks to behave with restraint showed that in spite of the accurate map, the careful plan, the confident speech, and the calm manner he really was a Babe in the Wood. Not yet, he had said. Did he intend later to use them not only for arson but for murder too? Could she imagine him inciting them to burn down Mrs Porteous's house, while Mrs Porteous and Margaret were in it? Yes, she could. She should be doing something to prevent it therefore. But what?

'Why didn't you bring big Molly, Mick?' she asked.

'She wanted to come. She wants to look after you, Duffy, while your mother's away. I said it was all right by me.'

'I'm leaving tomorrow night,' said Cooley. 'Tell her to come then. Duffy could do with some company.'

'It's for Duffy to say. What about it, Duffy?'

Duffy was leering at Cooley in a way that reminded her of his disciple Crosbie.

He's asking me if I'd be jealous if Molly came here, she thought. Well, would I? Would I want him to suck my wee hard pears instead of her big bags of haggis? I love him, don't I? But shouldn't he be introduced to the joys of sex by somebody like her who's all body and no brain. If his mind is inflamed and disordered by repressed desire, what better poultice than Molly's big soft white loving body?

'Sunday night, about eight,' he said.

After the shitty business in the church, thought Cooley.

'I'll tell her,' said Mick, grinning.

CHAPTER FOURTEEN

Lightburn Public Library was a new brick building all on the one level for the convenience of the many infirm old ladies who used it. Its front looked on to a quiet street consisting mainly of the backs of shops. Behind it was a wasteland of whins, broom, nettles, and long grass. At that time of day Lightburn became a morgue, especially on a chilly wet night. It seemed to Cooley they could have played bagpipes without disturbing anyone.

Leaving his hat and coat under a bush Crosbie went first. A practised shopbreaker, he climbed agilely on to Mick's shoulders. The window was easily pushed open. Though it was small he quickly squeezed through, head-first.

Cooley hoped he got his head stuck in the lavatory pan.

But they soon heard him saying it was a piece of cake.

It was then Cooley's turn. Since, as well as small boobs, she had narrow shoulders and a skinny arse she had no difficulty in wriggling through, but as she descended on the other side one of her arms went into the pan, soaking her sleeve to the elbow. Never had she felt such a fool, not even when she had discovered she had gonorrhoea. She could have killed Crosbie for tittering.

They heard Duffy repeat his instructions to Mick, who was to be back at five minutes to eleven.

'Mick'll not go to Chuck's,' whispered Crosbie. 'He'll go to Annie's.'

'Maybe Friday night's somebody else's turn,' she said. 'What does his mother say?'

'Christ, Cooley, she doesn't know. She'd cut off his balls if she did.'

'Somebody should tell her then.'

'Somebody will.' Crosbie chuckled, as if he intended to be the clype himself.

Cooley lit a cigarette.

'Duffy said we weren't to smoke.'

'Duffy can go to hell.'

'You shouldn't talk like that about Duffy.'

'You can go to hell too.'

But when Duffy came through the window nimbly, with hardly a hair out of place, he at once ordered her to put out the cigarette.

She was minded to mutiny.

'Duffy said put it out.'

She wouldn't have admitted it but she was afraid of this little runt. Maybe one of his headaches was coming on. It was these according to Mick that made him homicidal. Also she still had to get the ten pounds from Duffy. So after a few defiant puffs she threw the cigarette into the lavatory pan.

Duffy shone his torch. They saw it floating.

'Take it out,' he said.

'Take it out yourself.'

'Duffy said take it out,' said Crosbie.

Was it his knife that was prodding her in the back? She picked up the soaked cigarette. 'Where will I put it?'

'We should make you eat it,' said Crosbie, chuckling.

'Put it in your pocket,' said Duffy.

She had to do it. She had no confidence that he would be able to, or would want to, restrain his swan-killer.

They went through the swing doors into the library.

Duffy showed them what he wanted done. He took down a book, tore a page from the middle, dropped it into a black plastic bag, and then replaced the book. He did the same with three other books.

Thinking of it it had seemed stupid, seeing it done it seemed stupider still.

'Is that all, Duffy?' asked Crosbie.

'That's all, Johnny. Just one page.'

He allotted them their sections. Cooley's was **Romantic Fiction**.

Crosbie had already begun. He had been ordered out of the library several times. This was revenge, but what pleased him more was that he was obliging Duffy.

For the first dozen or so books Cooley herself found some satisfaction in that what she was doing, though stupid, would give annoyance to Miss Purvis.

Soon, however, she was imagining that she had done well at school and this was her working as a librarian. Her hair was tidily arranged and she was wearing sensible clothes and shoes. She was polite to the crabbed old cunts who grumbled because the books they wanted weren't available. She was respectful to Miss Purvis. After work was over she would go dancing with David Martin. They were to be married and inherit the shop. They would be members of St Stephen's church. Between the pages of her hymn-book she would keep leaves of lavender.

Her reverie was interrupted. On the other side of the shelves Crosbie was whispering. Duffy, busy at the History Section, was out of hearing.

'Cooley.'

'What do you want?'

'There's a money-box in the desk. Bluenose keeps the fines money in it.'

'I know that.'

'This is Friday. All the week's fines will be in it. Maybe a whole month's.'

'So what?'

'You want money to go to London. Here's your chance to get some.'

'The desk will be locked.'

'That's nothing. Force it open. I'll lend you my knife.'

She wanted nothing to do with that knife.

'If you like I'll do it for you.'

'What about Duffy?'

'You go and talk to him while I'm doing it.'

'How will we get it out without him knowing?'

'I'll hide it up my jouks.'

If Duffy found out he'd blame Crosbie.

'All right, Johnny. I'll go and talk to him.'

On her way over to Duffy she paused to look out of the window. All she saw were garbage bins outside shops, some lamp-posts, and rain stotting on the street. It was very dreary. Yet she felt sad. She was going to London, nothing would stop her, but she had been born in Lightburn and though she had told herself and it too many times that she hated its guts she could not help feeling sorry that she was leaving it, perhaps for good.

She stood beside Duffy as he tore a page out of book after book.

'All you're doing,' she said. 'is ruining books.'

'You'll never understand.'

'It'll break Bluenose's heart.' Unexpectedly she felt sympathy for the librarian. Purvis loved her books in the way that mothers loved their children. She was often seen clasping bundles of them to her breast.

'They'll think it was done by vandals,' she said. 'Weirdo vandals. Proper vandals would tear the books to pieces.'

She thought she heard a click as Crosbie broke open the desk.

'You didn't tell them about breaking into the church,' she said.

'I haven't made up my mind yet whether or not to do that myself.'

So anointing hymn-books with shit was too sacred a task for sinners like her, Crosbie, and Mick.

'Have you filled your bag yet?' he asked.

'No. I got tired.'

'Well, you've had a rest.'

'Aye, aye, sir.'

It was hard, she thought as she went back to her shelves, to keep your own sense of humour when you were dealing with someone who had absolutely none. What Duffy was doing now, and what he was going to do in the chruch tomorrow night, were comical, but he could not see that, any more than a blind man could see his own face. Purvis, Porteous, and Milne were like him. Laughing at other people and at yourself was necessary if you weren't to become shut-in and desperate.

'I've got it, Cooley,' whispered Crosbie. 'I haven't opened it but it's heavy. There could be pounds in it. It's all yours.'

'Thanks, Johnny.'

'You'd like me if you got to know me better.'

Tell that to swans and cats and Sally Cooper, she thought.

At last Duffy gave the whistle to stop. Cooley's hands and armes were sore and tired. The three bags were full. Baa-baa black sheep, she thought. She felt a bit delirious. Maybe it was something she'd caught at the coup, or she wasn't completely cured of the clap, or else it was simply too strong a dose of Duffy's nonsense.

Crosbie had a bulge under his sweater. Cooley screened him from Duffy. She had thought of a way to get rid of Duffy while the money-box was thrown down to Mick.

'Better take a last look round, Duffy. Maybe some pages were dropped.'

She had dropped some deliberately.

'All right.'

As soon as he was gone Crosbie stood on the lavatory seat and looked out. Mick was standing below. 'Catch this, Mick. It's the fines box. It's for Cooley. She needs money to go to London.'

'Shouldn't we share it?'

'No, it's for Cooley.'

'Does Duffy know?'

'No. Don't tell him. Hide it under bushes.'

Mick caught the box and then the three bags.

Cooley and Crosbie were out and down on the ground before Duffy appeared at the window.

'Did you find any pages, Duffy?' asked Crosbie.

'The desk was broken into,' said Duffy. 'Who did it? What was taken?'

None of them wanted to answer.

Duffy waited.

'Look, it's raining and it's cold,' said Cooley.

'What was taken?'

'Christ, Duffy, just a box with some money in it,' said Mick.

'Who took it? Was it you, Cooley?'

'No, it wasn't, and I told you not to call me Cooley. It was Crosbie if you want to know.'

'She asked me to,' whined Crosbie.

'Hand it up to me. I'll put it back.'

'We think we should keep it,' said Cooley. 'Three to one, Duffy. You're outvoted.'

'We didn't take a vote,' said Crosbie. 'I vote for Duffy putting it back.'

'Taking it was your idea, you creepy bastard.'

'You shouldn't call me names like that, Cooley. Mick votes for putting it back. Don't you, Mick?'

'Sure.'

'So it's three to one, Cooley, but you're the one.'

Mick handed up the box to Duffy who went off with it.

'What's the matter with you, Mick?' she asked. 'Are you frightened of him?'

'I'm frightened of nobody.'

Crosbie chuckled. 'Except your mother, Mick.'

'Duffy's my pal.'

'Some pal!'

'He's going to give me three quid for Molly.'

'Did you go to Annie's, Mick?' asked Crosbie.

'Sure. But don't tell Duffy.'

'Was she pleased to see you?'

'She could hardly wait.'

'Were the weans in bed?' asked Cooley. 'Or are they allowed to watch?'

'Tell us about it, Mick.'

'Don't bother,' said Cooley.

'What an arse she's got, Johnny!'

'What did she give you this time?' asked Crosbie.

'Just a can of beer but I'm going back. She said she'd have some supper ready for me.'

'Did you ask her if I could come? You said you would, Mick.'

'I did, Johnny. She said some other time.'

'She doesn't want you, you creep,' said Cooley. 'Nobody does.'

'You'll call me a creep once too often, Cooley.'

Duffy reappeared at the window. Mick solicitously helped him down.

'It was a good idea putting it back, Duffy. The cops will know it couldn't have been us. If it had been us we'd have taken the money.'

'Good thinking, Mick,' said Crosbie.

'Let's get out of here,' said Cooley. 'I'm shivering.'

'Will we make a fire of these bags and heat her up?' asked Crosbie.

'They've to be put among the dustbins outside the shops.' said Duffy. 'They'll be taken to the coup.'

'Not till Monday,' said Cooley. 'Dustmen don't work on Saturdays.'

Duffy hesitated. He had forgotten that. 'We could take them to the coup ourselves.'

Even Mick was shocked. 'Christ, Duffy, it's nearly a mile.'

'And it's pitch-dark and pouring with rain,' said Cooley.

'Just stick them under bushes,' suggested Mick.

Crosbie agreed. 'They'd never be found, Duffy. People often dump rubbish there.'

Duffy as leader asserted himself. 'We'll put them where I said. They'll be safe there till Monday.'

They sneaked out and deposited the bags among the dustbins.

It seemed to Cooley that a bag stuffed with pages would look suspicious outside a fruit-shop but she was eager to get away, so she kept quiet.

'What's next, Duffy?' asked Crosbie. 'In the war.'

'The war's over,' said Cooley. 'There's been an honourable settlement. Peace with honour.'

'I was talking to Duffy.'

'Come to my house tomorrow night at seven,' said Duffy.

'Will we bring Molly?' asked Mick.

'Duffy said he wanted her on Sunday night,' said Crosbie. 'Isn't that right, Duffy?'

'Yes.'

Then Cooley and Duffy watched as Crosbie and Mick slunk away in the shadows. Tomorrow night, she thought, the two terriers from North Ireland would be waiting round some corner ready to pounce. Mick wouldn't run the risk of having his precious dick given a permanent black-and-blue erection. He'd leave Crosbie to be savaged. Rats weren't loyal.

She and Duffy set off for Kenilworth Court.

'You didn't warn Crosbie not to go near the library tomorrow,' she said. 'That's the kind of stupid thing he'll do.' Only he wouldn't do it because he was stupid, he'd do it because he was treacherous.

She saw that Duffy realised he had made a mistake in trusting Crosbie. She felt sorry for him. He wanted to be clever but hadn't the brains for it. He only half-understood things. He liked to think he was interested in big ideas like truth and justice, while other boys his age thought only of girls and football. She compared him with someone really clever, who did understand books and politics and who had educated parents to advise him. Like Stephen Telfer, Margaret Porteous's friend. He did silly things too, like painting the statue in the town square; but that had just been a joke, to make people laugh. Cooley herself had laughed at Burns's red nose. He had got away with it because he had the intelligence to know what the limits were. Even Mick Dykes had more of that kind of intelligence than Duffy.

CHAPTER FIFTEEN

Detective Sergeant Angus McLeod, nicknamed Teuchter, unlike his colleague George Milne, believed that honest youngsters, in Lightburn and elsewhere, far outnumbered the rascals. He had three of his own, one still at school, whereas George had none. A burly, genial, red-faced crofter's son from Skye, he did not need his grandmother's gift of second sight to know that the Lowlanders he worked with thought him slow-witted, especially as his accent sometimes became almost unintelligibly Highland when he got excited. He was determined one day to astonish them all, but being canny he had mentioned this ambition to no one, not even in Gaelic to his fair-haired cheerful wife Flora who also came from Skye. He had never worn a kilt in his life but liked hairy tweed suits that looked and, some said, smelled like heather.

To him and his assistant Detective Constable Harry Black was assigned the investigation of the extraordinary graffiti that had appeared on the town hall wall. However, since there were also eighteen unsolved burglaries on the books, he was told not to waste too much time on it.

Having had a strict religious upbringing in the Free Kirk, McLeod suspected it was the work of some well-meaning but too enthusiastic sect, though these were not numerous in the district. George Milne on the other hand had given his opinion that the words were subversive and therefore some extremist political organisation was to blame. These too were very scarce locally.

The first clue was provided by Flora, thanks to her remarkable memory. When out shopping she had noticed the words on the wall and had remembered seeing them somewhere before. She had searched through a bundle of religious tracts that she had accumulated over the years, and sure enough there it was, yellow in colour, with the words in question printed in black capitals. This particular tract, she recalled, had been pushed through the letter-box about two years ago. She had not set eyes on the person or persons delivering them. Every house in the avenue must have got one.

Every house in the town, damn near, her husband discovered. The name of the sect responsible for disseminating them was given as The Church of Christ the Redeemer and Scourger of Wickedness. He had never heard of it before, nor it seemed had anyone else. A telephone call to the printers in Glasgow produced little useful information. They had no idea where the headquarters of the sect were. As far as they could remember an old man with a white beard had come in one day about two years ago and ordered ten thousand copies. He had paid in advance in cash and a few days later had returned in a battered blue van to collect the tracts. They had not seen or heard of him since.

Ten thousand copies weren't all that many for a religious tract. In Lightburn alone there were almost that number of households. The police of neighbouring towns could not remember any such tract ever having been distributed there, but they admitted it could have been: what was more forgettable than a religious tract? It seemed though that the old fellow had picked on Lightburn to receive his message. Was he a native of the town anxious to save its inhabitants from hell-fire? Very likely, said McLeod, who himself had been brought up to believe in the torments of hell. Black was discreetly non-committal. (To his lady-friend, Fiona Campbell, however, he was self-piteously outspoken: 'How would you like to work with somebody that wears hairy suits and believes in hell?')

McLeod quickly came to the conclusion **that** since after all the message was on the side of the angels, and since it had already been scrubbed off, the best thing to do was to forget it.

Chief-Inspector Findlay agreed. In his view, kept to himself, promotion to Superintendent was not likely to be achieved by the prosecution of religious cranks while burglars, muggers, and vandals went uncaught and unpunished.

On Saturday morning, at five minutes past nine, McLeod received a telephone call from Miss Purvis to report that the public library had been broken into during the night.

McLeod knew Miss Purvis, who lived in the same part of the town as himself. Chronic dyspepsia, which had given a bluish tinge to her nose, had also caused her temper to be short. She was outraged by his calmness.

'How do I know if anything's been stolen?' she screamed. 'I've had a shock. I smelled cigarette smoke. My desk's been broken into. Come at once, please.'

'Some misguided pranksters, Harry,' McLeod said, on their way to the library.

They found the library door locked. Miss Purvis was taking no more chances. They had to bang on it.

They had expected to find chaos and destruction, but no, the whole place was as tidy as a church, as it always was. People grumbled at that. In other libraries nowadays you could relax and chat, but not in Miss Purvis's. Large notices commanded silence.

'Well, I'm glad to see no damage has been done,' said McLeod.

'My desk's been broken into. Isn't that damage?'

Yes, but it had been neatly done. Inside, the first thing he saw was a black money-box marked FINES. It was heavy. It was full of coins. It was locked.

'How much is in it?' he asked.

'Six pounds and eighty-five pence.'

'Was anything taken?'

'No. They must have panicked and fled.'

He smiled. Whatever the explanation that wasn't it. The intruders had gone about their business coolly. But what in God's name had their business been? Did Miss Purvis have a secret diary that somebody was after, for blackmail purposes? He grinned. He had seen too many thrillers on television.

'It's nothing to laugh at, Mr McLeod.'

'No, it isn't. What about books? Do you have any that are especially valuable? First editions and things like that?'

'If I had do you think I would have been allowed to keep them? They would have been taken to headquarters.'

He knew the reason for her bitterness. Not long ago she had been passed over for the position of chief librarian in favour of a man ten years younger, less experienced therefore, and not any better qualified.

'Books are heavy to carry,' he said, 'and not worth much. Financially speaking, of course.'

'They have considerable second-hand value nowadays.'

'Is that a fact? Have you noticed any missing?'

'I haven't had time to check. It will take days.'

'How did they get in?'

'You're the detectives, not me.'

'We'll soon find out. You didn't forget to lock the front door, did you?'

'Do you think I'm a fool?'

'People have forgotten to lock up banks before now. Well, we'll have a look round.'

He searched inside, Black outside. After a few minutes they met at the lavatory window.

'This is where they got in, serge,' called Black. 'There's mud on the ledge and lots of footprints.'

'And the lavatory seat's dirty. Ah yes, the snib is off the window.'

'I'd say there were three or four.'

'Some kind of silly prank, wouldn't you say, Harry?'

'In that case what about the desk being opened?'

'There's always somebody goes too far. Remember they didn't touch the money.'

'That's so.'

'Scout around, Harry. They might have dropped something.'

He himself returned to Miss Purvis. 'They got in through the lavatory window. It cost me five pence to find that out.' It was a joke but she did not appreciate it.

'I've never approved of that lavatory. There was none for the public in the old building.'

'We must move with the times, Miss Purvis.'

He was still not taking it urgently enough for her. 'The library opens at ten, Mr McLeod.'

'We'll be away by then.'

'How long will it take you to catch them?'

He shook his head. She had been reading too many detective stories. The shelves were full of them. Real life was different. 'To be honest with you, Miss Purvis, I doubt if we ever will.'

She was shocked. 'Why not? That's what you're paid for, isn't it? They must have left finger-prints.'

'Not on the box. It was wiped clean. In a place like this there must be thousands of finger-prints.'

'Haven't you got a list of young criminals?'

George Milne had, quite a long one, of delinquents actual and potential.

Black came in, shaking his head. He had found nothing. He had got his shoes muddied.

'I think you're right, serge. A stupid caper. Maybe they saw something like it in a film'

'To be truthful, Miss Purvis,' said McLeod, 'you've been lucky. You've no idea the sights Harry and I have seen. Sheer wanton destruction. Filth, too.'

'I could give you some names myself,' she said. 'I don't let them come into my library and make nuisances of themselves. I order them out. They don't like it. They would break in just for spite.'

'If it was spite they'd have wrecked the place. There was a school in Aberdeen burned to the ground by a boy of twelve, out of spite. Damage estimated at a quarter of a million pounds.'

'That awful girl Cooley could have done it. She's had the impertinence to argue with me. She's used foul language. She's never out of trouble.'

'It's not the sort of thing Helen Cooley would do. Is it Harry?'

'No, serge.'

'In any case our information is that she's left the town.'

They heard then a thumping on the outside door. Miss Purvis had locked it again.

Black went and came back accompanied by James Gilliespie, the fruiterer, in a brown overall, and carrying a black plastic bag stuffed with something. McLeod thought, rather foolishly, of cabbage leaves.

'This was outside my shop this morning,' said Gilliespie. 'We didn't put it there. Do you know what's in it?'

'I'm afraid I don't, Mr Gilliespie.'

'Pages. Pages out of books. I thought Miss Purvis might be interested.'

Miss Purvis shrieked. She looked into the bag. If it had contained bloody human remains she could hardly have shown more horror. She picked up one of the pages, glanced at it, whimpered the name of the book from which it had been torn, rushed to the shelves, took down that book, opened it, and found she was right. She was right too with the next three pages. Looking at a book she would wail that a page was missing. It wasn't really for it was in her hand but they all knew what she meant. McLeod was impressed. Not many librarians knew their books so well.

'Better go and see if there are any other bags,' he whispered to Black.

Black went off with Gilliespie, explaining the situation to him.

Miss Purvis was now in that state of fluttering nerves known locally as having canaries. 'Did you know that lots of people have a grudge against books?' she cried. 'Not just illiterates and hooligans. Councillors, too. Books are luxuries, they say. Do you know what Milton the poet called books? He called them the life-blood of master spirits. Yet less than a penny per person is spent on them in this country. Did you know that? We don't deserve to be called a civilised nation. The sooner the birch is brought back the better,' she added, somewhat contradictorily.

'To go to all that trouble, for what, Miss Purvis? A stupid joke, I'm thinking.'

'I don't think it was just a joke. I think it was more sinister than that.'

'Sinister?'

'Somebody wanted to show contempt for books.'

In that case why not burn the lot, like the Nazis?

Just then Harry Black came in carrying another stuffed bag. There was a third one outside, he said.

Miss Purvis looked as if she was going to faint. The rest of her face turning white made the blueness of her nose very noticeable.

Ten minutes later the detectives thankfully took their leave.

Miss Purvis's two assistants had arrived. Ordering them about gave her back some of her confidence.

McLeod had offered some advice. 'There's a chance that one of them will come back to do some gloating. So if any suspicious-looking character comes in give me a ring.'

In the car on the way to the golf club where a burglary had been reported Black said, with a grin: 'Well, serge, what do you think?'

'What do *you* think, Harry?'

'What about those smart Alecs from the High School that call themselves intellectuals? Like Dr Telfer's son and Mrs Porteous's daughter. Wasn't it them that painted the statue?'

'That was never proved, Harry.'

The truth was, no resolute attempt had been made to prove it. Somebody high up had decided that clever young people should not have their careers ruined because of a silly high-spirited escapade.

McLeod then had a flash of what later turned out to have been second sight. He wondered if there could be any connection between what had happened in the library and the writing on the town hall wall. Unfortunately he had lived so long among sceptical Lowlanders that he no longer trusted his intuitions.

After an hour or so of fruitless enquiries at the golf club they had been back at the station only a few minutes when Miss Purvis telephoned to say that 'that horrible boy Crosbie' had come into the library and was gloating.

'If he's being a nuisance,' said McLeod, 'call the police.'

'Aren't you the police?'

'We're C.I.D. You want the uniformed branch, Miss Purvis.'

'But you told me one of them might come back to gloat. Well, he's gloating all right.'

'Miss Purvis, if it was Crosbie that broke into the library and left that money-box behind then I'm the Loch Ness Monster.'

'I still think you should come and question him. He's weak-minded, isn't he? It should be easy to get the truth out of him.'

About as easy as getting milk out of a bull. Unless of course Crosbie felt like shopping someone.

'Very well, Miss Purvis, we'll be along shortly.'

McLeod found Crosbie in the reading-room, gloating all right but it was over the big breasts of a young woman in a newspaper. A sniffy old man waited impatiently for his turn.

'Hello, Johnny,' whispered McLeod, into the not very clean ear. 'How would you like to come out to my car for a minute or two?'

'What for?'

The old man became Crosbie's ally. 'Who are you?' he demanded.

'Detective Sergeant McLeod of the C.I.D.'

'If it's against the law to look at these pictures it should be against the law to publish them. They're just a temptation for the likes of young fellows like this. What do you want him for?'

'I'm making some enquiries and I think he may be able to help.'

'Take him away then.' The old man seized the newspaper. The girl in the picture could have been his grand-daughter. He was already slavering over her.

McLeod felt disgusted. He had no sympathy for the lechery of the old. Flora was amused. 'Remember you'll be old yourself one day, Angus.'

They sat in the car, McLeod and Crosbie in the back, Black in front.

'What were you doing in the library, Johnny?' asked McLeod.

'Looking at books. That's what libraries are for, isn't it?'

'But you can't read, Johnny.'

Crosbie leered. 'Who told you that? This is what I'm reading. It's good. Would you like me to give it to you when I'm finished with it?'

He had taken from his picket a paperback on the cover of which was depicted in gaudy colours an act of copulation, in the manner of animals, by a man and woman both naked.

Black stretched forward to see it.

'Filth,' muttered McLeod. 'Where did you get this?' A few months ago he had succeeded in having a newsagent in the town fined fifty pounds for selling pornography like this. Mrs Porteous had congratulated him.

'A pal gave it to me.'

'Mick Dykes, you mean?'

'Biggest dick in town,' murmured Black.

'You're not often in the library on Saturday mornings, are you, Johnny?' said McLeod.

'It's a free country. I can go where I want.'

'When you broke into the library last night, you and Mick, why didn't you take the money-box? Your finger-prints are all over it.'

'I don't know what you're talking about.'

McLeod's questioning was half-hearted. He was convinced that Crosbie for once was innocent. 'Where *is* Dykes?' he asked. 'I thought you and him were inseparables.'

'Maybe he's paying Fat Annie a visit,' said Black. 'I don't think Johnny's welcome there.'

McLeod frowned. He knew about young Dykes and Mrs Burnet – it was a joke at the station – but he did not find it funny like the others.

'Who's Fat Annie?' asked Crosbie, slyly.

McLeod opened the door. 'Get out.'

'What about giving me a lift home? For wasting my time.'

'The talk is that Archie Cooper's coming home on leave this week-end, Johnny,' said Black. 'With a mate.'

'What's that got to do with me?'

'They say he's going to get even with you for what you did to his sister Sally.'

'I did nothing she didn't want me to. It's your job to protect me.' With that he slammed the door shut and ran off.

'Miserable creature,' said McLeod, in pity and anger. 'All the same it is our duty to protect him. I wonder if Sergeant Milne's going to keep an eye on Cooper. For Cooper's own sake, I mean. It would be very foolish of the young man to spoil his career in the Army because of a rascal like Crosbie.'

'Serge, nobody in the town would believe Crosbie if he said it was Cooper that had blacked his eyes and bloodied his nose and mangled his privates.'

'That's enough, Harry. The boy may be a depraved beast but he has a mother who loves him.'

'Yes, serge.' Black managed not to smile. That evening though when he was telling Fiona he would roar with laughter. So would she.

CHAPTER SIXTEEN

On Saturday evening Cooley was sitting on the sofa in Duffy's living room, sullenly smoking, in her outdoor clothes, with her Singapore Airlines bag at her feet. She hadn't been able to persuade him to give up the raid on the church, and if she didn't take part in it herself she wasn't to get the ten pounds he had promised her.

Shit in itself didn't scunner her: it was natural, like fallen leaves. She didn't believe in God so hymn-books weren't sacred to her. Anything that would disgust Mrs Porteous should have pleased her. For those reasons she should have been looking forward to the visit to the church, but on the contrary every time she thought of it she grued. This wasn't because Mick Dykes and Johnny Crosbie were to take part. Well, it wasn't altogether that. There was another reason that she felt like a pain in her mind but couldn't put into words.

Duffy had his eyes shut and his hands clasped, like a priest praying before a holy ceremony. He had been busy up to a short time ago making preparations. He had tried to keep these secret.

They were waiting for Dykes and Crosbie.

'You're not human, Duffy,' she said.

She had said it to him before and he had regarded it as a compliment, but she could think of nothing that would express better what she felt about him.

In spite of her own contempt for people she needed their company. It had been the loneliness at the coup more than the cold and discomfort that she had found hardest to bear, so much so that she had talked to the rats. The person she hated most was the one she would have most liked to be.

She wanted what Mrs Porteous had, plenty of money, a big house, two cars, pearls, and expensive clothes.

God knew what Duffy wanted.

'All right,' she said, 'everybody's selfish, everybody's a liar, and every bastard that's got authority abuses it. I should know. But what about yourself, Duffy? Nobody could be more selfish than you. You've never given that much of yourself to anyone.' She put two fingers so close together that there wasn't room for a flea. 'Maybe you don't tell lies but you think them.'

He opened his eyes and gave her another smile that chilled her blood. Could she imagine him using that kitchen knife on her if she provoked him too far? No, but she could almost imagine him getting Crosbie to do it for him.

The door-bell rang.

'Look, Duffy,' he said, 'if you're really set on doing it we'll do it ourselves, you and me. You don't want to have anything more to do with that crummy pair.'

It rang again.

'Open the door, Helen,' he said.

Don't call me Helen, she screamed within. Yet he wasn't to call her Cooley either.

Perhaps they had brought Molly with them. Wee Cathie too. They didn't know yet about the job in the church. They probably hoped they were coming to a party, with drink, sex, and dancing.

She went and opened the door.

They stood grinning at her, the big ape and the small rat. It was strange how grins could be so different and yet so alike. Mick's was eager, friendly, and pathetic. Crosbie's was sly, secretive, and pathetic.

'We're a bit late,' said Mick. 'Johnny had to come by all the quiet ways. Archie Cooper's in town. Wee Cathie saw him and his mate going into a pub.'

'I'm not frightened of them,' said Crosbie.

'He wants Duffy to hide him the way he's been hiding you, Cooley.'

'Duffy's got another job for you.'

'What sort of job?'

'He'll tell you himself. Don't laugh. He wouldn't like it.'

'Why should we laugh? Is he in a good mood?'

Somehow the ordinary phrase 'a good mood' hardly applied to Duffy. 'I don't know what kind of mood he's in,' she said, tartly.

They went into the living room. Dykes and Crosbie stood like soldiers awaiting orders. Duffy was now both general and priest.

'Sit down,' he said.

'Thanks, Duffy.' They sat down on the sofa.

Cooley snatched up her bag and retired to a chair in the background.

'Can we smoke, Duffy?' asked Dykes.

Duffy nodded.

Dykes and Crosbie lit up.

So did Cooley, though it was her third in the last hour. The more cigarette smoke there was in the room the more annoyed Duffy would be, and the more annoyed he was the more human he'd become. So she hoped, anyway.

'Why didn't you bring Molly, Mick?' she asked.

'It's tomorrow night she's to come. Isn't it, Duffy? I told her. You never saw anybody more pleased, the silly cunt.' The word was spoken fondly. 'She really goes for you, Duffy. Cooley said you had a job for us. Whatever it is you'll find us game. But Johnny's got something to tell you first. Go on, Johnny, tell him.'

'Tell him what?' asked Cooley. 'Have you killed another cat, Johnny?'

'We're not talking to you, Cooley,' said Dykes. 'We're talking to Duffy.'

'I went to the library this morning,' muttered Crosbie.

Though he cringed and tried to look ashamed he was really gleeful inside. Cooley wondered if Duffy saw that.

'I told you he would,' she said.

Duffy was as patient as a priest.

'I didn't tell them anything, Duffy.'

'Johnny would never shop you, Duffy,' said Dykes. 'He likes you.'

They didn't know the danger they were in, thought Cooley. They hadn't seen those paintings.

'Who's them, Johnny?' asked Duffy, quietly.

'Teuchter and Flash Harry.'

Cooley explained. 'Detective Sergeant McLeod and Detective Constable Black. Friends of mine, I don't think. Black's called Flash Harry because he dresses like a dude.'

'Teuchter came into the reading room and said he wanted to speak to me,' said Crosbie.

'What were you doing in the reading room, Johnny? You don't usually go there on Saturday mornings, do you?'

Crosbie leered. 'I was looking at boobs in the newspaper. Bluenose wanted to throw me out but she didn't.'

'She was keeping you there till McLeod came,' said Cooley.

'Why did you go to the library, Johnny?' asked Duffy.

'I wanted to see Bluenose's face. She'd been greeting. Her eyes were red.'

'What did McLeod say to you?'

'It's all right, Duffy,' said Dykes. 'They know that if it had been Johnny who'd broken in he'd have taken the box with the money. That's what you wanted them to think, wasn't it? Smart thinking, Duffy.'

Cooley had a curious feeling that there were two Duffies in the room, the one watching the other all the time. Perhaps she was thinking of the two faces in the paintings.

'Did they say anything about the pages?' asked Duffy.

'They never mentioned them, Duffy.'

'The bags are gone,' said Mick. 'The other garbage is still there but not the bags.'

'Maybe Teuchter's not so dumb,' said Cooley. 'You should have hidden them under the bushes, general. Anyway, what difference does it make?'

She knew very well that Duffy would think it made a

great difference. There would be no shocks for the readers of the books. They would not be suddenly jolted from the world of make-believe into the world of reality. They would not be forced to face the truth about themselves.

She herself thought that was a load of crap.

At any rate he should know better now than to trust a vicious clown like Crosbie.

'Cooley said you'd another job for us, Duffy,' said Mick. 'Whatever it is Johnny and me are game.'

Duffy hesitated. For a few seconds Cooley thought that he was thinking of abandoning his silly war.

'Tonight,' he said, slowly, 'we are going to break into St Stephen's church.'

Mick Dykes was not only astounded, he was also greatly alarmed. Cooley remembered how superstitious he was.

'What the fuck is there to steal in a church?' he muttered.

'We are not going to steal anything.'

'Are we going to tear pages out of Bibles?' asked Crosbie, sniggering.

At least it was a better idea than Duffy's. 'Wouldn't that be enough?' asked Cooley.

Duffy ignored her. 'What we are going to do,' he said, 'is to put a spot of excrement on all the hymn-books in the first twelve rows.'

Mick was like a dog confronted by a hedgehog. His mind reached out to consider the matter and then drew back, baffled. 'Excrement?' he mumbled.

'Shit,' said Cooley.

'I know what it is,' he said, peevishly. It was its relevance in relation to hymn-books that puzzled him.

'Who are the members of St Stephen's?' asked Duffy.

'Mrs Porteous is one,' said Mick.

Once, in Dirty Chuck's, braving many jeers, he had confessed that of all the women in Lightburn Mrs Porteous was the one he fancied most.

'That's the church big Milne goes to,' said Crosbie, 'him and his humphy-backed wife.'

'Miss Purvis is a member,' said Duffy. 'So is Chief-Inspector Findlay. And Dr Telfer. All the people in Lightburn who think that you, Mick, and you, Johnny, and you, Cooley, and me are dirt beneath their feet.'

Cooley had to agree with him, but to complicate things *she* thought Crosbie was dirt beneath *her* feet, and Mick too because of his treatment of Molly.

'I see what Duffy's getting at,' said Crosbie. 'They're all snobs. He wants to show them that they're as common as shit, like us. Is that it, Duffy?'

'That's it, Johnny.'

There was no doubt about it. If Duffy gave the order this disciple of his would cut throats.

Mick still had qualms. 'I don't like monkeying about in a church. It's unlucky. We'd have to go through the graveyard.'

'With all the corpses rising out of their graves and rattling their bones at you, Mick,' said Cooley.

'It's not funny, Cooley.' Seeking practical objections, he lowered his voice. 'Where would you get all the stuff?'

'Duffy's got it ready, in a biscuit tin with a picture of Bonnie Prince Charlie on the lid.'

'The arrangements have been made,' said Duffy.

'Is it worth it, Duffy? All that trouble? What would we get out of it?'

'Mick's right,' said Cooley. 'It might be worth it if we could be in church tomorrow to see their faces, but we can't. Anyway, I'm catching the bus for Glasgow tonight.'

'What will we put it on with?' asked Mick, with a shudder.

'Our fingers,' said Crosbie, gleefully.

'The arrangements have been made,' repeated Duffy.

Cooley could not resist saying, 'We'll let you do Mrs Porteous's, Mick.'

He cheered up. 'I'd like that.'

There were many queer ways of showing love, she thought, but surely none queerer than that.

CHAPTER SEVENTEEN

St Stephen's church had been built in 1846, three years after the Great Disruption in the Church of Scotland, when the prosperous seceders of Lightburn, determined to prove the sincerity of their allegiance to Christ the King and at the same time to confound their opponents, had erected the most massive structure they could afford, of grey stone, with a soaring steeple and solid, dignified, though hardly comfortable interior furnishings. In time, as bigotry waned, stained glass windows and an organ had been installed. The kirkyard was like a small wood, with some full grown trees. The roots of these gave trouble to the gravediggers as did the leaves in autumn to the caretakers, but the congregation liked to think of their departed relatives and friends as lying snug beneath the spreading branches, sung to by birds. It was the custom on dry days for worshippers to chat reverently amidst the trees, but on cold dark nights in March the kirkyard was deserted, save for homeless cats or foraging owls or even a wandering fox.

It was easy therefore for Duffy's small army to creep through the gates and among the trees up to the back door without being seen. He carried the biscuit tin wrapped in airtight silver foil. In his pockets he had the rest of the equipment: four small wooden spoons, the kind used for supping ice-cream, and four plastic cups that had once contained assorted yoghurt.

Gravestones came close to the back door. The nearest had an angel on top. Cooley slung her airbag over a wing. In the light from distant street lamps many other gravestones could be seen. Once or twice she thought they were moving towards her, but it was the effects of shadows.

To her amusement her hand was gripped by Mick's. His was cold and stiff, and his teeth were chittering.

Duffy and Crosbie were trying to open a small window at the side of the door.

'I don't like it here,' muttered Mick.

'Why not? It's nice and quiet and it's out of the wind.'

'It's not lucky to disturb the dead.'

'They can't be disturbed, Mick. They're just maggots and bones.'

'What about their souls?'

He had seen too many horror films.

Duffy and Crosbie had succeeded. Some dunts had loosened the catch. Though the window was narrow it was close enough to the ground for them to be able to squeeze through easily, except for Dykes whose difficulty was caused not so much by his bulk as by his being paralysed with superstitious fear. Cooley felt him. He was as rigid as a corpse. He couldn't speak. He couldn't even chew.

She felt sorry for him, especially as Crosbie was in a state of ghoulish delight. 'You'll be safer in the church, Mick; well, warmer anyway.'

They went through the vestry. By the light of Duffy's torch they saw the minister's black gown hanging from a peg. Crosbie put it on and began to snuffle through his nose in an imitation of Mr Cargill. Cooley couldn't help laughing. Mick though was appalled and showed it by trying to speak, like Frankenstein's monster.

As she went into the vast creaking church Cooley wished there was something she could do to excuse the intrusion and propitiate God if He happened to be there, hiding behind one of the great stone pillars. If she had been a Catholic she could have crossed herself. All she could think of was to put her fingers to her nose. It wasn't intended as a gesture of impudent defiance, though Mr Cargill and his parishioners would have seen it as such.

While Crosbie held his torch, Duffy, kneeling on the stone floor, unwrapped and opened the tin. As if it had contained myrrh, whatever myrrh was, he spooned portions into the four cups.

'Jesus!' Cooley held Mrs Duffy's handkerchief, soaked in scent, to her nose. She made up her mind to take no further part.

Like someone assisting a priest, Crosbie, in the black gown, came and handed Mick his cupful and spoon.

Cooley refused to take hers. 'Count me out. I'm going to be sick.'

'Duffy said you'd to take it.'

'Duffy can go to hell.'

He cried: 'Duffy, she'll not take it.'

Duffy came up to her. 'What's wrong?'

'My stomach's turning, that's what's wrong. You wouldn't ask Margaret Porteous to do this, would you?'

'Why did you come?'

Because I thought I could protect you, you nutter, she yelled within, and because I need that ten pounds. Outwardly she mumbled, through the handkerchief: 'I said I'd come but I didn't say I would play with shit. I stopped doing that when I was a year old.'

'We are not playing. This is war.'

'Balls!'

'In war the penalty for refusing an order is death.'

She looked closer to see if he was joking. He certainly wasn't grinning from ear to ear. 'You're an idiot, Duffy.'

'Johnny, have you got your knife handy?'

'Sure, Duffy.' Crosbie had it out in a flash. It glittered like his eyes.

'I don't believe this,' she said.

She got ready to knee Crosbie in the goolies as hard as she could.

The knife was almost touching her throat.

'You're going too far, Duffy,' she said.

'All you have to do is to say you will obey orders.'

'Who the hell do you think you are?'

'Duffy's the leader,' said Crosbie, giggling.

'Mick, aren't you going to do something?' she asked.

But Mick, all his bounce and brag gone, was no help.

'All right,' she said, giving in, not because she was afraid but because she wanted that ten pounds.

Duffy then demonstrated. He opened a hymn-book at random and put a small spot between the pages. Cooley was reminded of a Catholic friend of her childhood, Bridget Flanagan, who every Ash Wednesday had had ash daubed on her brow.

'Just that much?' asked Crosbie, disappointed. 'They'll never notice it.'

'And it'll take hours,' said Cooley.

She made up her mind then to bring some sense into the proceedings, or at any rate what would look like sense by comparison. 'Why not just pick a dozen or so of the worst bastards and make a decent job of their hymn-books? It wouldn't take long and it'd certainly be noticed. Porteous, to begin with. Milne. The minister. Rob Roy.' Mr McGregor was headmaster of the High School. 'Big Bella.' Miss Isabel McKenzie was senior woman adviser. 'Chalmers, the Fiscal. Guthrie, the lawyer. Councillor Grant who says school-leavers that can't get jobs should be put in the Army. That's eight. I'm sure they're all members of this church. Maybe you can think of two or three others.'

'Chief-Inspector Findlay is head of the police in Lightburn,' said Duffy. 'He is a member of the church.'

'So's Martin that owns the furniture shop,' she said. He was also David's father and had blamed Cooley for giving his son the pox when it had been the other way round. 'He's also in the Rotary.'

'Dr Telfer,' said Crosbie. 'He told my dad I just pretended to have headaches.'

'Do you?' asked Cooley.

'No, I don't. Sometimes I can't stand the pain. Ask Mick.'

'If I asked Mick his name he couldn't tell me.'

'What about Teuchter?'

'Teuchter's all right for a cop, and he's got a nice wife. Anyway he belongs to the Free Church.'

It had no steeple, no Cross, and no stained glass windows. Visitors to the town often mistook it for a warehouse.

'Let's get started,' she said. 'Maybe we'll think of somebody else.'

She felt relieved. It was now a more or less straight-forward, though still disgusting, act of revenge against some of the most conceited and snobbish people in the town. There was no nonsense about symbolical. It wouldn't make them more humble and less hypocritical. It would make them furious. Their self-esteem would get a shock though, especially if it became a joke in the town, like the painting of Burns's statue.

It was easy enough tracking down the hymn-books, for to every pew in the front rows was affixed a card on which were typed the names of its occupants. There was no hymn-book with Mr Martin's name on it but there were two with his wife's name on them: both of these were liberally spread with the foul-smelling jam. Handkerchief at nose, Cooley did not do any of the anointing herself – the word kept occurring to her – but left it to Crosbie and Duffy and, in the case of Mrs Porteous's hymn-book, Mick. She found herself laughing, a little hysterically, as she watched Mick plastering on the filth with loving care. Mrs Porteous's was the fanciest hymn-book there. Bound in a dark-blue velvety cloth it had an inscription in it: 'To my darling Elizabeth. John.'

Last to be given the treatment was the minister's big Bible, up in the pulpit. Crosbie offered to do it but Duffy wanted to do it himself. He did not immediately come down but remained for two or three minutes. He looked as if he was praying.

She had never felt more impatient with him. He was no more a mystery than she was or Mick or Crosbie. It was all put on. Though she wasn't yet seventeen she had long ago learned that people were easy to understand so long

as you kept in mind that in everything they did they were
seeking their own advantage. They tried to disguise their
selfishness in a great variety of ways, Porteous for instance
by appearing to be charitable and Councillor Grant by
professing to be patriotic. Duffy was no different. This
war of his was in revenge for his having no father, for
not having done well at school, for not living in a villa, for
not having Margaret Porteous as his girl-friend, and most
recently for having been rejected by Mrs Porteous. All his
talk about showing up hypocrisy and making people face
the truth was baloney.

'For Christ's sake, Duffy,' she shouted, 'we're in a hurry
to get away. This place stinks.'

Five minutes later they were out in the fresh air again,
and never had it smelled fresher. Cooley wiped her hands
on the wet grass. The angel had looked after her bag
faithfully. 'Thanks,' she said, as she took it down. She
really did feel grateful. The nightmare was over. In an
hour or so she would be on a bus for Glasgow.

Duffy was clutching the biscuit tin. In it were the soiled
spoons and cups.

'You'd better get rid of that,' she said. 'If the cops
stopped you they'd want to see what was in it. Wouldn't
they get a surprise.'

'She's right, Duffy,' said Mick, who was recovering now
that he was out of the church. 'They stopped me last week
and made me show them it was fish suppers I was carrying.
They stole some chips.'

'Toss it over the wall,' she said.

'I'll do it, Duffy.' Crosbie ran with it among the graves
to the high stone wall beyond which was a wood.

They crept towards the gates. There they paused under
a large yew-tree. Duffy was subdued. Cooley had to take
command.

'We'd better go one at a time,' she said. 'Patrol cars often
come along this avenue, looking after the property of the
toffs. You go first, Mick. Give Annie my regards.'

'O.K.'

'I might never see you again, Mick, so look after yourself. I hope your dick grows another two inches at least.'

He wasn't sure how to take that. 'I'll remind Molly she's to go and see you tomorrow night, Duffy.'

'I don't think she'll need reminding,' said Cooley.

They watched Mick creep out of the gates and along the avenue.

'Will he go to Annie's?' asked Cooley.

'He'll have to wait in the coal-cellar,' said Crosbie. 'Men visit her on Saturday nights. They bring her drink and pay her money. Mick's got to wait till they've gone.'

'She's just a fat whure.'

'Everybody knows about her and Mick except Mick's mother. They're frightened to tell her in case she kills Mick.'

'I expect you'll tell her yourself, Johnny. You'd better go.'

'You wouldn't like to give me a goodbye kiss, would you?'

'No, I wouldn't.'

He laughed and turned to Duffy. 'Will I come to your house on Monday night, Duffy?'

'All right, Johnny.' Duffy sounded as if it was he and not Crosbie that had the unbearable headache.

'Have a good time with Molly, Duffy.'

They watched him go through the gates and disappear.

'You didn't warn him to keep away from the church tomorrow,' she said. 'You're stupid if you have anything more to do with him. You'll end up murdering somebody. Are you feeling all right?'

'Yes.'

'You don't look it. What about the money, Duffy?' After all she'd earned it.

He took two five pound notes from his pocket and gave them to her.

'Thanks. These might save my life. Well, Duffy, this is goodbye.'

'I'll walk with you to the bus-stop.'

'No. It'll be safer if we go alone.'

'Will you be all right?'

'Who cares?'

'I care.'

'You've a funny way of showing it.'

'You have relatives in Glasgow, haven't you?'

'Don't worry about me. I can take care of myself. I wish I could say the same about you. Be kind to big Molly. Somebody has to be. Maybe I'll drop you a line some time. Give me a couple of minutes to get clear. So long.'

'Goodbye, Helen.'

She hurried away then, after a last long look into his face. She saw no affection there. Like her he had not let himself get into the habit.

She found there were tears in her eyes. Behind her she heard what she at first thought was him laughing. But she had never heard him laughing even quietly, far less screaming with laughter like that. It must have been a bird or an animal in the wood, perhaps a rabbit caught in a snare.

CHAPTER EIGHTEEN

He should have been glad that she was gone and he would never again have to endure her taunts and provocations.

'Maybe you don't tell lies, but you think them.'

'You wouldn't ask Margaret Porteous to do this, would you?'

'You've never given that much of yourself to anyone.'

'You'll end up by murdering somebody.'

When he had ordered Crosbie to threaten her with the knife a part of him had been in deadly earnest. She was not only a hindrance but also a danger. If she had thought he was going too far she might have betrayed him, for his own good she would have claimed. Therefore it was as well that she was gone.

Why then from this doorway was he watching her anxiously as she waited in the bus shelter? Why was he having to restrain himself from running across the street and begging her not to go? And why, when the bus at last came, after nearly forty minutes by the town hall clocks, did his feeling of desolation increase as he saw her get on, with her bag slung over her shoulder?

He needed her. Whenever he had been tempted to deceive himself she had made him face the truth.

The bus disappeared round the corner at Martins' big furniture shop. As clearly as if he had been sitting beside her he saw her grinning self-contemptuously at the dream she had had of marrying David Martin and living in comfort and respectability. Instead she had got VD and the blame of giving it to him. Yet she had made a joke of it. 'If I couldn't laugh at myself I'd go off my head. That's what's going to happen to you, Duffy.'

Those whose purposes were as serious as his could not afford to laugh at themselves. Nowhere in the Bible did it say that Jesus Christ had ever done so.

As he walked slowly home, he heard her voice, affectionate but mocking: 'Tell the truth, Duffy. You ruined the library books because you never won prizes at school like Margaret Porteous and Stephen Telfer. Remember that picture of her with armfuls? And in the church tonight you weren't trying to show them they were as common as shit. You did it because you envy them. I was wrong when I said you weren't human. You just won't admit it.'

Tomorrow night he was going to admit it, when Molly McGowan came to his house. He would do with her what Mick Dykes and Johnny Crosbie and many others had done. There would be this difference in his case: the act by which he would acknowledge his common humanity would also leave him purged of many impure longings.

He could not continue to wage his war against lies and arrogance if he himself was not truthful and humble.

He had been home less than fifteen minutes when the door bell rang. It could not be Mrs Munro this time for on Saturday nights she went to Bingo. In any case the thumb on the button was too gentle for hers, or for Cooley's. It could be Molly, too shy to press hard. Through over-eagerness and typical confusion she had come a night too soon. He was not ready for her yet. His mind had to be prepared with prayer or meditation.

It was Mrs Ralston, wearing a red dress and white slippers with red pom-poms.

'Sorry to trouble you, Duffy,' she whispered. 'Have you got company?'

'No.'

'I thought Helen Cooley was staying with you.'

'She's gone.'

'Oh. Well, if you've a minute to spare, Duffy, Jack would like to see you.'

'What for?'

She smiled. 'To say goodbye, I think. He's always liked you, Duffy.'

She breathed quickly, as if she had been running. There was something false about her smile.

He heard Cooley's voice in his mind: 'It's not Jack that wants you, it's the wee darkie herself. Look, she's just had a bath, she smells like roses, and under that dress she's got very little on: though that's not the only reason why she's shivering. She wants you to comfort her. And couldn't you do with some comforting yourself?'

'I'm just in,' he said.

'Take your time. Come up when you're ready.'

'All right.'

'I'll leave the door open.'

She gave him another false smile and then hurried upstairs.

In the bathroom he washed his hands, for the second time since his return home. He was thinking of Mr Ralston, who would be dead in a day or two.

A minute or two later he was knocking quietly on the open door.

'Come in, Duffy,' she called. 'Shut the door.'

He had been in her house before and had admired the bright optimistic colours of the wall-paper, carpets, and loose covers. His mother on the other hand, invited up for a neighbourly cup of tea, had said that the china geese on the wall and the big picture of a wood in autumn with Bambi-like deer showed vulgar taste. 'But what else would you expect from somebody from the Gorbals?' She had been envious of Mrs Ralston's slim figure, and had attributed it, like the swarthiness, to some disease. 'I don't trust people who are always cheerful when by rights they should be miserable and ashamed.'

Mrs Ralston asked him to sit beside her on the orange sofa, in front of the gas fire. In her cheap red dress she was more elegant than Mrs Porteous in her expensive tweed costume. She had tea ready, the pot inside a tartan cosy, the cups and saucers white with gold designs, and the small milk jug and sugar bowl silver. (Imitation silver, his mother had said.) There were chocolate biscuits and serviettes of white lacy paper.

Again he heard Cooley's voice: 'When Mick visits Fat Annie he has to drink beer out of cans.'

Amidst Mrs Ralston's perfume he smelled disinfectant. There was no sound from the dying man.

'Jack's dozed off again,' she said. 'He's due his medicine in another ten minutes.' She glanced at the gilt clock on the mantelpiece. 'It's to dull the pain. There's no cure. We're just waiting for what the doctor called a merciful release.' She smiled, as she poured the tea. 'See the photograph?' It stood beside the clock. 'Guess who they are?'

He knew it was her wedding photograph. In her white dress she was beautiful, with her hair blacker than it was now. How eagerly and courageously she was looking forward to her new life!

'I was just eighteen,' she said. 'Jack wasn't twenty. We were too young. Don't make that mistake, Duffy.'

She hadn't been able to prevent Cissie making it.

'They used to say my mother must have had an affair with an Italian,' she said. 'Because of my darkness. We went to Dunbar for our honeymoon. Jack would have preferred Blackpool, but I wanted somewhere quiet. I was very romantic in those days. Dunbar's a small fishing port on the east coast. It was June but freezing cold. There was a wall at the harbour with dozens of birds' nests in it: kittewakes. They flew about crying "Kittewake, kittewake." We were very happy there but somehow we never went back.' She smiled. 'We've been to Blackpool four times.'

They heard noises outside on the landing, stumbling steps, mumbles, and a door slamming shut.

'That's Billy Stuart getting back,' she said. 'He was at Dundee watching the Rangers. I see they won. Agnes will be relieved. It was a cup-tie. Billy's a nice young man and he's fond of her but when Rangers get beat he drinks too much and gives her a clout if she complains. Why do men think it's the most important thing in the world for their team to win? Jack was the same in his young days, only his team was Partick Thistle and they lost so often he got used to it. Not that he would ever have lifted his hand to me. You're not interested in football, are you, Duffy?'

'No.'

'You must be the only boy in Lightburn that isn't. You'll not have heard from your mother yet? No, it's too soon. This man she's gone with, he'd be a fool not to marry her. She'll be going off to live in Bearsden among the toffs. She'll hold her own among them too. So will you, Duffy.'

She gazed at him over the rim of her cup. Like his own her eyes were brown, but unlike his they revealed her feelings. She was again breathing quickly.

'I'm going to ask you a very cheeky question, Duffy. If you think it's none of my business just say so. But your mother's not here to look after you, and I've known you since you were a toddler of three, so maybe I have some kind of a right to ask it. Did you sleep with Helen Cooley while she was staying with you? I don't just mean sleep.' She smiled, finding it difficult to explain to a simpleton without having to use words too simple and therefore too crude. 'The reason I'm asking is that she's been attending the clinic in Lochinvar Street, where they treat VD. You know what that is?'

'I think so.'

She smiled. 'You're too pure-minded for this world, Duffy.'

'She said she was cured.'

'And you believed her?'

'Yes.'

'You would. You trust everybody. Poor Duffy. Well, if you did sleep with her, and if in a day or two you notice a sore or a discharge, you must go at once to the clinic yourself.'

'I didn't sleep with her, Mrs Ralston.'

'Well, that's a relief.'

He wondered if she was aware how loudly she was panting.

'Have you ever been with a girl, Duffy? You know what I mean.'

He hardly recognised her because of the falseness of her smile. What she was about to do, seduce him, was against her nature. He knew the stresses causing it: her husband's dying, her daughter's unsuccessful marriage, and her grand-daughter's fatal deformity.

The only way he could think of to let them both escape from this situation was by his being childishly naive.

'Could I have another chocolate biscuit, please?' he asked, in a voice that suited the request.

She stopped breathing altogether. When she resumed, after a sad-sounding gasp, she no longer panted, and her smile was genuine.

'Help yourself,' she said, passing the plate.

A minute later she got up, saying she would go and see if Jack was awake.

He nibbled his biscuit, making sure no crumbs fell on the carpet.

He had never before spoken to someone close to death. There would be no deceit on Mr Ralston's part: there must be none on his. It might be too severe a test of his truthfulness and humility.

Mrs Ralston came back. He noticed for the first time how much grey there was in her hair. 'You can come now, Duffy.'

The bedroom had been freshly sprayed with disinfectant. In the bed, in white red-striped pyjamas too big for him, Mr Ralston was shrivelled to the size of a ten-year-old child. He had always been quick in his movements, now even a wink was slow, requiring effort. His face was grey and hollow, but in his eyes were still gleams of recognition and humour.

'Hello, Duffy,' he said, in a low hoarse voice.

Duffy had to go closer. There was a bedpan covered by a white cloth. 'Hello, Mr Ralston.'

'Got a job yet?'

'No.'

Mr Ralston winked. 'What's more important, got a girl?'

Duffy wondered if, to be truthful, he should say yes, meaning Molly McGowan, considering her visit tomorrow night, but he shook his head.

'Duffy's got more sense,' said Mrs Ralston.' He's waiting for the right girl.'

'Take a chance, Duffy. Never be afraid to take a chance. How's your mother? The best-looking woman in Lightburn, bar one.'

'I told you she'd gone to Spain for a holiday,' said Mrs Ralston, 'with her gentleman friend the whisky salesman.'

'What a job!' Mr Ralston smiled. He was falling asleep.

'The medicine makes him sleepy,' said Mrs Ralston.

Here, thought Duffy, was another war being waged, with Mr Ralston's body the battleground. The enemy was invisible but deadly.

Not long ago Duffy had read about a new drug which it was claimed would be able to break down the defences that many disease-causing bacteria built up against all known anti-biotics. The chemists who had produced it had admitted that in ten or twenty years these bacteria would have acquired defences against their drug too. Duffy had wondered for what purpose bacteria had been given this uncanny power to keep adapting so that they could go on killing. It had seemed to him to call in question the purpose of life itself. But surely so remorseless and universal an enemy ought to have caused human beings everywhere to unite to fight it. They would do so only if they could be made to feel in their hearts kinship with and responsibility for one another.

That, he thought, was what I was trying to do in the church.

Mr Ralston managed to open his eyes. 'Will you come to my funeral, Duffy?'

Mrs Ralston shook her head, letting Duffy know that he needn't take this invitation on request seriously.

'Yes, Mr Ralston, I'll come.'

'Your mother's invited too.' Then he was asleep. Indeed Duffy thought he had died.

'The doctor said he'll just pass away like that,' said Mrs Ralston, as she made her husband comfortable. 'I hope so.'

They went back to the living-room.

'It won't be long now,' she said. 'It's to be at the crematorium in Flemington.' That was a town about eight miles away. 'There's to be no religious service. Sit down, Duffy. Keep me company for a wee while. You've got nobody waiting for you. Would you like another chocolate biscuit?'

'No, thank you.'

'I don't think I'll stay here, afterwards. My sister in Toronto wants me to go and live with her. I've been to Canada and liked it. Jack said I should go. I wasn't to waste my chances because Cissie's wasted hers. I'm still a young woman. He said I should get married again. What's happened to Cissie just about broke his heart but he's never blamed her once or even that little rotten beast she's married to. He was such an optimist. He believed that one day poverty and war would be abolished. Even when he was stone sober he still believed that. Yet he's been trying the football pools for twenty years and never won anything.'

It was cold but dry as he set off. Even if he had not been carrying a Bible anyone could have guessed that he was going to church, he was dressed so neatly, smiled so decorously, and walked so carefully. He did not want to arrive with his shoes sullied with mud or dogs' dirt. Most people attending St Stephen's went by car. None came from his part of the town.

After last night's visit to Mr Ralston he too felt optimistic. He was not going to St Stephen's as a spy to observe the enemy's rage and disgust but rather as a secret ally whose good services on their behalf they would probably not appreciate at the time but would do so afterwards in private, some of them at any rate, in particular Mrs Porteous. If the trouble that had caused her to weep had its origin in pride, which was very likely, then by humbling her he might well have consoled her too.

He passed three old women dressed in black. He would have known they were Catholics even if they had not been clutching rosaries. He had once heard Mrs Munro say, of a Catholic neighbour, 'she's got the map of Ireland in her face.' That was an exaggeration but it was true that, because of their self-imposed segregation and their belief that God belonged to them, Catholics had acquired a difference, not easily described, which even Protestants as crude-minded as Mrs Munro and Mick Dykes could recognise at a glance. Mrs Munro had vowed to disown her son if he married a Pape. Mick boasted that he would never have sex with a girl if she was a Catholic. Crosbie claimed that he only killed Catholic cats.

He was early. There were only three cars in the car-park

on the opposite side of the road to the church. They were all foreign, a Datsun, a Volvo, and a Saab. Well-off people who proclaimed themselves patriots seldom bought British cars, saying that they were not as good value for money. They said British workers were always going on strike for ridiculous reasons.

Money and class, like religion, divided people. So many things did. So few things brought them together.

In spite of these grim reflections he still remained hopeful. Cooley would have jeered that it was because he was going to see Margaret Porteous in a minute or two. So it was, but there were other reasons.

A green Citroen drove into the car park. In it were Mr McLachlan who owned Lightburn Motors which special-ised in Citroens, and his wife and daughter Maureen. Maureen had been a dunce at school. To save her from the shame of being put into 4Y along with girls like Cooley and Molly McGowan she had been taken from the High School and sent to a private school in Glasgow.

The McLachlans passed Duffy. He smiled but Maureen turned her head away. She hated him because he too had not done well at school. If he had been brilliant she would have hated him for that too.

He heard her explaining scornfully: 'His name's Duffy. He lives in Kenilworth Court. His mother works in the Caledonian Hotel.'

Her mother turned to give him an indignant stare but her father laughed good-humouredly. 'Hell, isn't a church supposed to be open to everybody? The boy's doing no harm. I've a good mind to ask him to join us.'

'Don't you dare, Daddy!'

'And watch your language, John,' snapped his wife.

Dr Telfer's car arrived. It was a yellow Rover. Five people came out of it, the doctor himself, Mrs Telfer, their two daughters, and Stephen who had been driving. Tall and fair-haired, he was Margaret Porteous's friend, a prize-winner, the present school captain, the next dux, and a future doctor. He was laughing at some remark he had made which his sisters, one aged twelve and the other fourteen, had apparently not found as witty as he thought they should. Duffy wondered if it had concerned him and had been malicious, but it couldn't have been for, catching sight of Duffy hanging about by himself, Stephen sauntered over, with a friendly grin. 'Hello. Your name's Duffy, isn't it? I remember you. You used to come to school debates, didn't you? Are you waiting for somebody? If you're on your own why not join us?'

'Thank you. I'm waiting for Mrs Porteous.'

Telfer was surprised. 'Good. They should be along soon. They're often late. It's a white Merc. Be seeing you,'

Duffy heard the older of the girls ask eagerly about him. 'He's awfully good-looking,' she said. 'Isn't he, Amy?'

Amy, peeping back, giggled.

Mrs Telfer, a big cheerful woman, gave Duffy a wave.

The church bells had begun to ring.

He had said that he was waiting for Mrs Porteous, and so he was; but he had omitted to say that Mrs Porteous might not be expecting him, or that, when she saw him, she might not be pleased. She had not really promised to take him into church with her.

Cars now kept arriving all the time. Among them was Mr Flockhart's ten-year-old Cortina. Mrs Flockhart was pregnant. As always she looked sullen and sorry for herself. It had astonished 4X that Mr Flockhart who knew by heart many lines of poetry about love and beautiful women should have married one so peevish, plain, and flat-chested. It wasn't any wonder, Duffy's mother had admitted, that Mr Flockhart showed interest in other women, though as a teacher he should be setting a better example. That morning Mr Flockhart was interested, though at a distance, in a young woman with auburn hair and shapely legs. She was Miss Bremner who taught French at the High School. She was chaperoned by her mother who wore a pink hat. Most of the older women, like Mrs Milne, bent double with rheumatism, wore hats.

The sun had begun to shine. The big yew-tree at the

gate glittered. People on their way into church paused to chat to friends. The elders in their morning dress were at their posts at the door.

Duffy began to be afraid that the Porteouses were not coming that morning. Perhaps Mrs Porteous felt too unhappy.

Then, while the bells were still ringing, the big white car appeared, travelling fast. Margaret was driving. She was bare-headed but her mother wore a green hat. She also wore a fur coat. There were many fur coats among the congregation.

He had resolutely placed himself where they must see him as they drove into the car park. They would have half a minute to decide whether to greet or ignore him. If they ignored him his mood of elation would surely dissipate. He dreaded what might take its place.

Mrs Porteous would have given him a cold stare and then walked past, but Margaret came straight up to him, with her hands in the pockets of her blue coat. She spoke sharply, as if giving an order on the hockey-field: 'Is your name Duffy?'

'Yes.'

'I'm Margaret Porteous. I believe my mother said you wanted to join us in church this morning.'

Her mother must have told her he was simple-minded.

'If you still want to come we'd better hurry.'

It was not a gracious invitation but it was her nature to be bold and straightforward. That was how she played hockey and made speeches. She was dark-haired, unlike her mother. She must take after her dead father, the lawyer. It was said her mother had wanted to send her to a private school but she had refused. Cooley had been wrong to call her snobbish: she should have said proud.

Mrs Porteous was still uncharacteristically unsure of herself. The crisis was not yet over. 'Good morning,' she said. 'I hope you have not been waiting long.'

'No.'

'We nearly didn't come,' said Margaret.

There must have been some disagreement.

As he walked with them across the street and up the drive towards the church Duffy bore in mind that when it was discovered what had been done to the hymn-books and the minister's Bible suspicion might fall on him since he was probably the only person there not a regular worshipper. He would have to be wary.

The elder who greeted them at the door had a white flower in his button-hole, but it was from his scented hair and moustache that the fragrance came. He whispered to Mrs Porteous: 'There's been some trouble, Elizabeth. I'm not sure yet what it is exactly. I think we've been broken into.'

'Good heavens!'

Inside the church, amidst other smells, of furniture polish, of flowers, of ladies' perfume, and gentlemen's hair-oil, that of human excrement was easily detectable. Everywhere noses sniffed and brows crinkled in puzzlement and disgust.

They reached their pew and sat down.

'There's a stink of shit,' whispered Margaret.

'For heaven's sake, remember where you are,' said her mother, who couldn't help sniffing with distaste herself.

'Whoever broke in must have used the church as a lavatory,' said Margaret. 'Filthy beasts.'

Mrs Porteous beckoned to a passing elder. 'What on earth has happened, Pater?'

'It seems some person or persons broke into the church last night and – would you credit it? – placed human waste on Mr Cargill's Bible. Also in some hymn-books, I believe. The depths to which human beings can sink is incredible.'

'*Your* hymn-book, mother,' exclaimed Margaret, who had opened it at the place. 'Ugh!' She quickly closed it again.

'Oh no,' whimpered her mother. 'It was a present from your father.'

'Maybe then what's been done to it is symbolical.' That was said with great bitterness.

Duffy wondered at her use of his word.

Whatever she meant by it her mother was deeply hurt. 'How dare you!' she whispered. Tears gleamed in her eyes.

Duffy pretended not to be listening to this very private conversation. It seemed that they were at odds over some matter that concerned Mr Porteous, though he had been dead for ten years.

Surreptitiously he took note of how some of the other owners of affected hymn-books were reacting.

Mr and Mrs Martin could not have looked more shocked and self-piteous when they had learned that their son and heir David had got gonorrhoea. David himself was not present.

Miss McKenzie or Big Bella had her arms folded and was gazing sternly upwards as if demanding from God why He had allowed such a thing to happen in His church.

Councillor Grant saw political advantage in his having been chosen as one of the victims. He could be heard saying that if he had been heeded and the birch brought back this would never have happened. If anyone wanted to know whether he was prepared to wield it himself the answer was yes, with great pleasure.

Chief-Inspector Findlay, a tall morose man who looked more like an undertaker than a policeman, and Sergeant Milne were going about self-importantly collecting the defiled hymn-books. Only Mr Chalmers the Fiscal showed reluctance to hand his over. It wasn't that he wanted to keep it as a souvenir, it was simply that, being the person in Lightburn who decided what was or what was not a case for prosecution, he did not like himself to be personally involved. However, commanded by his wife, he surrendered it.

As Sergeant Milne took Mrs Porteous's hymn-book he gave Duffy a frown of recognition and surprise.

'I want it returned, sergeant,' said Mrs Porteous.

'They'll all be returned, Mrs Porteous, after C.I.D. has examined them.'

'Who could have done such a disgusting thing? What could have been their purpose, for heaven's sake?'

'For such people filth itself is a purpose.'

'Do you think they'll be caught?'

'You can be sure we'll do our best.'

Duffy had noticed Margaret making a sign to Stephen Telfer who had made one back. She was asking him if he knew anything about this and he was telling her he didn't.

His father looked glum and dismayed. Unlike Councillor Grant he did not consider himself honoured.

Duffy heard many murmurs of outrage. There was no evidence anywhere of anyone being moved to pity and understanding.

All the while the organist played uplifting music.

At last the congregation settled down. Old Mr Cargill appeared and hirpled up into the pulpit. Medals glittered on his chest. He tried to look undaunted. He spent a minute or two in silent prayer.

When he began to speak he could not keep a girn out of his voice. 'For those who may not yet be aware of what has happened let me briefly explain. During the night some person or persons have broken into the church and seen fit to defile a number of hymn-books and my Bible. These have been handed over to the police for examination. As Christian men and women it behoves us to pray for and forgive those who trespass against us, but as law-abiding citizens it is also our duty to do everything in our power to assist in apprehending and bringing to justice the perpetrators of this despicable and meaningless act.'

He then called on the congregation to join him in prayer.

That was the time, thought Duffy, in the great silence, for the most intelligent among them to realise that humility and not a desire for revenge should be the truly Christian response.

The service then began with an aggressive singing of the psalm 'The Lord's My Shepherd'.

The sermon was on the subject: 'Gratitude for the good things of the earth.' The old man's heart was not in it. Several times he stumbled into incoherence, and he ended abruptly.

During the coughing, sighing, and shuffling that followed Margaret turned to Duffy: 'I believe your mother's on holiday in Spain?'

He nodded. He wondered who had told her.

'So you're on your own?'

He nodded again.

'Would you like to have lunch with us?'

He hid his joy. Was she just being kind to the poor simpleton left to look after himself? Or did she really like him? Or was she using him to attack her mother?

'If your mother doesn't mind,' he murmured.

She didn't say that her mother wouldn't mind.

A few minutes later she mentioned it to her mother.

Mrs Porteous looked as if she was seeking some way to cancel the invitation without appearing unChristian. She could find none. 'If he wishes,' she said, curtly.

He should have politely rejected so grudged an invitation, and he was afraid that Margaret might despise him for not doing so; but the joy of being with her longer, in the car on the way to the house and then in the house itself, was worth the humiliation.

If he could have her friendship he would give up his war.

The service was cut short because the minister felt unwell. Afterwards the congregation in the sunshine and among the graves eagerly discussed the outrage.

Councillor Grant gave another little political speech.

The Martins, aware by this time that some kind of distinction had been conferred on them, were happy to receive the congratulatory sympathy of friends.

Miss McKenzie and Mr McGregor the headmaster conferred with other teachers, including Mr Flockhart and Miss Bremner. No doubt they were discussing which of their pupils, present or past, were most likely to have committed such a horrible and yet such a peculiar crime.

Mrs Porteous and Margaret were addressed by an old gentleman with a red face and white moustache, and his wife whose hair was dyed purple and whose fur coat was motheaten. They were Major and Mrs Haliburton. They did not speak with Scottish accents. Duffy had seen them in the supermarket, at the wine shelves.

'They wouldn't have dared to do a thing like that in John Knox's day, Margaret,' he said, jovially.

'In John Knox's day, Major, they smashed statues and holy ornaments. John Knox urged them on.'

'Ah, but that was to get rid of idolatry.'

'Maybe this was to get rid of hypocrisy.'

'Don't be ridiculous, Margaret,' said her mother. 'Not to say offensive.'

'Well, isn't it hypocritical to say you forgive and at the same time be determined to punish?'

'I don't think that is hypocritical at all,' she said. 'Do you, Major?'

'Let's have a theological debate about the nature of forgiveness, among the gravestones. Shall we?'

'No, we shan't,' said his wife. 'Let's go, Charles. I've got a chicken cooking in the oven.'

'My namesake, Charles I, forgave his enemies before they had his head chopped off; *He nothing common did or mean/Upon that memorable scene/But laid his comely head/Down as upon a bed*. Lovelace.'

'Marvell,' said Margaret.

'Was it? Anyway, magnificent stuff. Well, must march if I'm not to eat charred chicken. See you soon.'

'I hope his car starts,' said Margaret. 'It often won't.'

It must have started for it shortly came rattling out of the car park. It was an old blue Mini.

The Porteouses were then joined by the Telfers. Mrs Telfer was indignant. Someone had asked her if the business in the church wasn't one of her son's dubious jokes. She had pointed out that her husband's hymn-book had been one of those polluted. 'Yours too, I told her, Elizabeth. Do you know what she said then? That it could have been to put everybody off the scent!'

'Appropriate phrase,' said Stephen. 'Well, it certainly wasn't me.'

'Nor me,' said Margaret.

'Did anyone notice,' he asked, 'that only the front rows were involved? Who sits there? The Lightburn Establishment.'

'Are you suggesting it was some kind of political act?' asked his mother. 'Like sending letter-bombs?'

'With moral undertones.'

'What on earth are you talking about?'

'Religious undertones too,' said Margaret. 'Whoever did it could have been letting us know that though we're members of St Stephen's and wear fur coats we're not any more special than anyone else.'

'Precisely,' said Stephen, winking at Duffy.

Duffy was amazed. They were joking and yet how close to the truth they were.

Mrs Telfer was wearing a fur coat. 'You two are too clever for your own good,' she said. 'Aren't they, Elizabeth?'

'They certainly are.'

'Suppose you're right, Stephen,' said his father, earnestly, 'though like your mother I'm sceptical, who in Lightburn would think of conveying such a message in such a fashion?'

'No idea, Dad. Perhaps we have a Savonarola in our midst.'

'A what?' asked his mother.

'Savonarola. A religious reformer in Italy in the 15th century. He went too far and was burned at the stake.'

'I'm not surprised,' said Mrs Telfer. 'Haven't you noticed, Elizabeth, how intellectuals hate simple explanations?'

'And what, mother,' asked Stephen, 'is the simple explanation in this case?'

'Some filthy creatures decided to give a demonstration of their filthiness.'

Meanwhile the two Telfer girls had been making eyes at Duffy. Having to smile back prevented him from listening to the conversation as avidly as he would have liked. He would have to look up Savonarola in his encyclopaedia.

The two families went together to the car park. Stephen chatted to Duffy.

'I believe you know the girl called Helen Cooley.'

Duffy wondered how he knew that. 'She's gone to London,' he said, cautiously.

'Has she now? Yes, it's the kind of thing she would do. They say she gave David Martin a dose of the clap.'

'She said he gave it to her.'

Telfer was amused. 'Probably he did. I once saw her do something I would never have had the nerve to do myself. Years ago. In the public park. A big Alsatian was running loose. Frothing at the mouth. It seized in its teeth a ball some little girls were playing with. Everybody kept well clear, me included, but she grabbed the brute by the scruff of the neck and tore the ball out of its mouth. Then she cleaned the ball on its back. She had a fag in her mouth.'

'Cooley's afraid of nothing.' Except affection. He remembered her seated disconsolately at the back of the bus.

'Well, I hope she makes it in London. Do you play badminton?'

'No.'

'If you'd like to try we're at the church hall every Tuesday from seven to nine. If you haven't got a racket we'll lend you one. Be seeing you.'

In the car park the two families went to their respective cars.

'I'll drive,' said Margaret, getting into the driver's seat.

Her mother sat beside her. Duffy got into the back.

They drove along Ballochmyle Drive.

'What were you and Stephen talking about?' asked Margaret.

He hesitated. He did not want Mrs Porteous to know he was Cooley's friend.

'If it's such a secret I don't want to know.'

'You're too inquisitive, Margaret,' said her mother.

'He was asking me if I played badminton,' said Duffy.

Suddenly Margaret braked hard. 'Did you see that?' she cried.

'For goodness' sake, Margaret, be more careful. See what?'

'That awful boy John Crosbie. Wearing an Australian type of hat.'

'He may be awful and his hat may be out of place but that's no reason for giving us the fright of our lives.'

'He was wiping his bottom. I mean, pretending to do it.' She increased speed.

'This is a 30 m.p.h. zone, Margaret. His making obscene gestures is no excuse for you breaking the law.'

'Don't you understand? He must have been one of those who broke into the church. He was going back to gloat. That's the kind of creature he is. I'm in a hurry to get home to telephone the police. If they come quickly they'll catch him.'

Mrs Porteous looked back but saw no one. Crosbie had dodged into the wood.

Duffy had seen him. Cooley was going to be proved right. Crosbie would destroy him.

'Did you see him?' asked Margaret, turning to look at Duffy.

'I didn't see anybody.'

'You must have seen him. He was on the pavement in full view.'

'I didn't see him, Margaret,' said her mother.

'You've got other things on your mind.'

'Don't be impertinent.'

They turned off the public road up the avenue that led to The Poplars.

Duffy's mouth was dry with fear. Nothing could save him. The police would pick up Mick Dykes too. One or other of them would be sure to give him away, in Mick's case because all the questioning would confuse him, in Crosbie's for God knew what reason.

His one hope was to find Crosbie before the police did and warn him to keep his mouth shut, or he would kill him. He would be able to say it as if he meant it, for he would mean it.

Outside the big stone house was a car, a dark green Daimler, with, Duffy noticed, a registration number that wasn't local.

His companions' reactions to its appearance were startling.

'Oh Christ!' shouted Margaret.

Mrs Porteous's cry was anguished but also joyful.

Duffy was forgotten. So was Crosbie.

'You said it was finished,' said Margaret, accusingly.

'So I did. So it was.'

'Then what's he doing here?'

'I don't know.'

'Don't see him. Drive away somewhere. I'll go and tell him you don't want to see him.'

'But I do want to see him.' Mrs Porteous got out of the car. She was weeping.

A tall grey-haired man in a blue blazer came running out of the house. A golden Labrador ran after him, barking happily. Evidently it knew him well. He was not a stranger.

He and Mrs Porteous kissed. Then hand-in-hand they went into the house. The dog wasn't sure whether to go with them or stay out with Margaret. It decided inside was warmer.

'Sorry,' muttered Margaret. 'Lunch is off. Another time maybe.'

'It's all right.' He got out quickly. If he hurried he might catch up with Crosbie.

'If you like I'll drive you home.'

'I like walking. Goodbye.'

'Goodbye.'

A robin accompanied him down the avenue, flitting from one poplar to another. He envied it. It had a right to be here. It had no other purpose in life except to enjoy being alive.

He had discovered Mrs Porteous's secret. She was in love with the grey-haired man. There was some obstruction. Perhaps he was already married.

CHAPTER TWENTY

He was walking quickly along Ballochmyle Avenue towards the church, his Bible in his hand, when he heard the tooting of a car behind him. It came alongside and kept pace with him. It was a police car. His heart racing, he looked to see if Crosbie was in it, on his way to the station; but no, its only occupants were two young policemen.

It stopped. One of them called: 'You there.'

He walked over, making sure his Bible was seen. Perhaps it would keep them at bay.

They weren't yet hostile. He was too well-dressed and he might come from one of the villas, with well-off parents.

Both of them studied him. He smiled, as if he had no reason to be afraid of them.

'What's your name?'

'Duffy.'

'Just Duffy?'

'Thomas Duffy.'

'Do you live here?'

'No.'

'Where do you live?'

'Kenilworth Court.'

Their attitude changed. Their voices became sharper, their eyes colder.

'You're far from home, aren't you?'

'Not very far.'

'What are you doing in this part of the town?'

'I was at church.'

'What church?'

'St Stephen's. It's just along the road.'

'We know where it is. Were you at church all by yourself?'

'No. I was with Mrs Porteous and her daughter Margaret.'

That stumped them. It was hardly likely to be a lie, and Mrs Porteous was a lady with much influence.

He could read their minds. They were only about six years older than himself. They were still learning how to use their authority. They were curious as to his connection with Mrs Porteous but had to be careful not to frighten him. He might complain to her.

'If you were at St Stephen's this morning you'll know what happened there?'

'Do you mean, about the hymn-books?'

They grinned. They were sure now they were dealing with a simpleton.

'We mean about some hymn-books being plastered with shit.'

Officially they would call it a sordid crime. In private they would make ribald jokes about it.

'You don't happen to have any ideas who might have done it, Duffy?'

He looked shocked.

'Well, coming from Kenilworth Court you might know a number of villains.'

'Such as Johnny Crosbie.'

'Johnny Crosbie doesn't live in Kenilworth Court.'

'We know where he lives. Do you know Crosbie?'

'I knew him at school.'

'What does your father do, Duffy?'

'He's dead. My mother works in the Caledonian Hotel.'

They looked at each other and laughed.

'Is her name Bell?'

'It's Isabel.'

'Bell's her business name. We know the lady.'

'She's a voluptuous blonde.'

He pretended not to know what the word meant.

They drove away, still laughing, convinced they had been talking to a half-wit.

Somebody else must have telephoned them about Crosbie.
If they did not pick him up here on the road they would go
to his home.

Duffy must find him first.

He set off for Dirty Chuck's. If Crosbie wasn't there
Mick Dykes might be. Together Duffy and Mick should
be able to see to it that Crosbie told the police nothing.

Dirty Chuck's was in a tenement that had been condemned, in the oldest part of the town. It was the only
place where the youth of the district could forgather. Efforts
were being made to close it down, for it was suspected by
the authorities that illegal activities went on in it, such as
pot-smoking, glue-sniffing, and the planning of burglaries.
How it had got its nickname was not known. The present
proprietor's name was not Charles and neither he nor his
premises were particularly dirty. Its registered name, painted
above the door, was The Skylark Café. The tables and chairs
were of metal but the clattering they made, and every other
noise, were hardly heard above the din from the juke-box,
which on that Sabbath morning was bellowing a pop song
on the subject of love. The customers, all teenagers, seemed
to find no difficulty in carrying on private conversations.

When Duffy entered, with his Bible hidden in his pocket,
he was greeted with a scream of rapture from Molly
McGowan, who was seated at a table with Cathie Barr
and another girl whom he recognised as Sally Cooper.

Neither Crosbie nor Mick Dykes was present.

Molly came over. 'Looking for me, honey?' she asked,
with a coy simper that did not suit her big coarse freckled
face. 'You're looking great.' She waited, anxiously, for
him to return the compliment. He didn't but she was
not discouraged. She pressed close to him so that he
could smell her rank body odour. 'Tonight, at seven,' she
whispered. 'I can hardly wait.'

She could also hardly keep her hands off him. Turning
her head, she gave all the other girls in the café a snarl of
warning. He was hers and she'd use her teeth on any girl
who tried to steal him from her.

'Buy us a coke, Duffy,' shouted Cathie Barr.

'You don't have to buy them anything,' said Molly. 'You and me can sit at a table by ourselves.'

He bought four cokes. 'I'm looking for Mick Dykes.'

'You don't have to worry about Mick, Duffy. He said it was all right for me to go to your house." She dropped her voice. 'I'm staying the night. That's what you want, isn't it?'

'Get some potato crisps while you're at it, Duffy,' called Cathie.

He bought four packets.

'You're too generous, Duffy,' grumbled Molly, as she helped to carry the bottles.

'Hello, Duffy,' said Cathie. 'I was saying to Molly you've been to church.'

'Look here, Cathie,' said Molly, 'I'm not having anybody take the mickey out of Duffy. From now on I'm looking after him. Isn't that right, Duffy?'

'Who's looking after you, Molly?' sneered Sally.

'Duffy and me are looking after each other.'

'I wasn't taking the mickey,' said Cathie. 'I just asked if he was at church. Were you, Duffy?'

He gave her his shy simpleton's smile. 'Yes.'

'What church?'

'It's none of your business, Cathie, what church Duffy goes to,' said Molly.

'St Stephen's,' said Duffy, with childish pride.

'Among the nobs!' said Cathie.

'It's the nicest church in Lightburn,' he said, 'and it's got the highest spire.'

Molly backed him up. 'So it has.'

'Which spire are you talking about, Molly?' asked Cathie. 'The one with the bell in it or the one Mick showed you among the graves, in the summer-time?'

Sally giggled, in a sneery kind of way, at the idea of Mick's spire, which she too had seen though not among the graves.

'Don't listen to them, Duffy,' said Molly. 'Me and Mick

only went once to the graveyard. Mick doesn't like graves. He thinks they're unlucky.'

'Who did you see in the church, Duffy?' asked Cathie. 'Did you see Margaret Porteous? Cooley said you fancied her.'

'Cooley was a fucking liar,' said Molly. Then she remembered her lover was present, newly come from church. 'I mean, she said a lot of things that weren't true. Maybe you and me will go to church together next Sunday, Duffy.'

'Not St Stephen's,' said Cathie.

'We'll go to St Stephen's if we want to.'

'But you haven't got a fur coat, Molly.'

'I don't need a fur coat. Do I, Duffy? Anyway, maybe I could borrow Duffy's mother's.'

'I thought Mick Dykes would be here,' said Duffy, shyly.

'He's not allowed,' said Cathie. 'His mother's found out about him and Fat Annie.'

'It must have been that wee rat Crosbie that shopped him,' said Sally.

'No, it was Mick's sister Nellie. When he came home last night after visiting Annie his mother was waiting for him. With a big belt. Have you seen Mrs Dykes, Duffy? She's big and fierce. She made him take off his jeans and then she leathered his bare behind. He can't sit down now. He's got a black eye too.'

'What's it to his mother if he's been fucking Fat Annie?' sneered Sally.

'It wasn't for the fucking he went to Annie's,' said Molly, earnestly. 'He said it was too much like hard work. He went because she let him sit in front of the fire and drink beer. His mother never lets him do that at home.'

'How do you know his mother leathered him?' sneered Sally.

'Cathie gets to know everything,' said Molly.

'I know something else,' said Cathie. 'Annie's up the

spout. It wasn't Mick, though. His mother says it was but it wasn't.'

Sally sneered. 'I expect you know who it was, Cathie.'

'Yes, I know but I'm not going to say. He's a married man with four weans.'

Duffy thought of Mrs Porteous. Was her lover a married man with children? She would despise Mrs Burnet and yet was just as immoral.

'Serves Mick right,' sneered Sally. 'Him and his big dick.' Her sneer became coquettish. 'I've never seen you in here before, Duffy. Have you come to size up the talent, now that Cooley's gone?'

'He came to see me,' said Molly.

On Cathie's wizened face appeared a witch's smile. 'You never said, Duffy, if you saw Margaret Porteous in the church.'

Casually he asked if Johnny Crosbie came there on Sunday mornings.

'Not this morning,' said Molly. 'He's keeping out of Archie Cooper's way.'

'He needn't bother,' said Sally. 'My dad says Archie's to leave the wee cunt alone. It would be stupid to ruin his Army career for the likes of Johnny Crosbie.'

'Besides,' said Cathie, 'Archie and his mate had to be brought home in a taxi last night from the British Legion hall, too drunk to walk.'

'Who told you that?' said Sally.

'Nobody needs to tell Cathie anything,' said Molly. 'She just knows.'

'Everybody wanted to stand them drinks,' said Sally. 'They're heroes. Every soldier in Northern Ireland is a hero. That's what my dad thinks.'

'You never told us what Johnny Crosbie did to you, Sally,' said Cathie.

'And I'm not going to.' She looked towards the door. 'Look who's here!'

They turned their heads. Mick Dykes had come limping in. He had his hand up at his face to screen his eyes. They heard him ask for two packets of cigarettes and a bottle of Irn Bru.

Duffy went over to him. 'Hello, Mick.'

'Hello, Duffy. What are you doing here?'

'I want to talk to you.'

'What about? I've to go straight back home.'

'Is it true that Annie's expecting, Mick?' called Cathie.

Everybody in the café was staring at Mick. There were guffaws. His nerve failed. He took his purchases and fled.

Duffy went after him.

Every step was painful for Mick. It was easy to believe his behind was lacerated.

'Johnny Crosbie was hanging about the church this morning, Mick. People telephoned the police. They're looking for him now.'

'He gets headaches, Duffy. He doesn't know what he's doing. What we did last night in the church was wrong, Duffy. I told Cooley it would bring us bad luck and so it has.'

'If Johnny was trying to hide from the police where would he go?'

'He's got a den in Crimea Street, in the house where he was born.'

'But all the buildings there are being pulled down.'

'That's right. It's dangerous. Sometimes he spends the night there. He's got a paraffin heater.'

'Will he be there now?'

'He could be. Don't go there with your good clothes on, Duffy. You'd get them ruined. If you see Johnny tell him I'll get in touch when I can.' He grinned, ruefully. 'Tell him I'm confined to barracks. That's what soldiers say, isn't it?'

Duffy then let him go on alone. Poor Mick tried to walk with his usual virile swagger but pain and shame crippled him.

CHAPTER TWENTY-ONE

Crosbie lived in an older superior council housing scheme
where the houses were only four to a block and had small
individual gardens. Many of these were well-kept but none
more so than Mr Crosbie's. A dour withdrawn man who
drove a lorry for the council's Roads Department he was
not popular with his neighbours who thought he paid too
much attention to his roses and cabbages and not enough
to his wife and son. In Johnny's case they understood and
forgave but not in his wife's. Mrs Crosbie was liked and
pitied even by those whose children Johnny as an infant
had terrorised and whose houses he had broken into. She
had told them all a hundred times that Johnny's was a
medical condition, she couldn't remember its big name,
but it would get better when he grew up. She had said
that when he was three, she was still saying it now that he
was sixteen. Nobody believed her but nobody blamed her
either. The general opinion was that he should have been
strangled at birth, when his poor mother wasn't looking.

About sixty yards from Crosbie's house the same police
car was parked, on a piece of waste ground.

Using a bus shelter as an excuse for waiting there, Duffy
watched from a distance. If Crosbie appeared the police
would pick him up and take him to the station. All
Duffy could do then was to pray that Crosbie did not
give him away.

He was aware of the irony. Crosbie would not betray
him because he wanted to do him harm, on the contrary it would be because he liked him and wanted him
as a friend and comrade. He thought he and Duffy
had the same grudge against society. Both of them had

nothing to look forward to except everybody's contempt and animosity.

If the three of them were arrested and charged, Crosbie and Dykes, who had been in trouble with the police before, would be sent to reform schools. Duffy himself would be let off because he was simple-minded: many would testify to that. It would be said he had been led into crime. All his life afterwards he would be regarded by everyone as not quite right in the head. Children would shout 'Daftie!' after him in the street. His very efforts to show that he was not only sane but also more intelligent than most would be taken as proof of his simpleness. That he could tell what happened at Thermopylae or how many were killed at Hiroshima would be put down to his having heard about them somewhere and, in a way peculiar to weak-minded people, he had remembered them, without of course having any idea of their significance. Mr Harrison would not marry his mother: he would not want a criminal imbecile for a step-son. Every other man Duffy's mother might want to marry would be repelled for that reason too. More bitterly than ever she would blame Duffy for ruining her life. In the end she would abandon him. He might well end up, as Cooley had prophesised, married to Molly McGowan, with half a dozen backward children, all of them supported by the State.

On the other hand if Crosbie kept silent and there were no arrests how different Duffy's future could be. Instead of Crosbie and Mick Dykes, Molly McGowan and Cathie Barr, he would associate with Margaret Porteous and Stephen Telfer and their friends. He would take part in conversations about poetry and history. He would learn cleverer and more respectable ways of opposing defilers of truth and abusers of authority. He would be a help and not a hindrance to his mother's marrying, if not Mr Harrison then someone just as eligible. It was possible he himself might marry Margaret Porteous one day.

Crosbie could prevent all that from coming true.

At last the police car went away. They must be feeling

hungry. There was no great hurry. They could pick up Crosbie any time.

Duffy waited another half hour but Crosbie did not come. It was a good sign that he was keeping clear of the police.

It was after two when Duffy got home, tired and hungry. He had hardly time to take off his raincoat before Mrs Munro was ringing the door bell. Her eyes were red and she was sniffing with grief.

'Poor Jack's passed on, Duffy. Some time during the night. Phemie said you were the last to speak to him.' Still sniffing, she gave him a sly look. 'You're all dressed up. Were you at church?'

'Yes.' He wanted to be alone to think about Mr Ralston's death.

'What church was that, Duffy?' As usual she spoke to him as if he was ten years old.

'St Stephen's.'

'St Stephen's! That's away over in the West End. Are you sure? What took you there? From what I hear they don't let just anyone in. That's the benefit of being a bit on the simple side, you get away with things a more normal body wouldn't. Was it some special service for deprived children or something like that.' She went further in and listened. 'I'm glad you've got rid of that besom Helen Cooley. Phemie and me think maybe we shouldn't tell your mother you had her staying with you. We know it wasn't your fault. You'd be no match for that pushy bitch. I hope it's true what you told Phemie about not sleeping with her. Miss Porteous wouldn't like it, would she, if you had VD.'

He didn't understand.

'You had a visitor while you were out, Duffy. Good-looking black-haired lassie about your own age. Wearing a swanky blue coat. Said her name was Margaret Porteous.'

'What did she want?'

'I heard her at your door so I came to tell her you weren't in. She asked me to let you know she'd called and she would see you on Tuesday, at the badminton. I didn't know you played badminton, Duffy. Well, that's the message. Maybe her mother sent her. Their kind like to help homeless cats and disabled soldiers and old donkeys. You would be lucky, Duffy, if they're going to take an interest in you.'

There were no coal fires in his house. It was not easy to burn anything. It had to be done in a metal litter-box, and if it was something like his jotter it took some time, page by page. If he had been asked why he was destroying those accounts of human cruelties he would have replied that it was for Mr Ralston's sake. Take a chance, Duffy, the dead man had said, meaning don't be pessimistic, more good things happened than bad. As if to prove him right, the door-bell rang, it was Mrs Munro again, come this time with a badminton racket that she had found at the back of a cupboard. She had bought it years ago at a jumble sale, she didn't know if it was any use or not, it had a string or two missing, but Duffy was welcome to it. He thanked her and she went off pleased that she, who had little money, was as concerned for the fatherless retarded lad as Mrs Porteous, who could easily afford it.

About ten minutes later she was back, saying, anxiously, that she had thought she had smelled burning. Fire frightened her. You were always reading about people getting trapped and burnt to death. He assured her that he had just been burning some paper in a metal box. Just the same, she said, she'd be happier if she could see for herself what he had been up to. So, pushing him aside, she went into the kitchen, where she inspected the ashes in the box. They seemed safe enough but she sprinkled water on them to make sure. She wanted to know why he had burned the papers. He could have put them in the rubbish bin or flushed them down the lavatory. The truth was, she said, in a kindly way, he couldn't be trusted to be left on his own. No boy of sixteen could, even with all his gripping senses.

When she was gone he burned the tract. Then he took down from the wall of his bedroom the two paintings which had so worried Cooley. Rolling them up neatly, he fastened them with rubber bands and put them under his bed.

All he needed now, to enable him to sleep soundly that night, and every other night, without nightmares, was Crosbie's silence.

As a philosophical proposition he contemplated the silencing of Crosbie by killing him.

He had once heard someone declare on television that the greatest lie of the twentieth century was that it regarded human life as sacred. Politicians, ministers of religion, judges, everyone in authority, proclaimed that sanctity, and yet they knew that in their own lifetimes many millions of people had been killed in wars and many millions more had died of preventable disease and starvation. They knew also, and gave it their blessing, that new and more powerful weapons were being invented, able to lay waste the whole world.

In his seemingly guileless way Duffy had pointed out the discrepancy to Mr Flockhart.

Taken aback, the teacher had at first resorted to flippancy. 'When anyone says life is sacred, Duffy, he means his own.'

Duffy had waited for a serious answer.

'It's an ideal, Duffy, and in practice we always fall far short of our ideals, in this respect very far short. We're in an early stage of evolution, morally speaking. Give us another thousand years.'

On the Lightburn War Memorial, under the long list of names of men killed in the First World War, was an inscription that he had never understood: Death is swallowed up in Victory. He had wondered what the Germans, who had been defeated, put on their memorials.

When he was five he had seen some bigger boys harry a hedge-sparrow's nest. They had taken out the blue eggs and smashed them. He had realised then, and later more clearly, that those eggs, so small and frail, nevertheless represented an achievement more wonderful than any that the cleverest scientists and engineers were capable of. Life, it had seemed to him, was a gift that should be received and preserved with gratitude and reverence. Afterwards, to his mother's amusement, he had gone through a long period of refusing to kill any living creature, even a fly.

Governed by his own standards he could not kill anyone; but those standards would be dismissed by most people as too extreme and idealistic. He was entitled to judge himself by the standards of civilised society.

In a nuclear war many millions of people, most of them innocent, would be killed. Everybody knew that, most were reconciled to it, a few protested, and nobody was sure whom to blame. Surely therefore it would be the blackest hypocrisy for anyone to pretend to be shocked by his killing of one person, who was evil and, if allowed to live, would do great harm.

By burning the jotter he had, in a way, made himself fit to be Crosbie's executioner.

Between thinking and doing there was, he knew, an infinite difference.

As he waited for darkness he kept telling himself that all he was going to do was satisfy himself that Crosbie would not give him away. Up to now he had never responded to Crosbie's offers of friendship, but suppose he did and was able to persuade him that he was sincere (though he would not be, not altogether) then Crosbie might feel so pleased and honoured that for once his love of treachery would be subdued. It would mean Duffy's having to continue being friendly with him, for a while at any rate, at a time when he was trying to cultivate the friendship of Margaret Porteous. It could be done, but wariness and patience would be necessary.

He was dressed as he had been when he had stolen out to paint the declaration of war on the town hall: black jeans and jerkin, black balaclava, black gloves, and black sandshoes.

Outwardly very calm he was inwardly nervous. Many

things could go wrong. He could be seen leaving the house by Mrs Munro, or walking along the streets by acquaintances. Molly McGowan could come early and find him not at home. Crosbie might not be in his hide-out or Mick Dykes might be in it with him.

Luckily, just as he was about to leave, he heard some people who had been up to condole with Mrs Ralston being waylaid by Mrs Munro and invited in 'for a dram and a blether.' They were Mr Logan the house-painter and his wife. Mrs Munro would be too busy entertaining them to spy on him.

From the window he made sure there was no one about in the street. Quickly he opened and closed the door and ran downstairs. The street lamp at the foot of the stairs had not yet been fixed. It would not be the only lamp out of order. Thanks to vandals half the town's streets would be in darkness. In any case on a Sunday night with all the shops shut they were always deserted.

It was just after six. He had to get to Crimea Street, settle with Crosbie, and return home before seven when Molly was expected. Eagerness would make her early. What was to be done about her would depend on how he had got on with Crosbie.

In the old part of the town where Crimea Street was situated some tenements had already been razed to the ground, others were partly demolished, and others again, like Crosbie's, were waiting for their turn. Complaints were frequently made that the demolition and restoration were taking too long: the excuse was that the council's money kept running out. The area was an eyesore, though in the summer masses of a wild flower called willowherb had flourished all over it. It was dangerous, especially to children, because of falling masonry, tetanus, and hungry rats. The hope was that one day it would be turned into a public park with grass and trees and playing fields.

Stepping carefully and now and then having to shine his torch Duffy approached Crosbie's close. A cat miaowed and came towards him. It was limping. It was so desperate for company that it forgot its fear of boys who threw stones or aimed kicks at it, and rubbed itself against Duffy's legs. It was black and had a white ribbon round its neck. Probably it was some old woman's pet and companion. It looked old itself. Duffy patted it and spoke reassuringly. Life was strong within it, old and hungry and lost though it was. He wished he had some food to give it.

It came after him, right up to the close and inside. He remembered Crosbie's hatred of cats. It would be better to keep it away from him.

In the close was a smell of cats' piss, but the strongest smell was that of washing-soda, tons of which must have been used by generations of women to scour the stone floor. The walls were not tiled as in tenements where better-off people lived, but were painted dark-brown. Scribbled in white was the slogan FUCK THE POPE. Efforts had been made to erase it, either by shocked Catholics or, less likely, ashamed Protestants.

The cat, pressing itself against his legs, made him stumble. As gently as he could he pushed it out of his way. It darted up the stairs in front of him.

The stairs seemed to shake. It was really his legs that were shaking. So were his hands. So, it seemed, was his brain. Yet never had it been more important for him to think clearly.

He passed a communal lavatory on the half-landing. The chain had been plundered, probably to be used as a weapon. The space was so narrow that someone with big feet like Mick Dykes would have found it hard to close the door.

One-up, middle door, Mick had said. The name-plate had been removed. Duffy knocked. Suddenly the cat was hampering his feet again. He must not let Crosbie harm it.

He knocked again more loudly and called through the slot where the letter-box had been: 'Johnny, it's me, Duffy.'

He heard the clump of Crosbie's high-heeled boots. The

door slowly opened. The cat ran in. Crosbie tried to kick it but missed. 'Fucking cat!' he cried, in what sounded like terror. He rushed in pursuit of it, heedless of Duffy.

The living-room, which had also been the kitchen, was lit by two candles. There was no furniture, except for a wooden box on which Crosbie had been playing ludo. The paraffin heater that Mick had mentioned wasn't lit. The room was cold.

Australian hat on head and knife in hand, Crosbie was searching for the cat, in this room and the other one. 'I'll kill it,' he kept panting.

'Leave it alone, Johnny,' said Duffy. 'It's doing no harm.'

'That's what you think, Duffy. Cats give me head-aches.'

Aware of its danger the cat kept quiet.

'It's lost,' said Duffy. 'It wants company.'

'Every time I have one of my headaches there's a cat about. Somebody sends them.'

Duffy was astonished. 'Cats don't obey orders, like dogs. Nobody could send a cat anywhere.'

'I know what I'm talking about, Duffy, I can feel it coming on.' He let out a scream. It could have been the cat itself, with his knife in it.

'I'll open the outside door,' said Duffy. 'If we keep still it'll run out.'

He went and opened the door. Almost at once the cat shot past him.

'It's gone, Johnny,' he said.

Crosbie was crushing both hands, one still clutching the knife, against his brow. He was whimpering.

'Hasn't the doctor given you something to lessen the pain?' asked Duffy.

'Nothing's any good.'

'How long does it last?'

'Sometimes minutes, sometimes all day.'

Duffy himself was still trembling. His pain, intense too, was not physical. He felt his soul being torn apart. He had meant to talk reasonably with Crosbie but that did not seem possible now. He himself could not think clearly and Crosbie had this paralysing headache. He could not wait for another opportunity. It had to be completed in the next ten minutes or never at all. It was now half past six. Molly McGowan could be knocking at his door.

'It's cold in here,' he said. 'Let's go to my house. We can talk there.'

'Wait, Duffy. Wait. I can hardly see, you know. I go blind.'

'I'll help you.'

'Wait. I think it's getting less.'

'Did the doctor say what causes it?'

'I heard him telling my mother it was a tumour in the brain. He said an operation would do no good. It could kill me all the quicker. If I don't talk sense, Duffy, don't worry. Sometimes I go mad. Mick gets scared. Sometimes I don't know what I'm saying or what I'm doing.' He took his hands away from his face. He was trying to smile. 'I can't see yet. Wait a wee bit longer, Duffy. We've got plenty of time.'

'Have you seen Mick today?'

'No. I've been expecting him. Maybe we should wait for him.'

'He'll not come. His mother's found out about him and Mrs Burnet. He's not allowed out of the house.'

'He's frightened of his mother. She leathers him and he'll not hit her back because she's his mother. He's got no brains. He said he had a dream once, his mother cut off his dick with a hatchet. I'm beginning to see now, Duffy, but you'll have to help me.'

'All right.'

'Are the candles still lit?'

'Yes.'

'Blow them out, will you? I see all kinds of lights.'

Duffy blew out the candles and then taking Crosbie by the arm led him out of the house and down the stairs.

They moved slowly. Crosbie kept his eyes shut. It made

the pain less, he said. It also meant that his faith in Duffy as a friend who would do him no harm was absolute.

They went out into the street.

'Is this Sunday?' he asked.

'Yes.'

'I get mixed up. Is Cooley staying with you?'

'She's gone to London.'

'That's right. She said she was. Is this the night big Molly's coming to your house?'

'Yes.'

'Mick'll not be there?'

'No.'

'Just you and me, Duffy. We'll have great fun with the stupid bitch. We'll fuck her in turns all night.'

It was then that Duffy struck the first blow. The weapon was a half-brick he had picked up. He thought, as he heard bone cracking, that Crosbie deserved it because of his cruelty to the cat and to Molly. He also thought that he was doing Crosbie a good turn in making sure that this headache would be his last. He was not an assassin or executioner but a deliverer.

'For fuck's sake, Duffy,' mumbled Crosbie,' what did you do that for?' He sank to his knees. His hat fell off.

If no other blow was struck and he was left here he would probably die before anyone found him. It would be thought that the tumour had killed him. The bruise on his scalp would be attributed to his hitting his head in a fall (Mick or his mother would testify that he went blind) or to a stone dropping on him.

He might not die, though. Bending down, Duffy heard him moaning.

So Duffy had to strike again, several times, until his glove was sodden with blood. He felt the pain himself, in his imagination, more perhaps than Crosbie did.

Suddenly his arm felt so tired and weak that he could not have struck again if he had wanted to. All of him was utterly exhausted. He wanted just to kneel beside Crosbie and wait there, for the rest of his life, longer than that, for the rest of time. He felt, dimly as yet, that he had done something so infinitely wrong that everybody in the world was diminished by it.

It did not seem to be himself, but someone else, who a few minutes later resolutely dragged Crosbie's body into a nearby close in a partly demolished building and there covered it with rubble, handfuls of dust, and pieces of rotten wood. But before he did that he placed in Crosbie's fist a metal hair-grip, one of the half dozen that Cooley had left scattered on the carpet in his mother's room. No girl in particular would be suspected. Such hair-grips were used by millions.

Then that someone else took off the dusty and bloody gloves and pushed them well down through a hole in the floorboards of one of the houses in the close, where they would never be found. If the demolition was resumed tomorrow morning the body itself would be hidden under tons of debris.

Duffy watched with horror all this being done. He knew intimately this cool, active, thorough, and resolute person in the black jerkin spotted with blood, but seemed to have no influence over him.

Together they ran home, Duffy panting and fearful, the other alert and silent.

It was ten past seven when they were back inside the house. Shrieks of laughter could be heard coming from Mrs Munro's: her own little private wake for Mr Ralston was still going on. Molly hadn't yet arrived. Perhaps Cathie Barr had instructed her that it wasn't mannerly to be too prompt.

There was time for hands to be washed and clothes changed.

CHAPTER TWENTY-THREE

She was carrying a small bag and chewing gum. Her smile of lewd fondness turned anxious and uncertain as she stared at him. 'Jesus, Duffy,' she said, as she came in, 'you look funny. I hardly recognised you. I thought it was somebody else.'

It was that someone else who had the presence of mind to say, sadly: 'Mr Ralston who lives upstairs died last night.'

'I hate to hear about people being dead. If it was left to me everybody would live forever.'

She took off her duffel coat with its many badges and hung it on the hall-stand. All she had on under it were dirty jeans and a thin black acrylic jumper through which her big white breasts showed. Wasting no time she grabbed him in her strong arms and slobbered him with kisses. She stank of sweat and cheap perfume. 'It's as well I'm here,' she whispered, 'to cheer you up.'

Eagerly she went off to explore the house, with cries of wonder. In the bathroom she said that if he didn't mind she'd like to take a shower, she seldom got one in her own house, her mother said electricity was too dear, and anyway with ten in the family there was always someone needing the bathroom. 'To tell you the truth, Duffy, I'd like to use the toilet now. I'm always needing. My mum says I should see a doctor, it could be my kidneys, but it's because I drink too much cold coke. If you want to stay you're welcome.'

He did not stay. When she came out she asked to see his mother's bedroom. Mick had raved about it. She had an infantile hee-hee of a laugh. She kept using it all the time, with variations.

In the bedroom it expressed her delight at the pink carpet

and the big bed. She took off her shoes and socks, bashfully apologising for her dirty feet, and lay down on top of the red quilt.

'I feel like a bride,' she said.

Jumping up, she rushed over to the wardrobe. 'Mick said your mother's got lots of dresses and nighties.' She hee-hee'd in ecstasy as she fingered the bright assortment, and then put her face among them, sniffing their scent. 'Could I try a nightie on?' she asked. 'I'll be careful.' She picked out one that was dark-red, silky, ankle-length, and low at the front. 'This should fit me, across the chest. I've got big boobs, as maybe you've noticed.' She hee-hee'd modestly. 'So has your mother. Have you seen Cooley's? No, you haven't, because she hasn't got any to speak of. Neither has wee Cathie. Me, I've got better ones, Mick says, than lots of film stars.' She realised that to mention her past lover to her present one might be displeasing to the latter. 'You don't have to be jealous of Mick. You don't have to be jealous of anybody. Mick's always bragging about his big dick but he's got no style. You've got style, Duffy. All the girls say so, even Sally, and she's a sour-faced cunt that praises nobody. Sorry, Duffy. I know you don't approve of swearing. I don't approve of it either. You should hear me telling off my wee sisters. I don't think I should try this on till I've had my shower. Will you come and show me how it works? I always get it freezing cold or scalding hot.'

In the bathroom she whispered: 'We could have a shower together. Like Adam and Eve under a waterfall. I saw that in a film once.'

It took her seconds to remove jeans and jumper. Her breasts were white and luscious; so too was her bottom which she proudly flaunted. On her belly was tattoo'd, in blue, the word LOVE: her umbilicus was the O. But what struck him was the contrast between her body, which had an innocence like an animal's, and her face which, for all its immaturity, was very human, in its coarseness, greed, and lust.

Rather impatiently she helped him to strip. 'Don't be shy with your Molly. She's all yours and you're all hers.' She hee-hee'd with relief when she found what she was anxiously looking for. 'Wee Cathie thinks she knows everything. She told me you wouldn't be able to manage it. She said you weren't interested in girls. Well, maybe you're not interested in other girls but this shows you're interested in me.' She stooped and kissed it, but not voraciously. She was too experienced to excite him too much too soon.

She was pleased that the soap was scented.

They stepped into the bath, under the warm water. She soaped herself all over and then him.

She explained about the tattoo. It had been done in Glasgow, months ago. She wouldn't say who had paid for it: she was finished with him. She was finished with them all, including Mick. She was Duffy's now, until death. 'Do you know what I wish, Duffy? I wish we were married and this was our house. We would have a wee girl with brown hair and brown eyes like you and a wee boy with red hair and blue eyes like me. They wouldn't have to be backward either, for our Morag's very bright: all her teachers have said so. What do you wish, Duffy?'

To save himself from having to consider, far less answer, that question, he pressed his face against her soapy breasts, with shudders and moans, seeking oblivion.

She thought desire was overwhelming him. 'So you can't wait, honey? All right, you don't have to wait. Molly's wide open, waiting for you. Come home, lover boy, come home.' Taking hold of him she let him slide into her. 'You're safe in there, honey. Take it easy, though. We've got all night. Molly's all yours. Nobody else is waiting for a turn. Nobody else is going to get a share. That's it. Nice and slow and easy. All the way home. You've got it now. Just keep that up. Jesus, I'm in heaven, do you know that, in heaven. I've been dreaming of this for years. Talk about Adam and Eve. You and me were made for each other. I've come twice already. Five's my record. I'm going to beat it easy with you. You're better than Mick, a lot better. Take a rest now. Look, you're still shivering. What are you thinking about, Duffy, I'll tell you what I'm thinking. This is our honeymoon. We were married today, in St Stephen's. I was wearing a gorgeous white dress and had an armful of lilies. The reception was in the Caledonian Hotel. Over fifty guests. Champagne for everybody to toast the bride and groom. Now this is us in the bridal suite. Let me do the work this time, honey. Put your hands here.' She placed his hands on her buttocks. 'Relax. That's it. Leave it all to your Molly. She knows what you want. She knows how to put you in heaven. You know, Duffy, I think you've been saving it all up for me. Isn't this marvellous? Just give my arse a squeeze if you want to take over. I know men like to finish it. I'm wishing I wasn't on the pill. I want your baby, Duffy, the wee boy with the red hair or the wee girl with the brown eyes.'

The door-bell rang, stridently.

'Never mind it,' she said. 'Keep going, honey, keep going. We'll finish together.'

The water began to turn cold.

'Jesus!' she reached past him to turn it off but turned it the wrong way. Icy water poured down on them.

'For Christ's sake!' she yelled, and this time turned it the right way.

The door-bell was still ringing.

'It's getting on my nerves,' she said. Not so whole-heartedly now, she returned to the love-making. 'I'd think it was Mick if his mother hadn't ordered him to stay in the house. That creep Johnny Crosbie wouldn't come without Mick. It can't be Cooley. You said she'd gone to London, though Sally doesn't believe it. You'd think it was cops, the way they keep on ringing. Anyway, this isn't against the law. I'm over sixteen and boys can do it at any age if they're able. I know two who can do it better than a lot of men and they're just twelve. Maybe it's kids playing at ringing door-bells. I used to play at it when I was a kid. Look, honey, maybe we should finish this in bed, where it'll be more comfortable anyway.'

He clung to her. He wanted this love-making as it was called, this ultimate defilement, this escape from self, to go on forever.

'O.K.' she said. With determination this time, she held him firm, heaved her strong hips, and soon brought him ruthlessly to climax.

His groan of despair she took to be of pleasure and appreciation.

'It was good,' she said, 'but it'll be better in bed. Go and get rid of whoever's ringing that fucking bell. See you soon.'

She stepped out of the bath, seized a towel, and ran towards the bedroom.

He felt as exhausted as he had been beside Crosbie's body. He put on his dressing-gown. It must be Cooley at the door. No one else would ring with such persistence. She had come back, afraid that without her to restrain him he would go too far. 'You'll end up murdering somebody.'

Only Cooley could help him now.

It was Mrs Munro wearing a black dress that smelled of moth balls. She was peevish and not quite sober. She had just suffered a severe disappointment in love. For years she had had a little affair going with Andy Logan, with occasional nookie in the back room of his shop in Wallace Street, amidst rolls of paper and the smell of paint, after Bingo. That evening he had made it all too plain, by ignoring her ogles of allurement, that she was no longer on his list. As a consequence when she shuffled on sore feet into Duffy's house she was in a mood of vindictive virtuousness.

'I can see I'm too late,' she cried. She pulled open his dressing-gown and revealed his spent state. 'Look at that. The one thing you had in your favour was your innocence and now you've lost it. Where is she? She didn't think I saw her but I did. Her mother's got seven others besides her and her father's a scrounger who hasn't worked for years. He comes into The Curly Lamb (that's the pub where Mr Munro's captain of the domino team) and cadges drinks.

How could I settle down to watching television knowing that you were being raped, for that I'm sure is what it amounted to. First it was that brazen bitch Cooley and now this trollop McGowan who, if what I hear is right, opens her legs to men of seventy and boys of fourteen alike. Why is your hair wet? What's been going on? Where is she?'

She looked in the living-room, then in the bathroom, and finally in the bedroom. What she saw there made her shriek. Molly, naked, was seated on the bed clipping her toe-nails. The red nightgown was spread out ready to be put on. She had brushed her hair, put on powder and lipstick, and sprinkled herself with scent.

Mrs Munro was flabbergasted by those bridal preparations. 'You impudent besom!' she cried.

Molly looked up, astonished. 'Who's this fat cow?' she asked.

'I'll fat cow you! Who gave you permission to come into this house and use it as if it was your own?'

Molly was on her dignity. 'Duffy did. Tell her, Duffy.'

'You know this boy's not right in the head. Neither are you, from all accounts, but you've got loads of slyness to make up for it. Look, your face is full of it.' But it was Molly's breasts that Mrs Munro found most provoking. They were too insolent in their jutting firmness (Mrs Munro's own without support sagged to her navel) too fresh and white (not like Mrs Munro's the colour of old paste) and too round.

Molly had encountered boozy jealous women before. 'Mrs, you're drunk,' she said tolerantly. 'Duffy, get rid of her, for fuck's sake.'

'How dare you use such language in my presence!' cried Mrs Munro. 'How dare you call me drunk!' She then saw the tattoo on Molly's belly. 'In the name of God what's that?'

'It's a tattoo.'

'I know it's a tattoo, but what does it say?'

'It says LOVE. It should have been MAKE LOVE NOT WAR

but it would have cost too much.' She smiled, prepared to be neighbourly. 'You don't have to tell his mother. Duffy and me are going to get married. Aren't we, honey?'

She turned her back then, modestly, to pick up the nightgown and put it on.

Mrs Munro could not resist. Though her feet were killing her she rushed forward and gave that big soft white backside a resounding skelp. 'Go and put your clothes on,' she cried, 'and get out of this house before I send for the police.'

Molly was more affronted than hurt. She rebuked Duffy. 'Are you going to stand there like a dummy and let her hit your sweetheart?'

Mrs Munro remembered that there was a dead man and a grieving widow upstairs. 'Keep your voice down,' she said. 'There's death in the building.'

'You're the one, Mrs, that's doing all the shouting. Me and Duffy were minding our own business, quiet as mice, bothering nobody, and you come in and start yelling your head off.'

'While his mother's away I'm taking her place. I'm Mrs Munro, her next-door neighbour. Get dressed and leave.'

'I'll leave if Duffy wants me to leave, and not because you tell me to.'

'Look at him. He's lost what wits he had. God knows what damage you've done him, girl. A boy so simple he hardly knew the difference between men and women, I'm referring to sex, and you come at him with those bosoms and that behind. Is it any wonder he's struck dumb? I don't have to ask what business it was you were minding. I had a look at his business when I came in. Poor Duffy. There's no hope for you now.'

'He wanted it as much as me,' said Molly. 'He was desperate for it. If you ask me he needed it.'

'What man or boy offered that body of yours wouldn't be desperate for it?' asked Mrs Munro, with a sigh. Except my Alec, she thought bitterly: he'd ask you if you played dominoes.

Molly appreciated the compliment. 'I'm going to spend

the night: to keep him company. To tell you the truth, I'm looking forward to a good night's sleep, for a change. At home I've to sleep with two of my sisters; sometimes three, for wee Jessie crawls in too.'

As one of a big family herself, brought up in a room-and-kitchen, Mrs Munro sympathised. She sat on the bed: her feet were painful. She wondered if it would rouse Alec to perform his marital duties more often if she had LOVE tattoo'd on her belly. Unfortunately it would never be seen in the rolls of fat. This girl, she had to admit, had an enticing body. If she had been a man herself she would have been enticed. The randiness she had felt two hours ago when Andy, with his smart patter and artist's bow-tie, had come into her house now returned. But Andy was lost to her forever. There was no one else she could think of, available and willing to assuage her. There was young Bruce Stuart, only twenty-one and in his sexual prime, able to serve ten women without losing power or interest. He would be able to make it last, too, unlike Alec with whom it was all over before she could say double-six. Billy of course couldn't be importuned: not because he was a neighbour's husband but because he would feel insulted.

She sighed again. 'Maybe you're right, maybe it was what he needed, to make him grow up, God help him.'

Molly had put on the nightgown. It was too tight across the chest and buttocks. Mrs Munro gave it a helpful tug.

'Duffy,' she said, 'Would you like to get me a wee whisky? Not all that wee. Glenmorangie, that your mother keeps for special visitors. No water.'

'I'll get it,' said Molly. 'I know where the whisky's kept.' She went out, with much waggling of her bottom.

'It's true, the lassie's never had much of a chance,' said Mrs Munro. 'Duffy, if I interrupted your education, I'm sorry. That's what Mr Munro told me I would be doing. It was on the tip of my tongue to say he had a lot to learn himself. What am I to do, Duffy? I know what your mother would want me to do. She'd want me to kick her down the stairs. But your mother's enjoying herself, isn't she, with a man in her bed that's not thinking of dominoes. So if you can keep a secret so maybe can I. Would you like her to stay the night?'

He nodded. He could not bear to spend the night alone. His monsters, as Cooley had called them, were on the prowl.

Mrs Munro had to laugh. 'Aren't you the young devil?'

Molly came in with the whisky. 'Why is he a young devil, Mrs Munro?'

'He wants you to stay the night. My God, lassie, this is a real stotter. Maybe you should go and pour some of it back.'

'That's all that was left.'

'Well, in that case I might as well finish it off. Here's to young love.' She took a generous sip.

'Why is he a devil because he wants me to stay?' asked Molly, earnestly. 'We'd be doing no harm.'

'Halleluijah to that, lassie. It's just that everybody, me included, was thinking he's a softie, left out of things, a bit backward – no offence, Duffy – and what does he get up to the minute his mother's back's turned? First it was that Helen Cooley he had staying with him.'

'He didn't sleep with Cooley,' said Molly. 'She's got the pox. I've never had anything like that. I'm very careful.'

'You're very lucky, more like. He swears he didn't sleep with her, though we don't mean sleeping, do we?' Then he's invited you, and on Tuesday night guess what? He's to play badminton with guess who? Margaret Porteous, her whose mother owns the pottery.'

This quick transition from a rival with pox to one that played badminton had Molly frowning. She had no gum in her mouth but champed as if she did.

'He doesn't know Margaret Porteous.'

'I wouldn't have thought so myself but she was at his door earlier today leaving a message that she would see him at the badminton on Tuesday.'

'How can he play badminton? He hasn't got a racket.'

'I gave him one. I bought it at a jumble sale years ago.'

'Porteous and her crowd will just laugh at him.'

'Maybe, but she didn't strike me as the kind who'd laugh at somebody with a misfortune.'

Mrs Munro had drunk the whisky too quickly. She rose and handed the empty glass to Molly. 'Jack Ralston used to say Duffy had the knack of keeping quiet. Hasn't he just? He's not uttered a word since I came in.'

'He doesn't speak much,' admitted Molly.

Mrs Munro indicated that she wanted Molly to see her out.

At the door she said: 'He seems to have something on his mind. Do you think he's worrying about his mother?'

Molly smirked. 'He's got me on his mind.'

'That could be it. I'm wondering if you're not too much for him.'

'I'll see he takes it easy.'

'You do that. Good-night.'

Mrs Munro shuffled across the landing into her own house, resolved to claim her rights. If Alec was still reading the *News of the World* or the *Sunday Post* she would take it from him, without apology. She would make it very clear she wanted to be made love to. If necessary she would strip naked in front of him. If he said wait till bed-time she would remind him any time was bed-time and any place was a bed for the purposes of love. She might even challenge him to do it from the back as, it seemed, Billy Stuart did now that Agnes was so big-bellied. However it was done it would be beautiful, even if her belly was rolls of fat and his legs ropes of varicose veins. To help her to see it as beautiful she would imagine Molly and Duffy doing it, the girl with her splendid body and the boy so young and handsome (his mind needn't come into it).

Before going back to the bedroom Molly took the opportunity to use the toilet again and also to satisfy herself that Duffy hadn't passed Cooley's pox on to her. Her private parts were as rosy and healthy as ever, and in very good working order.

The only blemish on her happiness was the mysterious

intrusion of Margaret Porteous. She would have to get Duffy to tell her about this invitation to play badminton on Tuesday. In any case she had nothing to worry about. Playing badminton couldn't be compared with making love, could it?

He was still where she had left him, against the wall, except that he wasn't standing but crouching. He was making whimpering noises. She was reminded of a collie pup her family once had. It had cowered like this, whimpering, when it had made a mess and knew it was going to get its nose rubbed in it.

She crouched beside him. He didn't seem to see her. He was shivering. She touched him. He was cold. Yet the room was warm.

'What's the matter, honey?' she asked. 'She's not going to tell your mother. What if she did? We're going to get married, aren't we?'

He didn't seem to hear her either. She couldn't help grinning. She'd never had this effect on anybody before.

'Is it because she told me about Margaret Porteous? Don't be daft. I couldn't be jealous of her. She's not in our class, Duffy. She thinks you and me are common as shit.'

She began to feel worried. Maybe Cathie had been right and making love to a woman was dangerous for him: some men were like that, Cathie had said. But he had been willing, hadn't he? She had had to tell him to take it easy. He had wanted it to go on all night.

'Say something, Duffy, for Christ's sake.'

But he said nothing.

Perhaps he took fits. She wouldn't like it if any of her kids took fits. She imagined that little boy with the red hair taking a fit like this, unable to see or hear or speak.

'I didn't know you took fits, Duffy.'

In Dirty Chuck's girls had often discussed his peculiar backwardness. Nobody had ever suggested it could be because he took fits.

'Is there any medicine you take for it?'

Apprehensively she took his hand and with it rubbed her

warm breast. It had no effect. She might as well have been
made of wood. She wondered if she should go and bring
Mrs Munro.

'I don't know what the hell to do, Duffy.'

CHAPTER TWENTY-FOUR

On Tuesday morning when Mrs Crosbie crept meekly into
Lightburn Police Station to report that her boy Johnny
was missing she was received with courtesy and kindness,
though everybody she spoke to thought privately that if the
young bastard never turned up she would be a lot better-off.
She was passed on to Detective-Sergeant McLeod who had
been looking for Crosbie to question him in connection
with the defiling of the hymn-books. In the station as in the
town itself there had been some hilarity over that escapade:
none of the victims was all that popular. McLeod, however,
as a Free Kirk adherent, had seen nothing funny or fitting
in what he kept calling a sacrilege.

Interviewing Mrs Crosbie he was kindly and patient.

'Is he in the habit of not coming home?' he asked.

'For one night sometimes, never for two.'

In a hat shaped like a chamber-pot, with artificial flowers
round its brim, she represented, he thought, truth, far
better than marble statues he had seen, of beautiful young
women with bare bosoms and laurels in their hair. She
would not knowingly tell a lie to save her own life or,
what was more precious to her (such was the miracle of
motherhood) her worthless son's.

'You see, Mr McLeod, Johnny and his father have never
got on. Mr Crosbie is a very proud man. He thinks Johnny
has brought shame on him.'

Well, to be fair, so he has, thought McLeod.

'He's not religious but he believes that Johnny is a
judgment on him.'

McLeod belonged to a church that saw judgments
everywhere.

'Johnny has a tumour on his brain.' She said it so humbly that at first McLeod didn't grasp its enormity.

'Did you say a tumour?'

'Yes.'

But there were tumours and tumours. Flora had had one, about five years ago, in her uterus. Thank God it had not been malignant and had been cut out with no harmful consequence. The brain was a trickier area.

'Is he receiving medical attention?' he asked.

'Oh yes. Dr Telfer's our doctor. He's been very attentive. But nothing can be done. It is malignant and it can't be operated on.'

McLeod was stunned. His villain, before his very eyes, had been turned into a victim, deserving pity.

'It gives him terrible headaches. That is why he does such crazy things. Sometimes he goes blind.'

'I must say, Mrs Crosbie, I didn't know that about your boy.'

'It's been my fault, Mr McLeod. I've told everybody that one day he would be cured. I said it because I hoped it was true, only I knew it wasn't.'

McLeod didn't know how to say it. He coughed instead.

She understood. 'Any time.'

So he could be lying somewhere dead.

'Have you any idea where he might have gone, Mrs Crosbie?'

She began to haver. 'He often says he would like to see the world. He looks at maps a lot.'

McLeod himself had no such wish. Two summers ago he had gone on holiday to the Costa Del Sol. He had not enjoyed it. It had not been his idea of pleasure and relaxation to sit on a hot beach surrounded by women with bare breasts. Given the choice of retiring to Barbados or Skye he'd choose the island of rain and mists any day. But really anywhere would do, so long as you did not have a tumour in your brain.

'He keeps saying he'd like to see London.'

'Is that so?' McLeod himself had no inclination to visit

that sinful and alien capital.

'He could be lying dead somewhere,' she said, 'here in Lightburn.'

So he could, if the tumour had burst, if that was what tumours did.

'Well, Mrs Crosbie, I assure you we'll do everything we can to find him for you. It's a bit early yet to classify him as an officially missing person but if he doesn't turn up in a day or two we'll put out a nation-wide appeal. His description will be given to every police station in the country.'

'I'm not sure Johnny would like that . . .'

When she was gone McLeod sought out Detective Constable Black. He could not bear to tell him about Crosbie's tumour. Such things depressed Harry, who did not have the consolation and spiritual strength given by religious faith. Harry indeed was living in sin with Fiona Campbell, a physiotherapist at the local hospital. It amazed McLeod that a man so pernickety about dress and personal cleanliness – Harry liked a fresh shirt on every day – and so antagonistic towards law-breakers, should be so lax in his own morals, for he also smoked and drank.

Together they set off to pay a visit they did not look forward to. Mick Dykes, Crosbie's pal, was the most likely person in Lightburn to know where he might be. Unfortunately Mick's mother was a lady best avoided. Formidable at any time, she was said to be in a furious frame of mind because she had found out that her son Mick was the lover of Mrs Burnet, alias Fat Annie, a married woman with three children. Rumour had it that she had threatened to chop off his trespassing dick with a hatchet. At no time however would she welcome representatives of the law.

'What the fuck do you want?' she asked.

A cigarette hung from her mouth. Her sleeves were rolled up, revealing arms as massive as a wrestler's. She was wearing a lumpy purple jumper with holes in it. Her hair was shaggy, her eyes fierce.

McLeod tried very hard to keep calm. If he got excited or angry his pronounciation of English suffered. It would be humiliating to hear this termagant speaking the language better than himself.

'We would be obliged, Mrs Dykes, if we could ask your son Michael some questions about his friend Johnny Crosbie, whose mother has reported him missing.'

'She should be saying good riddance. He's broken her heart a hundred times. I don't see how Mick will be able to help you because he's not been over the door since Sunday. But you can come in. Make sure you wipe your feet on the mat.'

Whatever her sleeves had been rolled up for it couldn't have been to tidy or clean her house. It was a mess and stank of tobacco, alcohol, sweat, anal odours, rancid fat, and other dubious substances. McLeod felt sorry for Harry, whose nose was more fastidious than his own.

The two older sons were seen sneaking into a bedroom. There was no sign of Mick or Mr Dykes, senior.

'Dykes is down at the public library,' said Mrs Dykes, 'getting a free read at the newspapers. Either it's to find out what's going on in the world or it's to keep out of my way or maybe it's both. Mick's in the shunkey, where he spends half his life, tossing himself off, I shouldn't wonder. Well, didn't you do it yourself, sergeant, when you were his age? There's no law against it, so far anyway, though there's bound to be some interfering bastard somewhere thinking one up. Why the hell are you bothering about Johnny Crosbie? If he was found with his throat cut nobody would grieve, except his mother, poor sod. Have you asked Archie Cooper? He was going to tear off Johnny's balls for what he did to his sister Sally, though according to Mick she asked for what she got.'

'Mr Cooper has been questioned. We are satisfied that he knows nothing about Johnny's disappearance.'

'You're telling me. Him and his mate have never been sober during their leave. Everybody wanted to stand the heroes a drink. Heroes my arse. The Brits have no fucking right in Ireland. You ask Dykes: he knows the history. I'll tell Big Dick you're here.'

They heard her banging on the bathroom door and bawling that Teuchter and Flash Harry had come to ask him about Johnny Crosbie.

'If she was my mother,' said Black, 'I'd drown myself.'

She came back laughing. 'Do you think I could get him into the police force? He's big and stupid enough.'

McLeod and Black did not join in her laughter.

'He'd do anything he was ordered to do, so long as the money was good. That's how you fellows look at it, isn't it? Dykes says you've got no opinions or principles of your own. You're just the bosses' bully-boys.'

McLeod could hardly point out that she was referring to the uniformed branch. It would have looked as if he was agreeing with her.

They heard the cistern being flushed. Soon young Dykes appeared, sheepish and anxious.

'What about Johnny?' he muttered. 'What's happened to him?'

Before he could prevent her his mother pulled from under his pullover a pornographic magazine. She opened it. There were coloured pictures of hard-faced women with huge breasts.

Black looked with a grin, but McLeod turned his eyes away. He would have liked to ask where the boy had got this filthy thing but his rule was, keep to the matter in hand, which was Crosbie's whereabouts.

'He can't get enough of it,' Mrs Dykes was saying. 'If he was a Derby winner we'd make a fortune hiring him out.'

'Michael,' said McLeod, 'have you any idea where Johnny might be? His mother has reported him missing. He left the house on Sunday morning about ten o'clock, without saying where he was going. He was seen two hours later in Ballochmyle Avenue, near St Stephen's church. Since then he seems to have disappeared. We thought that since you're his best friend you may have some idea where he may be.'

'How do I know where he is?' mumbled Mick. 'I've not been out of the house since Sunday.'

'I can vouch for that,' said his mother.

'Mrs Crosbie mentioned a possibility that he might have gone to London,' said McLeod.

'It's Cooley that's gone to London.'

'You mean Helen Cooley?'

'She's one whose spirit you bastards will never break,' said Mrs Dykes.

'She wouldn't go with Johnny. She doesn't like him.'

'Who does, you big sumph?'

'I like him. He gets bad headaches. Nobody's fair to him.'

McLeod did not want to hear any more about those headaches. They were not his business. Finding the boy who suffered from them was.

'Have you any definite reason to believe Helen Cooley has gone to London?' he asked.

'She asked me to ask my uncle Fred if he could get her a lift. He's a lorry-driver. He gave her a note to give to a mate of his in a depot in Glasgow. I don't know if she went.'

'This is the first I've heard of this,' said Mrs Dykes, 'though his uncle Fred happens to be my brother. It's not a crime, is it, to help somebody get a lift?'

'Is it a crime to help an absconder to avoid arrest, though it is possible your brother was not aware that that was what he was doing. It may be necessary for us to question him.'

'He'll tell you bugger-all. Fred's not fond of your kind. If Dykes was here he'd tell you you were a shower of Fascists, well-paid to protect your masters, them with the money and property. He'd tell you that the biggest thieves in the country are the financiers and speculators. I'd be obliged if you'd get the hell out of my house.'

She did not merely show them to the door, she shoved them towards it.

CHAPTER TWENTY-FIVE

The detectives had hardly left before Mick was pleading with his mother to let him go out. He was sure he knew where Johnny was hiding. He wanted to warn him that the cops were looking for him.

She was pleased with him for having the gumption to withhold the information from McLeod, and she was also feeling a bit sorry for having leathered him in the presence of his brothers and married sisters, not to mention his six-year-old nephew, though luckily wee Malcolm had been asleep. She had had too much to drink and had lost her temper. Besides she had since learned that the wean Fat Annie was expecting couldn't be Mick's. Also he was her youngest. Though he was six feet tall and endowed like a bull she could remember wheeling him about in a pram. He had been a good baby: stick a dummy in his mouth and he'd be quiet for hours. It was in his favour too that he was loyal to his pal, even though that pal, headaches or not, wouldn't hesitate to shop him.

'All right, son. Will it take you long?'

'Just half an hour.'

'Where do you think he is?'

'He's got a den in Crimea Street, in the house where he was born.'

'They're knocking it down,' said Tam, his oldest brother.

'They've not started on Johnny's yet.'

'I wouldn't be so sure about that. Yesterday they were knocking down everything in sight. It was like a war down there. We'd to pack it in because of the stour and noise.'

Tam attended a pitch-and-toss school in that part of town.

Mick was alarmed. What if they demolished Johnny's building with him in it? They would think there was nobody there. He might have one of his headaches and not know what was going on.

'I'd better hurry,' said Mick, making for the door.

'Just a minute,' cried his mother. 'You might as well bring me a few things while you're out. Half a stone of tatties. A pint of milk. Half a pound of marge. A large plain loaf.'

'Fags,' said his other brother Jim.

'If you want fags you'd better give him the money.'

Grumbling, Jim went to his bedroom to search through his pockets.

'Hurry,' shouted Mick.

'You're making me suspicious,' said Tam, with a wink at his mother. 'You're making me think you want to get back to that fat cow. You're like a bull pawing the ground. Isn't he, ma?'

His mother raised her fist. 'Tam's not right, is he?' she cried.

'No, he isn't.'

'Just as well for you.'

'I just want to warn Johnny, that's all.'

'You think more of that obnoxious little bastard than you do of your whole family.'

'No, I don't. He's my pal, that's all.'

Jim came back with some money. It wasn't enough. He had to cadge the rest from his mother. She was reluctant. It took time. Mick was getting desperate.

At last he was allowed to go. He had the string-bag for the groceries stuffed into his pocket. He hated to be seen going errands.

He ran all the way. Before he was near Crimea Street he saw that Tam was right. After weeks of idleness the demolishers were back at work and were going at it as if they were on piece-work. There were great clatters and clouds of dust. If Johnny was found crushed to death it would be Duffy's fault. It had been his idea breaking into the church.

Mick had known it would bring bad luck. Look what had happened to him. Johnny too was missing. Cooley would get caught in London and sent back. The worst punishment ought to be Duffy's, for he had been the leader.

When Mick arrived, panting, amongst the great heaps of bricks, masonry, and wall-papered plaster, the huge iron ball was being swung against the building next to Johnny's. Johnny's, thank Christ, was still standing, though, as Mick stared at it in terror, it seemed to shoogle.

A middle-aged workman wearing a yellow hard hat stopped him. 'Where do you think you're going?' he shouted. 'This is a danger area. Do you want to get killed?'

Mick had to shout too. 'My pal Johnny Crosbie's in that building.'

'What the hell are you talking about? There's nobody there. Everybody was cleared out months ago.'

'I know but Johnny's got a den he sometimes sleeps in, in the house where he was born. Up that close. I've come to warn him.'

'He must be stone deaf.'

'He takes headaches. He wouldn't hear anything.'

'Is this a joke?'

'No. He could be in that building. I swear it.'

'That close?'

'That's right. First storey. Middle door.'

'The foundations have been loosened. The whole place could collapse.'

'I'll run up and see. It'll not take a minute.'

'No, you won't. Maybe I ought to tell the gaffer. All right. You wait here. First storey. Middle door.'

Mick ran after him. 'Let me come. He knows me.'

'What's your name?'

'Mick Dykes.'

The man grinned. 'Malky Dykes' boy?'

'Yes.'

'You're the one they say has the biggest dick in town.'

Three days ago Mick would have beamed at that jocular tribute. Today he scowled.

In the close the workman took off his helmet and put it on Mick. It was much too small. It perched ludicrously on the sandy curls.

'You're big in every department,' said the workman.

Mick raced up the stairs ahead of him.

The door was open. He ran in. 'Johnny!' he shouted.

'Not so fucking loud,' muttered the workman behind him. 'Do you want to bring the place down about us?'

They heard the great thump of the iron ball.

The ludo board was spread out on a box. On it were red and blue men, and the ivory dice that Johnny was so proud of.

'You see, he's been here,' said Mick. 'He was playing ludo.'

'That's a kid's game. How old is he?'

'Sixteen.'

'And he still plays ludo. He must be a head case. But let's get out of here quick.'

Mick slipped the dice into his pocket. He left the ludo board and the men.

As he went down the stairs he remembered how Johnny liked to play ludo with Mick's nephew and niece, aged six and four respectively. He never cheated them.

'Beat it,' said the workman. 'I hope the gaffer hasn't noticed.'

The potatoes were needed for dinner which had to be ready for one o'clock, but instead of making straight for the shop where his mother got groceries on credit Mick headed for Kenilworth Court. He was sure now that Johnny was at Duffy's. Probably he had spent the night there, helping Duffy to screw Molly. Thinking of the three of them in the big soft bed Mick, even as he ran, felt the old strong stirring in his loins and was greatly relieved. After all he had to suffer during the past three days, the pain and the shame, he had been afraid that his virility was weakened forever. Looking at those pictures of the tarts fingering their twats had not had the usual effect. In fact for some reason he could not understand it had depressed, not stimulated him. He had for the first time noticed their faces, how hard and cynical these were.

He was nervous as he rang Duffy's bell. Cooley had told him about the inquisitive neighbour.

When Duffy's door opened he walked in without waiting to be asked. He wasn't usually rude like this, it showed how keyed-up he was. At first he noticed nothing odd about Duffy.

In the living-room he sat down, again without being asked. He heard no noises. Perhaps Molly and Johnny were still in bed. He should have asked about Johnny first but somehow he put it off.

'Is she still here?' he asked. 'Molly.'

'No.'

'Oh. When did she leave?'

'This morning.'

'So she was here all night?'

'Yes.'

It was then that Mick noticed how pale Duffy was, how large and dark his eyes were, and how every now and then he shivered, though the room was warm. He couldn't have got much sleep. A night with Molly must have taken a lot out of him.

Mick felt he should give him some advice. 'Don't let her become your regular girl-friend, Duffy. Behind your back she'd give it to anybody for a packet of chewing gum.'

Duffy said nothing.

'Where's Johnny, Duffy? Did he spent the night here too? Is he still here?'

Duffy shook his head.

'Hasn't he been here at all?'

Again Duffy shook his head.

'Are you sure?'

Duffy nodded. He seemed too exhausted to speak.

'Then where the hell can he be? I was sure he would be here because he wasn't in his den that I told you about. I went there. I've just been. I took his dice. It's real ivory.' He brought it out of his pocket and showed it to Duffy.

'You see, Duffy, Teuchter and Flash Harry came to my house this morning to ask me if I knew where Johnny was. His mother's reported him missing. He's not been home since Sunday. He was last seen in Ballochmyle, near the church. I don't know what he was doing there. You told him not to. I thought he would be here, with you and Molly. They're knocking his building down.'

'Are the workmen there now?'

'Sure. You should see the place. You'd think a bomb had hit it. The cops think that Johnny's gone to London with Cooley, but do you know what I think? I think maybe he's hiding in the church. He likes creepy places. We shouldn't have done it, Duffy. Look what's happened to us since. Cooley's gone to London, I've been in trouble because of Annie, and Johnny's disappeared. It could be your turn next, Duffy.'

'Are you sure all the buildings are being knocked down?'

The question surprised Mick, but he put it down to Duffy's brain being still shaken after his night with Molly. 'Johnny's was the only one standing but they'll have started on it now.' He got to his feet. 'I'll have to go now.' He almost said that he'd to buy potatoes for the dinner. Duffy himself of course didn't mind going messages, and look how tidy the house was. He was a bit of a jessie. No wonder Molly had been too much for him.

'If Johnny comes, Duffy, tell him the cops are looking for him. We don't want Teuchter asking him questions about what happened in the church.'

Duffy saw him to the door.

Before he went out he whispered: 'If Molly's coming back tonight, Duffy, do you mind if I come too? Just for an hour or so.'

'I'm going to a funeral this afternoon.'

'Who's dead?'

'Mr Ralston, who lived upstairs.'

'I've never seen a dead person. They wanted me to look at my grandfather in his coffin but I wouldn't. I was just eight at the time. What about tomorrow night, Duffy? Could I come then?'

Duffy hesitated and then nodded.

Running down the stairs Mick found himself whistling cheerfully. He would get a row for being late with the potatoes, his arse was still sore, Johnny was missing, he would never again drink beer at Annie's fireside, maybe God still had it in for him, but he was young and alive and, let them laugh if they liked, he had the grandest dick in Lightburn.

CHAPTER TWENTY-SIX

The crematorium used by the people of Lightburn was in a neighbouring town eight miles away. A bus passed the gates and Duffy had intended to take it but Mrs Ralston insisted that he accompany her and her family in the black limousine hired from Paton the undertaker. She was concerned about him, he didn't look well. She thought he was upset by Jack's death and also was missing her mother.

In the big opulent car Mrs Ralston, Cissie, and Duffy sat on one side, while opposite them sat Cissie's husband Albert, Sid, Jack's brother from Motherwell, and Angela, Sid's wife.

Cissie wept all the way, not only because her father was dead and her baby in hospital was dying, but also for remoter reasons not clearly known to herself. Albert, like an American marine with his crew-cut hair and pale skinny face, chewed gum, picked his nose, and scowled out at the rain. Mrs Ralston, in black, puffed sadly at her veil. Sid kept whispering, out of the corner of his mouth, to his wife to keep quiet. She was scandalised that there was to be no religious service. She had a pudgy face, huffy mouth, crafty eyes, and girning voice. Albert's dress also displeased her. She did not think a mauve suit with wide lapels, a floral shirt, a black tie like a shoelace, and high-heeled boots, appropriate for a funeral. She herself wore a black hat, black gloves, and black shoes, but her fur coat was brown. Fur, she had said, of any colour was suitable for any occasion.

'People will think the Ralstons are heathens,' she said.

'Jack didn't want a minister to be present,' replied Mrs Ralston.

'When he was too ill to realise what he was saying.'

'His mind was clear enough.'

'It's all right for him, Phemie. He's not here to bear the affront. Heathen scruff, that's what they'll think we are, with good reason too.' She glared at Albert.

'At least they'll not think we're hypocrites.'

'Well said, Phemie,' said Sid.

'She's not,' said Sid. 'far from it.'

'I'll answer for myself, Sid Ralston, if you don't mind.'

'You never go. You're always saying that those who do go are a lot of hypocrites.'

'So they are, most of them. A person can be a good Christian without ever stepping inside a church.'

'I doubt if the Pope would agree with you, Angela,' said her husband, with a wink at Duffy.

Albert showed interest. A supporter of Glasgow Rangers, he was a fanatical anti-Papist.

'Is there to be no service at all?' asked Angela. 'Are we just to sit and look at one another?'

'What's wrong with that, if we're remembering Jack?' said Sid.

'Is he just to be burnt like a sackful of rubbish?'

'He'd have been the first to admit that's all he is now.'

'Show respect for your brother, Sid Ralston. Maybe he didn't deserve it when he was alive – he was a bit of a reckless scamp, wasn't he? – but he's entitled to it now that he's gone. I hope there's going to be sacred music at least.'

'Pipe tunes,' said Mrs Ralston. 'Slow airs. That's what the reckless scamp wanted.'

'They'll never allow that. It would lower the dignity of the place.'

'If you wanted jazz they'd give you jazz,' said Sid. 'It's a business like any other. The customer gets what he pays for. See this car? The more luxurious it is the more the undertaker can charge.'

'At your funeral, Sid Ralston, we'll all go in a lorry.'

He chuckled. 'It wouldn't bother me, Angela.' He gave Duffy another wink.

'You mentioned the Pope, Sid. Well, as good Protestants we know we don't need his approval to get into heaven or keep out of hell, but we do have to have some Christian words spoken at the funeral.'

Her husband winked at Duffy again. This time he meant that he and Duffy were too wise to worry about heaven or hell. Being alive here on earth was all that mattered.

'Councillor Adam McPherson's going to say a few words,' said Mrs Ralston.

'I suppose it would be too much to hope that he's a Conservative?'

'Jack would spin in his coffin if a Tory was to speak at his funeral.'

'See how bitter these socialists are. They carry their spite with them into the grave.'

'You know Jack was never bitter or spiteful. He was never envious either. He didn't mind other people having more than he had. What made him angry was when some Tory with a landed estate and millions in the bank accused men without tuppence of ruining the country with their greed.'

'This is supposed to be a funeral, Phemie, not a political meeting. I just hope this Councillor McPherson's not one of those that want a revolution.'

'He's dying himself, of lung cancer.'

'I expect he's a heavy smoker. I thought so. Well, he's brought it on himself. You'd wonder at somebody that can't manage his own life sensibly would have the impertinence to tell us how the country should be run.'

'If you were to delve into any politician's life, Angela,' said her husband, 'you'd say the same thing. Look at Lloyd George. He couldn't see an attractive woman without wanting to go to bed with her and yet he was said to be the wisest statesman of his time.'

'Sid, remember there's a juvenile present.'

'President Kennedy too. Didn't he say he had to have a woman a day to keep himself in vigorous health?'

'That's crap,' said Albert. 'It makes fuck-all difference to your health. They used to tell boxers in training to keep away from their wives because fucking would weaken them. Doctors say it makes no difference.'

'Don't use such disgusting words in the presence of ladies,' cried Angela.

'What ladies?'

'One of them happens to be your wife.'

'Leave him alone,' said Cissie. 'You're always getting at him, Aunt Angela.'

Angela was choked with indignation.

'Let's all think our private thoughts,' said Sid, with another wink at Duffy.

Think of anything, except Crosbie. Think of the badminton tonight. Think of what to wear: would clean jeans do? Think of a racket: the one Mrs Munro had given him had strings missing, but Stephen Telfer had said he could borrow one. Think of who else might be present.

Someone was speaking to him. 'You!' It was Angela. She did not approve of him, not a member of the family, travelling with them. 'Where was it you said your mother was?'

'Spain.'

'Spain's a big place. Whereabouts in Spain?'

'Torremolinos.'

'March is a funny time to go for a holiday.'

'Duffy's mother's very busy during the summer,' said Mrs Ralston.

'Why didn't she take you with her? You don't look as if you could be trusted to be left on your own.'

'Duffy's managing very well.'

'Just the same it's very selfish of her to go off by herself.'

'Who said she's by herself?' Albert grinned and winked at Duffy.

'So she's got a friend with her.'

'You could call him that.'

'So that's the way of it! I might have guessed. Wherever you turn nowadays there's immorality.'

'Leave the boy alone,' said Sid, with a note in his voice that Angela, though she bridled and tightened her lips, nonetheless heeded.

CHAPTER TWENTY-SEVEN

The notice in the *Glasgow Herald* had said: No flowers. Friends welcome.' On the coffin therefore was only one flower, a dark-red rose, the dead man's tribute to his wife, and the small reception hall was crowded. During Jack's last days not many had come to see him because they had not wanted to watch him suffer and in any case they had their own lives to live, but they were all here now to do him honour. Duffy knew most of them. He was given his share of neighbourly nods and smiles.

Present from Kenilworth Court were Mrs Munro, red-eyed and with her shoes slipped off; Alec her husband, peeping at his hands now and then as if weighing up his chances; young Billy Stuart, wearing his Rangers scarf under his raincoat; Mrs Stuart, pale-faced and tearful; Mr Duncanson, a dustman, who lived up the adjacent close; Mrs Duncanson, who sucked peppermints as if she was in church; and several others.

Among those from other parts of the town was Mr Logan, with a black bow-tie and his hair, dyed black, gleaming with scented oil. His fat wife was not with him. She had known that one of his lady-loves came from Kenilworth Court and had always suspected Phemie Ralston. It would have been hard to convince her it had been Maggie Munro who, with her ruined figure and misshapen feet, was no more bedworthy than herself.

Some of the women enquired after Duffy's mother. He heard one whisper to another: 'Poor lad, he always tries to look as if he knew what was going on.'

He paid them all as close attention as he could, lest he

should slip again into that state of paralysed terror which
had so frightened Molly.

An opinion shared by many was that Jack had deserved
the best but all the same the money spent on that swanky
coffin with the brass fittings and silk tassels would have
been more sensibly used to provide for the widow. It was
however generally believed that she would not remain a
widow for long, being still a young woman and bonny
with it.

Another general belief was that *that* wasn't the box that
would go into the furnace. Out of sight a cheap one of
pinewood would be substituted.

All the time in the background there was music: a pipe
band played slow airs, commemorating sad events such
as enforced departures from ancestral islands. There were
tears on tough Celtic faces.

At last Councillor McPherson arrived, apologising for
being late. His dress at least must have pleased Angela,
for he wore a dark suit and black tie. So too would his
appearance, for he was grey-haired and ill-looking, with
clapped-in cheeks and hardly enough energy to stand up
straight far less overturn society. He certainly did not
look like the firebrand who in his younger days had
advocated the abolition of Royalty, the House of Lords,
the Judges, and the Established Churches, as well as the
Stock Exchange. Nor did he sound like it either, for he
spoke in a weary voice often interrupted by coughing.

That afternoon it was Death he was for abolishing. 'I
could give you a hundred memories of my friend and
comrade Jack Ralston. So could every one of you here.
Put together, surely they would represent him at his best.
We give one another immortality. Only a person loved
and remembered by no one ever dies. There is no such
person . . .'

Realists all, they weren't sure that they agreed with
Adam, as their frowns and grunts indicated. In a few
minutes all that would be left of Jack was a shovelful
of ashes. He would never again trundle a bowl towards

the jack or drink a pint of heavy in The Auld Hoose or carry a hodful of bricks or cheer a goal scored. They would remember him doing all those things but it wouldn't be the same as seeing him do them. As a politician Adam had to talk like that. They knew better. In the end memories faded, everybody was forgotten. Death always had the last laugh.

When the councillor finished, his voice hoarse, and dying for a smoke, he called upon other friends of Jack to stand up and say a few words. They sat still. They were not used to speaking in public, especially when stone-sober. They did not want to make fools of themselves. Later, in The Auld Hoose or The Covenanter or The Curly Lamb or another of Lightburn's fifteen pubs, when they had had two or three halfs and half-pints they would tell the whole world what they thought of their mate Jack Ralston. Here in this bleak crematorium, with the polished coffin and the red rose and the homesick music and their critical wives and, to be frank, some people present they didn't care much for, it would be a tongue-tied ordeal.

Archie Duncanson was first to get to his feet. A small burly man with a big purple nose, he told of how he and Jack had tried football pools together for over eight years and hadn't won so much as a tosser. They'd wondered if it was a record. If you wanted to know what a man was worth you couldn't do better than check a coupon with him and find that instead of the magic twenty-four points you had only eight, the miserable minimum, and therefore instead of half a million quid not a sausage, well if he could see the joke of it and laugh, as Jack had, then he was indeed a friend worth cherishing.

Others decided they could do as well as a beery-nosed dustman. They got up in their turn and praised their dead friend.

CHAPTER TWENTY-EIGHT

The same car took the same passengers to the Caledonian Hotel where refreshments were to be served in a private room to a specially invited few.

Angela had a new grumble: the drinks were to be alcoholic, and free.

'Tea would have done, Phemie, with some scones. Alcoholic drink at funerals is out of fashion nowadays, among the better class of people anyway. If they want whisky let them pay for it.'

'Do the better class of people ask their guests to pay?'

'This is a funeral, Phemie, not a party.'

'It's a good old Scotch custom,' said Sid.

'Well, it's one you're not going to observe, Sid Ralston, for you're driving me home tonight, remember.'

Cissie spoke. 'Dad always wanted people to enjoy themselves.'

'It's not as if he left you well provided for, Phemie,' said Angela.

'How could he?' said Sid grimly. 'He was ill and out of work.'

'I'm just stating a fact. All his life Jack was never a saver. He was a heavy smoker: look what it did to him. He was too fond of a drink: look at the price of whisky. He must have squandered hundreds of pounds on those football pools. I thought it was disgraceful that coarse-looking man mentioning them. But what can you expect from a dustman?'

Mrs Ralston gave her an answer. 'From Archie Duncanson you can expect civility, sensible advice, and help when you need it.'

'I can see, Phemie, living in that run-down place has caused you to lower your standards.'

'You know, wife,' said Albert, in a friendly enough voice, 'you do fuck-all but grumble.'

If she hadn't had her own standards raised by living in a bought bungalow among other bought bungalows she would have clouted him with her handbag. 'Are you going to let that rubbish insult your wife?' she cried to Sid.

'Who are you calling rubbish?' said Albert, aggrieved that his friendliness had been repaid with abuse.

'If he's rubbish then I'm rubbish too,' said Cissie.

'All of you,' said Mrs Ralston, almost in tears, 'please remember we've just come from cremating my husband.'

They were all sorry.

Cissie though looked as if she would never forgive her aunt Angela.

Later in the hotel Mrs Ralston and Mrs Munro were seated in a corner of the private room drinking whisky-and-water and discussing in confidential whispers the former's future. Duffy sat near them sipping coca-cola. He was so quiet they and everybody else forgot he was there.

At the other side of the room Angela was chatting to Jack's last employer, Mr Whiteford and his wife. She had been amazed that so well-to-do a couple had accepted the invitation.

'So you've still got it in mind to go to Toronto?' said Mrs Munro.

'In Kate's cable she and her man Bobby said I'd be very welcome. As you know, Maggie, I liked Toronto.'

'You saw it in summer, Phemie. At this time of year it'll be knee-deep in snow.'

'The houses are all centrally heated. The shops are lovely. You should see Eaton's Centre.'

'I don't think it's the shops that would take you there.'

'Maybe not. It's got other attractions.'

'You met a man there, didn't you? I've always had that impression.'

'Yes, I did. Now that Jack's gone and can't be hurt I can talk about it. This man fancied me.'

'Lots of men fancy you, Phemie. There's Whiteford. He can hardly keep his eyes off you.'

'He had a good job, chief security officer at a big college.'

'He'd be a big fellow then, not like Jack.'

'Yes, he's big, but he's cheery, like Jack. He has a fine house on the college campus, a lovely place with grass and trees and lots of black squirrels.'

'I never knew squirrels could be black. It's a different world over there.'

'I'd miss my friends,'

'They'd miss you, Phemie. Is he a bachelor? I hope not, for they get set in their ways.'

'He's a widower.'

'Any family?'

'Two. Both married and off his hands.'

'Not too old, I hope?'

'He's just fifty.'

'You say he fancied you. Did you fancy him?'

'Yes, I did, very much.'

'That was two years ago. He could have found somebody else since.'

'Kate says he's still single. Every time he meets her he asks after me; so she says.'

'I expect he earns more than Jack ever did.'

'I never compared them.'

'Speaking in confidence, Phemie, did you ever visit him on your owny-oh?'

'Yes.'

'Enough said then.'

'Enough said.'

'What about Cissie? And wee Mary?'

'Wee Mary's not got much longer to live and Cissie's got her man.'

'He's a disaster.'

'We think so, she doesn't.'

'He's young of course. He could improve.'

'I hope so.'

'Have you considered asking her to go with you?'

'I've suggested it. She told me her place was with her man.'

'God help her. Look at that, Phemie. Andy Logan's got his hand on Jessie Duncanson's behoochy again. She's not objecting either. What can he see in her, for God's sake? She's no chicken and she's no oil painting.'

'She's got a fine figure.'

'Do you think so? Are you sure she's not wearing falsies? I wish Archie would notice and blacken his eye. What is it about a funeral makes people randy?'

'I didn't know it did.'

'Where are your eyes? Look at them, all desperate to go to bed with anybody but their husband or wife. Except my Alec. He's wondering if his team will be top of the domino league this year like they were last year. It's funny, Phemie, he never was keen on it. It must be misplaced hormones or something like that. Even on our honeymoon. Nowadays if I drop a hint he tells me to be my age, which is forty-two, as you know, and not eighty-two, as he seems to think.'

'He's a good man in every other way.'

'So I should bite my nails and think myself lucky?'

Angela then approached with Mr and Mrs Whiteford who wished to take their leave and thank their hostess. They did it graciously and Phemie was gracious in return.

'They're the kind of people you should try to keep in with, Phemie,' said Angela, when they were gone. 'They admire you, did you know that?'

'*He* admires her, anyway,' said Mrs Munro. 'He fancies Phemie. He's made approaches.'

'That's enough, Maggie,' said Phemie.

'I should say it's enough,' said Angela, shocked. 'It's a very serious allegation. I'm waiting to hear you deny it, Phemie.'

'Suppose I can't?'

'You're not hinting it's true?'

'Are you surprised, Angela?'

'I'm dumbfounded. He's such a gentleman.'

'Princes and beggars are all the same when they've got houghmagandy on their minds,' said Mrs Munro.

'What a disgusting word, Mrs Munro!'

'A very expressive word, Angela. Burns was fond of it.'

Angela then noticed Duffy within earshot. 'What on earth is that boy doing here? He should have been sent home long ago.'

'There's nobody at home,' said Mrs Ralston. 'I told him if he waited he'd get a lift.'

'You know, I've not heard him say two words. I expect he's been warned to keep his mouth shut. That way he can pass for normal.'

Duffy then went up to Mrs Ralston. 'I think I'll go now.'

'We'll all be going in another half hour. I believe it's still raining.'

'It doesn't matter. I'd like to walk. Thank you for inviting me. Good evening, ladies.'

As he walked away he heard Angela saying: 'He's copied that from films.'

In the foyer he was stopped by Mr Rowan, the proprietor of the hotel.

'You're Bell's boy, aren't you? Mrs Duffy's, I mean.'

'Yes, sir.'

'Were you at the funeral?'

'Yes. Mr Ralston was a neighbour.'

'You won't have had word from your mother yet?'

'No.'

'It's a bit early. How are you managing on your own?'

'All right, thank you'

'Well, if you need anything just come and let me know. I'd do a lot to oblige your mother. We think very highly of her here.'

'Thank you, Mr Rowan.'

It was not possible not to think of Crosbie, and yet thinking of him was very dangerous.

It was as if Duffy had soaked his clothes with paraffin, like a Buddhist monk he had seen on television. Thinking of Crosbie was like striking a match.

Suppose the body was never found. There would be no prolonged and determined search. Only Mrs Crosbie would bother the authorities. They would treat her with sympathy and, whether or not they believed it themselves, assure her that Johnny would turn up sooner or later. Hundreds of young people like him ran away from home every year.

Trying to think of something else was becoming harder and harder.

On his way to the church hall he wondered about Cooley, where she was and how she was getting on. He knew what she would have said to him: 'You were going to save the world and instead you're a murderer. Maybe you should give yourself up. They'd put you in a madhouse but at least it would keep you from murdering somebody else, yourself most likely. The more you hate yourself for what you did the more likely you are to do it again.'

It was strange how well Cooley had known him.

That monk in Saigon had been protesting against the Vietnam War. Millions had seen him do it. His sacrifice had been in vain. The war had gone on.

If Duffy made the same sacrifice and burned himself to death, in front of the town hall, say, what cause could he claim to be dying for? If he was to say that it was in expiation not only for the one death in the derelict building

in Crimea Street but also for the millions of deaths during
the War, he would be told that between his one killing and
those many killings there was a profound difference: his
threatened civilisation, those had helped to save it.

As he approached the church hall it occurred to him
that Margaret Porteous might not be present that night,
the trouble at home having prevented her. He stopped.
Without her to introduce him the others would think
he was an interloper. Stephen Telfer might greet him
cheerfully but that was all: he wouldn't want to spoil his
evening looking after somebody he didn't really know and
wasn't much interested in. No one would be rude to him,
most of them would smile, but he would feel out of it. But
then he *was* out of it, and out of everything, for the rest of
his life. Not even Margaret Porteous could get him back.

Suppose the body was discovered. The police would
think that the injuries to Crosbie's head had been caused
by the mass of bricks and stones falling on him. When they
learned about his tumour they would be confirmed in that
opinion. During an attack he had crept into the close, not
seeing where he was going, and had died there or fallen
unconscious. If the hair-grip was still in his fist it would
puzzle them but not enough to make them change their
verdict that his death had been a gruesome accident. No
one would ever suspect Duffy, except perhaps Cooley. So
far as the law was concerned he would get away with it.
There was though that sentence of exclusion.

Why did he still have this absurd belief that Margaret
Porteous could have saved him? She owed him no special
loyalty. To her he was just a lonely misfit whom she had
pitied, an opportunity for her to show her contempt for
the commonplace morality of her mother and her mother's
friends. She would be as horrified as they if she knew that
he had killed Crosbie. She would join them in keeping
him out.

Another car arrived at the church hall. He saw its
three occupants, a boy and two girls, dressed in white,
hurrying into the hall out of the cold. He heard them

laughing and joking. They were friends. They trusted one another.

Crosbie had trusted him. He had laughed, in utter astonishment, after the first blow. It had been inconceivable to him that Duffy, his friend, could have been so treacherous and cruel.

Even people like Angela who had no generosity, or like Albert who had no compassion, were safe within the fold. They were not liked or admired or respected but they were accepted.

He went forward to the parked cars. Neither the Porteous' white Mercedes nor their green Escort was among them. Perhaps Margaret had come with Stephen Telfer. He opened the door and at once heard happy cries, laughter, and the thud of sandshoes on the wooden floor. He crept upstairs to the small balcony where he sat in a corner in deep shadow looking down at the badminton court. A foursome was in progress. Stephen Telfer and Margaret were playing David Martin and Ellen Findlay. The rest were seated on benches watching and chatting. They were at ease among themselves. It was a respite from studying for the Leaving Certificate Examinations which would take place soon and in which they hoped to do well. Afterwards most of them would go to University. Their futures were secured. But what struck Duffy most was something that they weren't aware of themselves, all their lives they had taken it for granted: it was their dependence on one another, not for anything in particular but for their acceptance as members of society. He realised then how much people gave to one another without knowing that they were doing it. You had to be excluded to know it.

Margaret Porteous was dressed in a short white skirt and a white sweatshirt with an inscription on it that he could not make out. Her bosom was smaller than Molly McGowan's and her thighs more muscular. There were patches of sweat under her oxters. She played as if her life depended on it, leaping and running at speed, smashing the shuttle as hard as she could, and shouting with annoyance

when she mishit. All her life she would love competition
and hate losing.

They were all an immeasurable distance from him. If
he shouted they would look up, not seeing him in the
blackness behind the lights; but he might as well be on
another planet, he was so far out of their reach.

After only two or three minutes he crept down the stairs
again, so quietly that the two in the entrance hall, in a
recess, kissing passionately, did not notice him.

They heard him opening the door. The girl said,
anxiously: 'Who was that?' The boy replied, 'I didn't
see anybody. It must have been the wind.'

At home there was a can of paraffin, used for lamps when
there was a power failure.

CHAPTER THIRTY

Many of the people moving out of the old dirty dilapidated tenements with stairhead lavatories into new houses with bathrooms and in some cases gardens had left behind those of their belongings that were worn and done, such as scuffed armchairs with broken springs, chamber pots of chipped enamel, torn rugs, soiled mattresses, pots and pans with holes in them, broken electric fires, and a miscellany of other household articles, including a whole piano. All these came tumbling down with the walls and were scooped up with the rest of the debris in the huge mechanical shovel and loaded into lorries to be dumped into a quarry outside the town. The shovel-operator, Rab Kemp, and his mates soon gave up laughing at the surprise items that came up with almost every shovelful. Therefore on Thursday afternoon when he saw a cowboy boot sticking out of a mass of plaster covered with yellow wall-paper he paid it little attention until, with a swing of the shovel its contents shifted and he realised, with a shock that as he said afterwards sent a chill through his heart, that the boot was attached to a foot and the foot to a body.

'Jesus fucking Christ,' he muttered, feeling sick and by no means blasphemous. He could not believe it but there it was, a body, a human body, with the face still hidden under the yellow wallpaper.

As gently as he could he lowered the shovel to the ground. Then, green-faced, and with all the strength gone out of his legs, he climbed down and took a closer look. It was a body all right, bent and battered. Feebly he shouted and waved.

Mates saw and came running. Among them was the

middle-aged workman who had spoken to Mick Dykes
two days ago. His name was Peter McLean.

Yesterday the body of a black cat had been unearthed
and there had been jokes about bad luck, but this was
different, this was one of their own species, this was a
matter of supreme seriousness.

The gaffer had gone off an hour ago. In his absence they
did not know what to do. They were to be paid a big bonus
if the job was completed by tomorrow afternoon. This delay
might prevent that, which would be unfair for it wasn't their
fault. The police would have to be sent for and they might
order work to be stopped for the rest of the day. Come to
think of it though, would they want to go on working? Well
yes, they would. They had worked hard for that bonus: it
would be a pity to lose it. The boy – but girls too wore
cowboy boots and jeans – had not been killed by Rab's
shovel or Bert's iron ball. He must have been lying dead
in the building before it was knocked down.

Peter McLean then told about his meeting two days ago
with Mick Dykes: how they had gone into not this building
but the one next to it looking for Mick's pal. It seemed that
they had looked in the wrong place. Mick had said his pal
wasn't well: something wrong with his head.

There was something a lot more wrong with it now.

'Poor cunt,' muttered one, and the rest nodded and
bowed their heads. They had their caps off, though it had
begun to rain.

The police had to be sent for. They were suspicious
bastards and would want to know why they hadn't been
notified immediately. Peter McLean was deputed to go.
He agreed, with reluctance, but objected to having to walk:
it was over half a mile. So he was driven in a ten-ton lorry
half full of debris.

His mates stood well back from the big bucket. They
thought they could smell the body now, though many
dubious smells were encountered in the demolition of old
buildings where people had lived for over a hundred years.
Their cigarettes, lit by shaky hands, tasted of stink.

Detective-Sergeant McLeod was in his office in the station when the big lorry clattered into the courtyard. He was writing out a report on the golf-club break-in. Two culprits had been found, not owing to any skilful detection on his part but because of an anonymous telephone call. Honest people often benefited when thieves fell out.

George Milne knocked and looked in. 'You'd better come and listen to this, Angus. It looks as if your friend Crosbie's been found.'

McLeod had dared to say a word or two in Crosbie's favour: he was young, only sixteen, and he had a tumour on his brain. This wasn't the first time George had sneered at him for it.

'Is he all right?' he asked.

'I would say he's all right. He's dead.'

McLeod was to say to Flora that night that he had known George Milne for eight years but hadn't realised until that moment the depth of George's unhappiness and disappointment. Only a man in despair could have been so callous.

'How did it happen?' asked McLeod.

'You'd better come and hear it from the fellows who found him.'

In the room where suspects or witnesses were interrogated there were two workmen, one middle-aged in dirty dungarees and tackety boots, the other younger, smoking a cigarette.

McLean told his story again. He did not do it well but McLeod was experienced in sorting out incoherence.

He conferred with George.

'It sounds like Crosbie all right,' he said.

'It does.'

'Though lots of boys wear cowboy boots. We shouldn't jump to conclusions. If I go on ahead, George, will you let the boss know?'

Chief-Inspector Findlay had given instructions that he was to be consulted only on matters of consequence, by which he meant those that might bring him promotion.

Less profitable and more humdrum matters he was content to leave to his underlings.

There would be other things to see to, such as the removal of the remains to the hospital mortuary, where the autopsy would be done. There was also the breaking of the news to the parents.

'That's a job for you, Angus.'

'Yes.' Let George or anyone else be sarcastic. It was a job for a man who believed in divine mercy.

He took Harry Black with him. The lorry came thundering behind.

'If it is Crosbie,' said Harry, grinning, 'we'll never find out who put the shit on the hymn-books.'

McLeod frowned. The young lacked compassion. They prided themselves on their toughness and honesty. In the age of the nuclear bomb life was cheap, they thought: it was humbug to pretend otherwise. If you didn't look after yourself nobody else would; on the contrary everybody that could would do you down. Their trouble was that they did not believe in God. McLeod's own children were affected. 'You don't really think, Dad, that the meek will ever inherit the earth?' He didn't but then his God was stern Jehovah not gentle Jesus. The good would be rewarded, the wicked punished, if not on earth then certainly in heaven or hell. Even Flora did not take religion seriously enough nowadays. Teasing him, she had said that the Free Kirk God reminded her of George Milne, except that George did not have a long white beard. She should have said except that George never forgave, however penitent the sinner.

'I hope this isn't going to keep us late,' said Harry. 'I promised Fiona I'd take her out to the Blue Lagoon this evening.'

The Blue Lagoon was a disco, run by Chinese.

It was a typical example of the selfishness of the young.

They had to leave the car and walk almost a hundred yards over heaps of rubble. It was raining too. Harry grumbled about getting his shoes and raincoat dirty.

McLeod noticed the derisive smirks exchanged by the

workmen. He knew that his reputation in the town was that of a good-natured Highland stot. Harry's was even less complimentary: he was thought to be a conceited upstart.

It was unjust but inevitable. Guardians of the law by the very nature of their task were not given many opportunities to reveal their more likeable qualities.

'It wasn't my fault,' said Kemp, the shovel-operator. 'How was I to know a body was there?'

'Were any precautions taken before the buildings were knocked down? Did anybody shout up the closes? Or blow a whistle?'

'The buildings were lying empty for months.'

'I was just asking.'

'If he was dead he wouldn't have heard, would he?' asked McLean.

McLeod approached the big rusty bucket, resolutely. He was a tall man but even so had to stand on tip-toe to look in. He recognised the boot: the cowboy swinging a lasso was stamped on it. Inside it, or the other one, would be a knife. He reached in and gingerly pulled aside a lump of plaster covered with yellow wallpaper. Red marks on it could have been parts of the original design, or blood. Revealed was what was left of one of the most insolent faces he had ever seen. It was now a bloody, squashed mess, but undoubtedly Crosbie's. His stomach heaved. The ruddiness fled from his face.

Careful not to let his raincoat touch the rusty iron, Harry Black took a quick look. 'It's Crosbie all right,' he said. 'I'd know that face anywhere.' He stepped back, wiping his hands with his handkerchief.

Just then Chief-Inspector Findlay, accompanied by Sergeant Milne, arrived. Findlay was satisfied with McLeod's account but Milne had to see for himself.

They were all agreed it must have been an accident. Crosbie had felt an attack coming on. He had crept into a close. There he had either died or fallen unconscious. No one was to blame. There would have to be a post-mortem but it would be a matter of course: the same with the Sheriff's inquiry.

Policemen were now present in force. The workmen were kept well back, as were also some members of the public who had somehow got to know something untoward had happened. Dr Telfer, the police surgeon, preceded the ambulance by a couple of minutes. He had time only for a cursory examination before having to supervise the digging out of the body and the carrying of it on a stretcher under a white sheet to the ambulance.

'It's young Crosbie all right,' he said. 'He was a patient of mine. God help his mother. She doted on him.'

'Angus here tells me he had a brain tumour,' said Findlay.

'That's right. Inoperable. He could have died any time.'

'There is no doubt in your mind that it was an accident?'

'Well, when they knocked the building down they couldn't have known he was in it. I expect he was dead then, anyway.'

'He had a lot of enemies.'

'So I believe. Well, since there's nothing I can do here I'd better get back to my patients. Will they send somebody from Glasgow to do the p.m.?'

'I expect so, doctor, but in our local interests I think you should be present.'

'Just let me know when it's to be.'

As the doctor went off the foreman came forward.

'Will it be all right for us to get started again?' he asked. 'We're scheduled to have it finished by tomorrow night.'

'It's raining,' said Findlay.

'We're used to working in the rain. We like it. It lays the dust.'

'Just as long as you don't find any more bodies.'

McLeod took that remark seriously. 'Wouldn't it be a good idea to blow a whistle or sound a siren before starting to knock a building down. Small children could be playing in some of the closes or houses.'

The foreman went off to give the order to resume work. He was annoyed with Detective-Sergeant McLeod. 'That bloody Hielandman,' he said, 'with the heather growing out of his ears, thinks we should blow a whistle or sound a siren.'

'It's a wonder he didn't say Gabriel's trumpet,' said one, who knew that McLeod was a member of the Free Kirk.

CHAPTER THIRTY-ONE

Now that they were certain the body was Crosbie's it was time to inform his parents.

'Why us, serge?' grumbled Harry. 'Let somebody else do some of the dirty work.'

'I do not regard it as dirty work, Harry.'

He regarded it as a sacred duty. He intended to invite the distressed mother to join him in prayer. He had been doing a bit of lay-preaching recently, embarrassing his family but, he hoped, pleasing God. He might be too long-winded, as both Flora and Mr McGeachan had hinted, but they were forgetting that in the old, more devout times, sermons in the Highlands had lasted two hours and longer.

Harry's presence would be inhibitory.

Therefore in the car outside the Crosbies' gate he asked Harry if he really wanted to be present.

'I can't think of anything I'd hate more,' said Harry.

Though relieved, McLeod made a note to deal with Harry's hardness of heart, in some future prayer.

Mrs Crosbie was wearing outdoor clothes, which included the black hat. She was just going out, she said, to look for Johnny. She was so humble that McLeod's own heart melted in pity.

'I'm afraid I've got news of Johnny,' he said. 'May I come in?'

'You're welcome, Mr McLeod.'

Her house reminded him of Mrs Dykes' pigsty, by being spotlessly clean and obsessionally tidy. She was the kind of housewife who polished the castors on chairs.

She took him into the kitchen and showed him a place

set at the table. It was for Johnny when he came home. He would be very hungry.

In the living-room on the mantelpiece and the wall above it was a whole gallery of photographs of Johnny, from the time of his birth to the present day. It was fascinating to see how his insolence had progressed as he got older. She was in some of them with him, smiling fondly.

There was no sign anywhere of Mr Crosbie, a man in whose existence McLeod found it hard to believe, though he had spoken to him once.

'Please sit down, Mrs Crosbie,' he said. 'Prepare yourself for a shock. It's bad news, I'm afraid. Johnny's been found, dead. A dreadful accident.'

He hadn't expected her to shriek and then weep frantically: she was not that kind of woman. But he hadn't expected her either just to sit and stare at him in silence, the black hat on her head and her small feet, in black shoes, close together and very still, like a pair of sleeping kittens.

She could not have understood. 'Johnny's dead, Mrs Crosbie. A sad accident.'

'I heard you, Mr McLeod. Who killed him?'

'Nobody killed him. It was an accident.'

'They were saying they were going to kill him.'

He supposed she meant the Coopers. 'That was just talk, Mrs Crosbie.'

'They were jealous of him because he was too clever for them.'

He noticed, for the first time, that she too had eyes of a different shade of blue.

'Listen to me, please, Mrs Crosbie. Johnny was found in one of the derelict buildings in the Calton area.'

'He was born there, in Crimea Street.'

'As a matter of fact it was in a building in that street. He must have gone there suffering from one of his headaches. He must have passed away there, peacefully. Dr Telfer said it could have happened any time, anywhere.'

'Don't mention that man's name to me. He never wanted Johnny to get better.'

That accusation, monstrously unfair McLeod knew, was whispered shyly. So was the next one: 'You were all in it together. You all wanted my Johnny dead.'

There was in that just enough truth to keep McLeod from denying it as positively as he would have liked. If ever a woman was in need of God's help it was her. Yet he hesitated to offer it.

'Why did they send you to tell me?' she said. 'Why didn't Mr Findlay come himself? He's the one in charge, isn't he?'

He couldn't very well say that the Chief-Inspector regarded such a duty beneath him. Nor could he, on the verge of prayer, tell a lie. So he changed the subject.

'Johnny's at the hospital, Mrs Crosbie. Either you or your husband will be required to identify him.'

'Crosbie would spit on my boy's face. He would rejoice.' She smiled sweetly.

The foundations of McLeod's faith shook, both as a believer in God and as a detective who over the years had acquired a knowledge of human nature. He had never had the luck – from the point of view of prospering in his profession – to capture a murderer, but he had arrested a number of thieves who had looked and spoken like honest persons, but in none had he ever been more mistaken than in Mrs Crosbie. In his perturbation he did what he had been trying hard not to do: he fell into his lay-preacher's way of speaking. It got him laughed at by his colleagues, behind his back. He had been warned about it by Flora. He himself thought it too solemn and a bit pompous. But when it took possession of him he could not stop it.

'There are times, Mrs Crosbie, in this life of affliction, when our only comfort is the mercy of God. God is merciful. That is the greatest truth we know on earth.'

'It is the greatest lie, Mr McLeod. God is cruel.'

Never had atrocious blasphemy been uttered so quietly and with such assurance. There could be only one explanation. The devil was speaking through her. There should have been horns poking through that black hat, a tail should have been seen under her chair. Instead of neat false teeth there should have been fangs.

Sometimes he had doubted when Mr McGeachan had told the congregation that the devil still existed, able to assume any shape he pleased. For the rest of his life McLeod would remember Mrs Crosbie's meek smile as she said 'God is cruel' and he would know that he had looked upon the devil.

She stood up, so softly that it was as if the kittens had awakened.

'Did you come in a car, Mr McLeod?'

'Yes.'

'Would you take me to Johnny?'

'There is no need to go now, Mrs Crosbie.'

Findlay had said, give them time to clean up the face a bit.

'Tomorrow morning would do.'

'I want to go now.'

She had not shed a single tear. But then who had ever heard of the devil weeping?

'It might not be convenient.' Even as he said it, trying to be kind, he knew it sounded heartless. That was the way the devil twisted things.

'If you don't want to take me I shall walk.'

Was this how the meek were going to inherit the earth, with the devil's help?

Outside in the street when she saw Harry Black in the car reading a newspaper she said: 'No thank you. I'll walk.' And off she went, meek as a mouse.

She must have heard that Harry had miscalled her Johnny, as indeed he had, more than once.

McLeod got into the car. He was still shaking.

'Where's she off to?' asked Harry.

'The hospital.'

'But she wasn't to go there till tomorrow.'

'That's what I told her.'

'It's quite a distance. Shouldn't we have offered her a lift?'

'I did. She preferred to walk.'

'How did she take it? No hysterics? She looked calm enough.'

'She thinks we all killed him.'

'She would think that, wouldn't she?'

'What do you mean?'

'Well, none of us went out of our way to help the poor young bastard, did we?'

No, they had not.

'We can't let her go to the morgue by herself,' said Harry. 'We'll have to go after her, serge. One of us has got to be there to make the identification official.'

'Would you like to be the one, Harry?'

'I wouldn't like it but I'll do it if you've had enough, serge. You look as if –' he was about to say 'as if you had been kicked in the balls', a very apt description of McLeod's pale face and anguished snorts.

'Do you know what she said, Harry? She said she did not want her husband to go and see the boy. She said he would spit in his face.'

'People who have had a shock say things they don't mean.'

It was humbling, and also exasperating, for a man who believed in God's mercy to be outdone in sympathy and understanding by a man who did not believe in God's very existence.

Black glanced at his watch. 'I'll be able to have a word with Fiona,' he said, happily.

They would later go to the Blue Lagoon, eat sweet and sour pork, drink wine, and dance. Afterwards they would make love. Harry would not lie beside his Fiona, fair-haired like McLeod's Flora, and ponder that terrible saying of Mrs Crosbie's: 'God is cruel,' as McLeod would. For in the depths of his soul he had now and then a great fear that it might be true.

CHAPTER THIRTY-TWO

In many Lightburn households the evening meal coincided with the Scottish television news which came after the main news, at six o'clock. Often not a great deal of attention was paid to it, most of the items being considered dull and parochial. This looked to be the case that Thursday, in the Dykes household. Moreover, a dispute was going on between Mick and his mother as to the amount of strawberry jam he was allowed to spread on top of his bread and margarine. They were only half listening therefore when it was announced towards the end that the body of a boy, identified as John Crosbie, missing since Sunday, had been found by workmen demolishing some old buildings, in Lightburn. A view of the town hall was shown for a few seconds.

Mick stopped in the act of reaching out again towards the jam pot. 'Did she say Johnny had been found?' he asked, incredulously.

His mother had been too intent on policing his knife. 'Do you know how much strawberry jam costs these days?'

'Did you hear, Tam?'

Tam had been thinking of his girl-friend who had told him, mendaciously he hoped, that she was pregnant. He had not heard.

Behind his newspaper Mr Dykes was not to be disturbed.

Luckily Jim, having nothing else to occupy his mind, had been listening and watching. 'She said they've found your pal Crosbie's body, Mick.'

'Did she say he was *dead*?'

'Bodies are usually dead,' said his mother.

'But how could he be dead?'

'Ask the cats he killed. Maybe somebody stuck a knife in him.'

'It must have been Cooley.'

'I thought she'd gone to London.'

'She must have sneaked back and done Johnny in. She didn't like him.'

'Who did?'

'Me. I liked him.'

'You're the only one that did.'

'There's somebody else.' He meant Duffy.

'Who?'

'I'm not saying.' Mick gulped down the last of his bread. 'Can I get going out?' He was desperate with anxiety and also, though he didn't realise it yet, with grief.

'No, you can't,' snapped his mother. 'Your week's not up. You'll stay in and wash the dishes.'

'But Johnny's dead, mother.'

'According to your father you shouldn't believe everything they tell you on television.'

From behind the newspaper Mr Dykes said, sagely: 'I was referring to political issues. On such issues it is the voice of the English Establishment and therefore not to be trusted.'

'There's somebody I've got to talk to about Johnny,' said Mick.

'Who?' asked his mother.

He knew Duffy would not want to be named. He shook his head.

'It's not that cow Burnet?'

'She didn't like Johnny.'

Her voice softened but not much. 'Is it Crosbie's mother you want to talk to?'

'No.' Mrs Crosbie didn't like him and had ordered him to keep away from Johnny. In his desperation he appealed to a higher court. 'Can I go, Dad?'

Mr Dykes lowered the newspaper. He hadn't shaved for three days. Two of his front teeth were missing. His spectacles had wire frames. He had a low opinion of the judges of the land and frequently criticised their verdicts and pronouncements, but he was fond of adopting judicial attitudes himself. 'I see no reason why not,' he said, after a pause.

'Just a minute,' said his wife. '*I* said he couldn't.' She gave the table a bang, making the dishes jump.

'Clear the ring,' said Tam, grinning.

'What I said,' said Mr Dykes, 'was that I could see no reason why he should not go out.'

'I'll tell you why not. Because I said he couldn't.'

'I was not delivering a judgment. I was merely airing an opinion.'

'The one thing I'll not tolerate is having my authority in this house undermined.'

'Those that assume authority, Nellie, have to be very sure that they do not use it unjustly.'

That was what Duffy had said. Abusers of authority, he had called them.

'Are you calling me unjust?' demanded Mrs Dykes.

'That is not for me to decide, Nellie. It is for you yourself. For my part I simply wished to put it on record that I see no harm in letting him out for a prescribed period to talk to whomever he pleases about his departed friend.'

'Just for an hour,' said Mick.

'Not for a minute,' said his mother. 'Why should you go out when I can't? I can't show my nose in any pub in town because of you and that fat cow Burnet.'

'Another drawback is a shortage of funds,' said his father.

'It's not fair,' muttered Mick. There was no private place in the house he could escape to to endure his misery and frustration. His brothers would not let him into their room, or his mother into hers. If he stayed in the bathroom longer than five minutes one of them would thump on the door. In any case he had been forbidden to snib it.

He could not help tears coming into his eyes. He felt in his pocket for Johnny's dice. If only he could have spoken to Duffy. He remembered how calm Duffy had been in the library and the church. For a few moments he thought of Molly and her boobs but even if they had been accessible they wouldn't have comforted him. If he had had a girl friend whom he really liked and who liked him she might have comforted him, but he hadn't.

He began to clear the dishes off the table and carry them into the kitchen. His mother and brothers settled down to watch television. His father went off to the bathroom with his newspaper.

'I didn't know Crosbie was as ill as that,' said his mother.

'I told you but you didn't believe me. Nobody believed me.'

'We all believe you now,' said Tam.

'All right,' said his mother. 'When you've done the dishes you can go. Be back in an hour, mind.'

'Don't let him take his dick with him,' said Tam. He and Jim roared with laughter.

His mother laughed too. 'You two shut up,' she said.

Even if he had known that the rain was so heavy and the night so dark he would still have wanted to visit Duffy. He had no cap and no raincoat and his shoes let in worse than ever, but he did not mind the discomfort, he was too concerned about Johnny, and besides Duffy's house would be bright and warm.

Perhaps Cooley had been driven to do it, by mysterious forces angry with them all for what they had done in the church. They had turned her into a kind of were-wolf. It could be that she had been ordered to kill him and Duffy too, and then herself. He had seen a film once with a story like that.

He kept to lighted streets all the way until he came to Duffy's which was in darkness near Duffy's close. He slunk cautiously, looking all about him. It was the sort of place a killer under a spell would lurk, with a long sharp knife or an open razor. So keen was his fear, he felt a sharp pain in his throat.

He was panting and terrified and drenched to the skin when at last he rang Duffy's door-bell. He was afraid the nosy woman would come out and tell him he had no business there; but he was still more afraid that Cooley, transformed in some awful unimaginable way, would suddenly rush down the stairs at him, her hands and mouth bloody.

There was Johnny too: his ghost wouldn't rest and be peaceful.

The door opposite opened. She looked out. Nobody tonight seemed human. 'You here again?' she asked.

'Duffy's my pal.'

'Some pal you are. You're Dykes, aren't you?'

'Yes.'

'We don't want your kind here. Did you hear the news on the televison tonight?'

'About Johnny?'

'He was here with you the other night, wasn't he?'

He wondered how she knew. Was she in the devil's plot against him and Duffy?

For Christ's sake, Duffy, he thought, open the door.

'You were here last night too, weren't you? Duffy's mother wouldn't be pleased. She doesn't want him associating with your sort.'

To his great relief Duffy's door opened. But Duffy did not cry, 'Come in, Mick.' Instead he stood staring like a zombie, his eyes dark in his pale face. It was as if Cooley had got to him first and drained all the blood out of him.

'Did you hear on the news what happened to Johnny?' muttered Mick.

Duffy just stared.

Mick lowered his voice so that Mrs Munro wouldn't hear the pleading whine in it. 'What about letting me in, Duffy? I'm soaked, I want to talk to you about Johnny.'

Duffy shook his head and then, to Mick's consternation, shut the door.

Never in his life had Mick felt lonelier, more miserable, and more sorry for himself.

'You've had your answer,' said the fat bitch, very pleased. 'Now off you go and never come back.' Her door closed too.

'For fuck's sake,' muttered Mick, trying to express his bewilderment. He couldn't understand why Duffy had rejected him. Was it because Molly was in the house and he wanted her for himself? Had he looked like a zombie because she had had him on the job too many times? Or was it Cooley the vampire that was in the house with him?

Not sure any longer what was real and what was imagination Mick crept down the stairs. Shivering with cold, he lingered at the closemouth. The rain was as pitiless as ever.

There was nowhere for him to go except back to his own house where there was no place for him to go either. If he had had any money he could have gone to Chuck's. He had scrounged cokes before but he couldn't tonight when they would all be talking about Johnny. He must be proud, for Johnny's sake.

He had an idea. The cops could tell him what had happened to Johnny. He could go to the station and ask them.

But big Milne might be there, with lots of suspicious questions. Because he was so unhappy, Mick wouldn't be on his guard and might give himself away and Duffy too. Duffy hadn't let him in but he was still a pal and pals must never be betrayed.

He had another idea. He would go to Teuchter's house and ask him. Teuchter himself was all right for a cop but it was his wife who gave Mick hope. Even his mother admitted that Mrs McLeod wasn't the stuck-up bastard she could easily have been.

He ran all the way, gasping more than he should have. He smoked too much. Johnny had often warned him about it.

The McLeods lived in a new residential area. Their house was a bungalow called Blaven.

Shivering, Mick pressed the bell button. He heard the chimes, and thought that if he ever had a house of his own he would have a door bell like this.

Mrs McLeod opened the door. She was wearing a tartan skirt and fair-isle jumper. There was a pleasant smell of home off her.

'Is Mr McLeod in, please?' he asked.

She stared at him curiously but not offensively. 'Who are you?' Her voice was homely too: it was warm and friendly.

'I'm Mick Dykes. Johnny Crosbie was my pal.' To his chagrin he sobbed. If people were hard he could be hard too, but if they were kind — it didn't happen all that often — he went soft.

'You'd better come in. You're drookit.'

'I'll make puddles on your carpet.'

'That doesn't matter.'

It mattered to him. He had his pride. 'It's all right, Mrs McLeod. I just want a word with Mr McLeod and then I'll go away.'

She went in. He heard her saying: 'Angus, there's a boy, Mick Dykes, to see you.'

McLeod must have protested for she said: 'Don't be silly, Angus. Of course you must talk to him. He's very upset.'

She came back to the door. 'He'll be here in a moment. Are you sure you won't come in?'

He shook his head. 'Thanks just the same.'

Suddenly there was Teuchter, with a pipe in his mouth. 'It's yourself, Mick. What's the matter?

'I heard the news on the television, Mr McLeod. About Johnny. Johnny Crosbie. Could you tell me what happened to him? Was it an accident?'

'I'm afraid I'm not at liberty to say any more than what was given out in the news. A further statement will be made in a day or two.'

'Was it his tumour that killed him?'

'You knew about that?'

'Oh yes.'

'Tell the boy,' said Mrs McLeod, from within.

'Tell him what?'

'Tell him the truth, that's all he wants to know.'

Everybody hid behind lies. Defilers of truth, Duffy had called them.

'Nobody knows the truth,' said McLeod. 'Not yet. There will have to be an autopsy.'

'What's that?' asked Mick.'

'A post mortem. To find out what caused his death.'

'Could somebody have killed him?'

'Why do you ask that?'

'Archie Cooper was saying he was going to get Johnny.'

'Archie Cooper had nothing to do with it.'

'Maybe somebody else did.'

'Have you somebody in mind?'

'Maybe I have.'

'Lots of people didn't care for him.'

'That's enough, Angus,' said Mrs McLeod, behind the door. 'The poor boy's dead.'

Yes, Johnny was dead. He would never play ludo again, or sing 'The Sash', or chase cats, or assemble model aeroplanes, or stand Mick cokes in Dirty Chuck's.

'Sorry for bothering you, Mr McLeod.'

Mick was about to turn away when Mrs McLeod opened the door wider. She had a raincoat in her hand. 'Take this,' she said. 'It's an old one of my husband's.'

He was appalled and couldn't help showing it. They had laughed at him because he had been to bed with Fat Annie, they would laugh louder and more nastily if they heard that he had been given a cop's raincoat. He would as soon have worn a crucifix belonging to a Pape. Yet it had been offered to him out of kindness.

He stumbled off into the rain, more bewildered than ever.

CHAPTER THIRTY-THREE

Chief-Inspector Findlay was taken aback (but in his secret heart not displeased) to receive a telephone call from Dr Imrie, the renowned pathologist from Glasgow, who was carrying out the post mortem on John Crosbie, in Lightburn hospital. It was to the effect that in Imrie's opinion the boy's death had not been caused by the building being knocked down on top of him or by the tumour on his brain, though this would have killed him soon enough. What had caused it were some vicious blows on the head, with a stone or brick with sharp edges. He could not of course be a hundred per cent positive, considering how many stones and bricks had descended on him, but he was pretty sure that it was a case of murder, and he gave some pathological evidence, obscure but impressive. To obtain a second expert opinion he had sent for his colleague Dr Lindsay. 'Also there was something clutched in his fist. Did you know that? I think you'd better come and see for yourself.' Seven and a half minutes later Findlay, accompanied by Inspector Hogg, Detective-Sergeant McLeod, and Detective-Constable Black, arrived in the hospital morgue.

They did not attempt to assess the significance of the marks on the boy's head: they were glad to take the doctor's word for that; but they examined with intense and devout interest the small metal hair-grip that had been forcibly extracted from the boy's fist.

The last murder committed in Lightburn had been eight years ago, before Chief-Inspector Findlay's time. An old man had taken a hammer to the head of his wife of thirty-five years because she had arrogantly switched off his favourite television programme. Then he had walked to the police station and given himself up. No detective work had been necessary and no commendations had resulted.

Dr Telfer stood by, wearing a white overall and looking left out.

Findlay and his colleague carried the hair-grip back to the station with them, in a small box lined with cotton wool, as if, Black was to say to Fiona that evening, giving her a fit of the giggles, it was John Knox's foreskin.

A conference was held in the Chief-Inspector's office to make preparations in the event that Dr Imrie's opinion was corroborated and a murder hunt had to be organised.

'It is a pity,' said Detective Sergeant McLeod, his accent at its thickest because of excitement, 'that we did not think to inspect the contents of the big bucket more closely.'

The Chief-Inspector was not grateful for that observation, shrewd though it was. If they did not themselves solve the crime quickly officious experts would be sent from Glasgow. These would say with asperity what McLeod had said modestly.

'We have the advantage of local knowledge,' said Findlay. 'Are we all agreed that what probably happened was that Crosbie attacked some girl with intent to rape her, as in the case of Sally Cooper, but this time met more than his match?'

'We should bear in mind, sir,' said McLeod, 'that nowadays many boys wear their hair long and some may well use hair grips.'

'A good point, Angus. We'll keep it in mind. But is there really any doubt in anybody's mind that the person we are looking for is a girl?'

They all nodded, except Harry Black.

'Do any names occur to you?' asked the Chief-Inspector.

'What about Sally Cooper?' asked Inspector Hogg. 'I heard her say she was going to get her own back. She actually said she would kill him.'

'She wouldn't have the strength,' said Sergeant Milne.

They waited for George to say whom he suspected. His

knowledge of the town was prodigious. But he kept quiet. He could have been thinking that whoever had got rid of Crosbie had done the town, and George himself, a good turn, for George was known to have detested the dead boy. Still, it wouldn't be like George to be tender towards any criminal, however obliged he might feel.

'What about big Molly McGowan?' asked Black. 'She's got the strength.' Especially in the thighs. He had joined in lewd jokes at the station about Molly's fuckable qualities. All the same, even as he was proposing her name, he was thinking that Molly, wise girl, would have let herself be raped, on the principle that one more fornication would make little difference.

'She has not got the viciousness,' said McLeod. 'I will tell you who has, and also the strength. Helen Cooley.'

Black was doubtful. Cooley was a bitch but not that sort of bitch. He should have held his tongue but he said: 'Didn't Mick Dykes tell us she's gone to London?'

McLeod explained. 'In the course of our enquiries, sir, relating to Crosbie's disappearance, we interrogated Michael Dykes, Crosbie's crony. He could not tell us anything about Crosbie or at any rate was not prepared to tell us anything, but he did offer the information that Helen Cooley had gone to London. His uncle Fred, a lorry-driver, got her a lift from Glasgow, early on Monday morning. If you recall Crosbie went missing on Sunday. Dr Imrie said he had been dead for at least four days. Cooley could have done it before she left for Glasgow.'

'What do you think George?' asked the Chief-Inspector.

'I would put her at the top of the list.'

'If you like, sir,' said McLeod, eagerly, 'I could trace all Cooley's movements since Sunday.'

'You'd have to be discreet, Angus. Pretend she's wanted for absconding.'

'Yes, sir.'

Some grinned, behind their hands. Angus was about as discreet as a Highland stot in a field of corn.

They were then all exhorted to keep their eyes and ears

open and consult their contacts. If Crosbie had been murdered there would be whispers naming the culprit.

On their way to question Mick's uncle, Mr Fred Meiklejohn, Black expressed his doubts. 'Honestly, serge, I can't see it as murder.'

'Dr Imrie is an expert in his field, Harry.'

'I know, but if there was a trial the defence would find other experts to contradict him.'

'What about the hair-grip?'

'That's right, serge, what about it? How did it get into his hand? He could have had a seizure and he held on to it in his pocket. It could just as easily have been a coin. Isn't that more likely than him snatching it out of the hair of somebody attacking him with a brick, especially if that somebody struck him from behind? I wouldn't be surprised if it turned out to be natural causes.'

'Do you know who came to my door last night, in the pouring rain?'

'Crosbie's ghost? Sorry, serge. No idea.'

'Mick Dykes.'

'What did he want?'

'He wanted to know what had happened to Crosbie. Do you know what he said? He said he thought Crosbie had been attacked and he had an idea who had done it. What do you think of that?'

'To be honest, serge, not much. Mick's not the brightest of lads. He liked Crosbie, God knows why, so he'd be upset and confused.'

'He was upset and confused, yes, but he knows Crosbie's enemies. We'll have a talk with him afterwards.'

Fred Meiklejohn lived in a council housing scheme, not far from the Cooleys. The small front garden seemed to have been planted with the rusty parts of cars. Among others were two wheels, an axle, a wing mirror, and a radiator.

Mrs Meiklejohn came to the door, a busy-looking small woman with dyed carroty hair in curlers and a cigarette hanging from her mouth. Short-sighted, she stretched forward to make sure they were who she thought they were before giving them a hearty sneer. She did not remove the cigarette. 'What do you two want? Nellie was warning us about you.'

Nellie was Mrs Dykes.

'We'd like to have a few words with your husband, Mrs Meiklejohn,' said McLeod.

'Well, you can't. He's in bed. He's just back from Felixstowe. He was driving all night and he's dead beat. Come back next month. What's it about anyway?'

'We want to ask him if he arranged a lift for Helen Cooley, from Glasgow to London, on Monday morning.'

'What do you want to know that for?'

'Helen has disappeared. Her parents are anxious.'

She laughed scornfully. 'I don't believe that. I know her parents. They're a pair of shits. If they heard she'd got her throat cut they wouldn't be anxious.'

McLeod felt discouraged. This hostility towards the guardians of the law was so unreasonable. Mrs Meiklejohn and her kind seemed to have imbibed it with their mother's milk. Little girls of three screamed abuse at police cars.

'Fred and me have a lot of time for Helen,' said Mrs Meiklejohn. 'She doesn't give a bugger for anything or anybody.'

Hardly an admirable attitude, McLeod would have thought.

'I'll see if he's asleep,' said Mrs Meiklejohn.

She was back in less than a minute. 'He says Helen got a lift on Monday, as far as Rugby. That's not very far from London.'

'Could your husband give me the name of the driver who gave her the lift?'

'He could but I don't think he will.'

She went and soon returned. 'He wants to know what you want the name for?'

'We may have to question your husband's colleague.'

'What for? What are you up to? There would be no

hanky-panky, if that's what you're thinking. He's a married man with three children.' She grinned. 'Anyway, just to put him and anybody else off the notion she told them she'd just been cured of a dose of the pox. The lassie's gone to make her fortune. Why don't you leave her alone?'

Off she went again. She came back shaking her head. 'He says I've to tell you nothing else. He doesn't trust you, Mr McLeod. Nothing personal. He doesn't trust any policeman. He's got his reasons.'

She shut the door on them but not too angrily or contemptuously. They were bastards doing a job that only bastards would do, but still they were human beings and McLeod had a wife and dapper Black a girl friend and they were her guests though she had kept them on her door-step: therefore, all things considered, they should be shown a small degree of tolerance.

Back in the car McLeod said, plaintively: 'Do you ever feel, Harry, that you are part of an army of occupation?'

'All the time, serge.'

'It seems to be getting worse.'

'It's because we're getting better paid. We'll get nothing out of Mick if that mother of his is there.'

'Don't forget Crosbie was his friend.'

'She'd break his teeth if he told us anything. We'd have to get him on his own.'

Mrs Dykes was instantly belligerent. Before McLeod could open his mouth she stridently accused him of getting her house a bad name with his visits, and when he said civilly that he only wanted to ask Michael a question or two concerning John Crosbie she accused him of persecuting her son.

They were not invited in. She brought Mick to the door, like a lioness her cub. 'He's hoarse. The silly bugger went walking in the rain last night.'

'We are investigating the disappearance of Helen Cooley,' said McLeod. 'Her parents are anxious about her.'

'My arse they're anxious. Relieved's more like it. Him especially. Some people should never have weans.'

Was it possible that she saw herself as a caring mother?

'I thought you were going to ask about Crosbie,' she said.

'In good time. When did you last see Helen Cooley, Michael?'

'On Saturday.' He really was hoarse.

'What time on Saturday?'

'About eight o'clock.'

'Where was this?'

'In the main street. She was waiting for a bus.'

'Did she tell you she was waiting for a bus?'

'Yes.'

'Was she going to Glasgow?'

'That's what she said.'

'Did you actually see her get on?'

'No. Johnny and me didn't wait.'

'So Johnny was with you?'

'Yes.'

'What did you do afterwards?'

'Johnny went home.'

His mother intervened. 'And *he* paid a visit to that fat trollop Annie Burnet. I expect you've heard about that. What's this all about anyway? Are you trying to connect Helen Cooley with what happened to Crosbie? I thought that was an accident.'

'It may well have been, Mrs Dykes.'

'That wouldn't suit you, would it? You want an excuse to hound that poor lassie. Dykes says why don't you go after the rich guys that don't pay their taxes. We have them in Lightburn too, you know.'

With that she dragged Mick in and slammed the door shut. Unlike her sister-in-law she made no allowances.

'That boy suspects Cooley,' said McLeod, in the car.

Black shook his head. 'I just can't see her going to Glasgow on Saturday night, returning on Sunday, bashing Crosbie's head in, leaving him for dead in a close, returning to Glasgow, and getting a lift to London on Monday morning. It doesn't make sense.'

'Murder seldom makes sense, Harry. But never fear. I am keeping an open mind.'

By three o'clock that afternoon McLeod's mind was closed, as regarded the manner in which Crosbie had met his death. Dr Imrie's colleague confirmed his findings: Crosbie had been murdered. The Glasgow police were immediately requested to trace the driver of the bus which had taken Cooley to Glasgow. By six o'clock they had found him. He remembered Cooley because of the Singapore Airlines bag she had been carrying, and also because of her woe-begone expression. She had come off at the terminus and so far as he could see had not been met by anyone. No driver, however, could be found who remembered her on his bus on Sunday, and no ticket clerk remembered having sold her a rail ticket.

It was given out to the news media that the investigations were continuing. Nothing was said about murder. Anyone with information was asked to come forward. The Lightburn police were particularly concerned that a local girl, Helen Cooley, should get in touch with them as soon as possible. It was believed she had gone to London. A photograph of her, making her look every inch a murderess, appeared in some national newspapers.

Detective Sergeant McLeod's first stroke of luck in the Crosbie case had been his happening to be in the station when the workmen had come to report the discovery of the body. The second was his being in the station on Sunday morning when the telephone call came. The third, and best, was that the call was for him.

On his way back from church he went into the station to find out if there had been any fresh developments. He was not surprised to find George Milne in charge. Already a number of telephone calls had been received, mainly from cranks and troublemakers, claiming that Helen Cooley had been seen in places as far apart as Aberdeen and Plymouth. Nothing so far had been heard from the London police.

George had taken command of the telephone. When it rang he picked it up and switched on the recorder. McLeod heard the voice in the ear-piece: it sounded female and angry. He felt justified in listening in on the other phone.

'Is this Lightburn Police Station?'

'It is,' said George. 'Who is calling?'

'Who am I talking to?'

'This is Sergeant Milne.'

'I thought so. I don't want to talk to you. Can I talk to Teuchter.'

'There is no one of that name here. Who are you?'

'You know who I am. Teuchter's his nickname. McLeod's his real name. I know it's Sunday but if he's not at the station give me his house number.'

'I cannot put you in touch with Detective Sergeant McLeod until I know who you are and what your business is.'

'You know who I am all right. I'm Helen Cooley.'

It certainly sounded like her, being young, female, Scottish, and aggressive.

'Can you give proof of your identity?' asked Milne.

'What do you mean, proof?'

'Any girl could say she was Helen Cooley.'

'She'd be a bloody fool to say that if she wasn't. There's nothing special about being me.'

'Where do your parents live?'

'32 Alloway Street.'

'Can you give me the name of the chairman of the Children's Panel?'

'Tight-pussy Porteous. For Christ's sake, get McLeod or tell me his number. This call's going to cost me a fortune.'

'Where are you phoning from?'

'Do you think I'm daft? Look, I'm going to hang up.'

McLeod then took over 'Hello, Helen. This is Detective Sergeant McLeod. What is it you want to tell me?'

'First, I want to tell you that I had fuck-all to do with Johnny Crosbie getting killed. You've got it in the newspapers that I did it. I'm thinking of suing.'

'No one has accused you. It was merely stated that you

might be able to assist us in our enquiries. What you should do, Helen, is to go at once and report to the nearest police station.' His heart sank. Here he was helping others to gain the glory.

'No thanks. I'm keeping well clear of police stations. I didn't do it. That's the first thing. The second thing is, I know who did it. I wish I didn't.'

'Did what?'

'Killed Crosbie.'

'No one has said that Johnny Crosbie was killed.'

'I can read between the lines. Anyway, I know what must have happened. I'm not saying all this for your sake, don't think that, if it had been anybody else that had done it I'd have let you find out for yourselves and hoped that you didn't. I've never shopped anybody in my life, not even people I've hated.'

He had to speak responsibly. This conversation would be listened to and assessed by his superiors.

'Giving information to the police is not shopping. It is doing your duty as a citizen.'

'To hell with that. Just a minute.'

She put more money in. He wondered where she was phoning from. Detective-Constable Anderson was trying to find out.

'This is somebody I like. Somebody I like a lot. Somebody I'd die for. That sounds like crap but it's true.'

This palaver and hesitation were typically feminine. Flora too could be slow in coming to the point.

'He's got himself into one hell of a mess,' she said.

'Who has?'

'I don't think I can bring myself to tell you. Maybe I'll just put this phone down and forget it.'

'Don't do that. What you should do, for your own good and that of your friend, is to go to the nearest police station and explain who you are. They will arrange for your journey back to Lightburn.'

'Come into my parlour. No thanks. What I'm afraid of is that somebody else might get killed.'

Was the silly girl suggesting there was a murderous lunatic at large in the town? She sounded very serious.

'Such as Tight-pussy.'

'Who?'

'Or her daughter.'

'Who are these people?'

'Mrs Porteous and her daughter Margaret. What happens if a person's mad and kills somebody?'

'It would depend on the circumstances.'

'Maybe I should think about it a bit more. The trouble is, the person he's most likely to kill next is himself. Do you know how he'll do it? He'll burn himself to death. You've seen pictures of people doing that. That's what he'd do. All right. I'll tell you. His name's Duffy. You won't have heard of him. He's never been in trouble. He lives in Kenilworth Court, number 86.'

She was wrong. He had heard of this Duffy. Constables Green and McHarg had reported questioning a boy of that name in Ballochmyle Avenue near St Stephen's church last Sunday. He had been well-dressed and well-spoken, though a bit on the simple side perhaps. He had claimed to have been at church with Mrs Porteous. Green and McHarg had made enquiries and found that he had been telling the truth.

What connection could there be between Cooley and such a boy? Had she pestered him with her affection and been repulsed.

'Everybody thinks Duffy's simple, but that's because he wants them to think it. He's the very opposite of simple. That declaration of war on the town hall, it was Duffy who did that. Abusers of authority. Defilers of truth. He hates them. It was his idea to tear pages out of the library books and put shit on the hymn-books. Acts of war. Symbolical, he said. He wanted to show everybody what hypocrites they were. As if they needed to be shown! He got Johnny Crosbie to help him. That was his big mistake. Make use of evil to bring about good, he said. He got rid of Johnny because he didn't trust him. I warned him it would come to that.'

After a pause she went on, while McLeod listened in
open-mouthed amazement and Milne in scowling incredulity: 'He said that if you declared war anything
you did after that wouldn't be a crime. I don't know if
he believed it or not. It's true, isn't it, that when countries
are at war they drop bombs and kill lots of people but they
don't think of themselves as murderers. It must have been
Flockhart the history teacher that put the idea into his head.
Flockhart told him about a famous writer who said judges
should have a roll of toilet paper in front of them when
they were sentencing people. That gave Duffy his idea of
putting shit on the hymn-books.'

McLeod had heard of Mr Flockhart's imprudent opinions but not that they included the advocacy of terrorism.
'You are not asking me to believe that Mr Flockhart
encouraged this boy Duffy to commit crimes?'

'No, I'm not. Don't blame Flockhart. But he did tell
Duffy that books tell lies.'

Surely no sane teacher ever told a pupil any such thing?

'Look, Mr McLeod, I've told you. It's up to you now.
You'll have to do something quick before he kills someone
else. Like Mrs Porteous. Or himself.'

'Why on earth should he want to harm Mrs Porteous?'

'She's the biggest hypocrite in town, isn't she? For
Christ's sake, look after him.'

Those were her last words. She seemed to be weeping.

McLeod found it hard to imagine the Helen Cooley he
knew in tears.

He and Milne stared at each other.

'What did you make of all that, George?'

'We know she's a liar, we know she does not like the
police, so it would be foolish to believe her.'

'But she couldn't have made all that up.'

'Liars have fertile imaginations.'

'Yes, but all that stuff about declaring war and hypocrites
and books telling lies and Duffy burning himself to death,
she couldn't have made that up. Do you know anything
about this Duffy, George?'

'I spoke to him once in the main street, the day that rubbish was painted on the town hall. He struck me as a quiet inoffensive boy.'

'That's what Green and McHarg thought. Was he by himself?'

'Crosbie and Dykes were with him. I got the impression he did not want their company.'

'You think they were taking advantage of him because they know or think he's a bit simple?'

'Yes. His mother is a barmaid at the Caledonian Hotel. She is highly regarded there. She is at present on holiday in Spain.'

'So he's on his own. He didn't give you the impression that he was capable of all those things Cooley accused him of?'

'He did not.'

Detective Constable Anderson then came in to confess that he had not been able to trace the call. 'London somewhere. A public call-box. Very difficult to trace. Sorry.'

When he was gone again McLeod remarked he couldn't understand how Mrs Porteous came into it.

'She may well be the biggest hypocrite in town.'

McLeod was startled. 'She's one of the pillars of society.'

'Which is why her private life should be above reproach.'

'Isn't it?'

'It is not, and has not been for some time.'

'What do you mean, George?'

'She has a lover.'

McLeod remembered Cooley's lewd word tight-pussy and felt embarrassed. He wasn't sure what George, a bigger prude than himself, meant by a lover. 'Well, she's a single woman.'

'He isn't. He is a married man. Therefore she is an adulteress.'

Could a woman who wasn't married commit adultery? Surely her sin was fornication.

'Is he a local man, George?'

'He is a well-known Edinburgh lawyer. His wife is a Catholic and will not give him a divorce.'

'He can't be very young.'

'He is about fifty.'

And she was about forty-five. Both of them well past the age of hotblooded and reckless romance. 'I had no idea,' said McLeod.

'It is a very well-guarded secret.'

'So how do you know, George?'

George would have been an important man in John Calvin's Geneva. He would be an important man today in Brezhnev's Russia.

'But Cooley wouldn't know it, or this boy Duffy.'

'I hardly think so.'

Still, Duffy must know her, Mrs Porteous I mean, if she had him at church with her.'

'I know nothing about that.'

'Suppose it's all true, George. At this very moment he could be prowling about Mrs Porteous's house. It's just as well she's got that big yellow Labrador.'

'She also has her paramour, who used to play Rugby.'

Flora says I've got little sense of humour, thought McLeod. She also says George has none; in his case she's right.

In all his forty-six years of membership of the Free Kirk of Scotland (having been enrolled at birth) under a succession of ministers to whom sexual immorality was anathema, McLeod had never heard anyone use the word paramour.

'I think we should go and have a talk with Duffy,' he said.

'This is a C.I.D. matter, Angus. Take Black or Anderson with you.'

'I'd rather you came, George. You heard what Cooley said about him.'

Like much else of Lightburn Kenilworth Court was a bit run down, with the roadway pot-holed, the pavements cracked, some street lamps smashed, and the closes in need of repainting. Many of the inhabitants, however, still clung to respectability and did not necessarily regard the police as enemies. McLeod and Milne therefore, though the latter was in uniform, were in little danger of being reviled from distant corners or having the hub-caps removed from their car.

The name on the small brass plate was I. Duffy. McLeod rang the bell.

As he waited he tried to look relaxed and friendly. Milne was as tense and stern as ever.

The door across the landing opened. A woman showed her face. It was hardly welcoming but it was not quite hostile either.

'I'm Mrs Munro,' she said. 'I promised Duffy's mother that I would keep an eye on him while she was away. She's in Spain on holiday. I hope nothing's happened to her.'

'Not that we know of, Mrs Munro,' said McLeod, smiling. 'It's the lad we'd like to have a word with.'

'May I ask what about?'

'It's a private matter. He doesn't seem to be at home.'

'He's gone to church.'

'Did you see him go? Did he tell you he was going?'

'He didn't have to. He was dressed for it and he was carrying a Bible.'

'Did he say what church he was going to?'

'He didn't, but last Sunday he went to St Stephen's. He seems to have made friends there.'

'Have you any idea when he'll be back?'

'He could be visiting his friends, couldn't he? He was carrying something else, wrapped in brown paper. It could have been a cake.'

'A cake?'

'That's right. You wouldn't believe it but he's a good baker. Is it about these rascals that have been pestering him that you want to see him?'

'Who are they, Mrs Munro?'

'First it was that Helen Cooley, then Dykes and that boy Crosbie that's been found dead, and worst of all if you ask me that big trollop Molly McGowan. She spent the night with him.'

'Have all these visited him recently?'

'They have. His mother would be very angry if she knew. She's quite a lady body, Mrs Duffy, though she's only a barmaid.'

'I see. Well, thank you very much, Mrs Munro. You've been very helpful.'

In the car, which still had its hub-caps and windscreen wipers, McLeod said: 'Just what has been going on, George? Have they been taking advantage of him because he's a simpleton?'

'It would look like it?'

'Or is Cooley right and he's not a simpleton at all? I think we should go and have a chat with Mr Flockhart. If anyone can tell us about Duffy it's him.'

Chief-Inspector Findlay's three-bedroomed bungalow was in the same new housing estate as Flockhart's two-bedroomed semi-detached. McLeod was aware that he ought to go there first and report Cooley's telephone call. There was a point when initiative on the part of subordinates became unpardonable presumption. He was already past it. If his luck did not hold he would be censured, not praised.

'Perhaps I should warn you, Angus,' said Milne, 'that we may find Mr and Mrs Flockhart not on the friendliest of terms.'

More scandalous gossip. George really was what Flora called him, an old sweetie-wife.

'Why is that, George?'

'She is pregnant.'

But wasn't that supposed to draw a couple closer, not drive them apart?

'She suspects him of associating with other women, particularly with Mrs Veitch of the Careers Office.'

McLeod knew Mrs Veitch and thought her very attractive, though too flamboyant in her dress. 'Is there anything in it?'

'Not in Mrs Veitch's case. She has another admirer whom she considers herself engaged to: a man from Aberdeen, in the oil industry. In some other cases I would say Mrs Flockhart's suspicions are justified.'

'So he fancies himself as a ladies' man?'

'He is not fit to teach children. If I had my way he would be dismissed.'

But if George had his way thumb-screws would still be used.

Mrs Flockhart came to the door, a small dark-haired woman, greeting-faced and obviously pregnant. She was dressed for Sunday. Perhaps she wasn't long back from church. She wasn't pleased to see them.

McLeod introduced himself and Milne. He explained that they wished to talk to her husband. They were sorry to have to come on Sunday. It was rather urgent.

They could hear a child bawling within.

'What's it about?' she asked, crossly. 'He says he's got a headache. Any excuse to get out of going to church.'

'We'll not keep him long.'

'Has it to do with the school? You've no right to bother us at home. Those crummy pupils of his, he thinks he can help them but he can't even help himself.'

Ungraciously she invited them in, no doubt because neighbours were watching.

She showed them into a room that was seldom used. The child was never allowed in here to drop jelly pieces on the white carpet or break the glass birds scattered about, as if in an aviary. McLeod liked the robins best.

'Sit down,' she said, wincing, for their trouser seats would sully the virgin moquette. 'I'll tell him you're here.'

Milne sat upright in one of the armchairs, with his cap on his knees. McLeod carefully inspected the birds from close up. They had been made in Italy where, he had read, many thousands of migratory birds were slaughtered every year on their way south to Africa. He wondered who collected these, Flockhart or his wife. Perhaps they had done it together, in earlier happier days.

Flockhart came shuffling in. His carpet slippers had holes at the big toes. His green cardigan hung loosely on him. His eyes were bleary, his black beard had crumbs in it, his hair was lank and thin on top, his fingers were stained with nicotine. He looked more like a failed prophet than a successful lecher. He had the hang-dog air of a man finding that contrition was never enough: more and more was always demanded. It was a situation to be found in many households. Often it dragged on for years. Sometimes it erupted into marital murder, as in the case of the old man who had hammered his wife to death.

McLeod thanked God that Flora had never found pleasure in humiliating him. She had had as many opportunities as most women but had taken very few.

'Well, gentlemen, what can I do for you?' asked Flockhart. He took out his cigarettes but put them away again. 'No smoking in here,' he said, with a grin that showed his bad teeth and humiliation.

'We're sorry to disturb you, Mr Flockhart,' said McLeod, 'especially on Sunday, but a serious situation has arisen and we hope you may be able to help us.'

The child screamed with rage. Its mother shouted. Flockhart closed his eyes and shuddered.

McLeod was glad his own three were grown-up. Perhaps George was feeling thankful that he had never had any.

'I hope you're not going to ask me to betray my pupils'

confidence,' said Flockhart. 'You wouldn't ask a priest to tell you the secrets of the confessional, would you? Why shouldn't a teacher be entitled to the same privilege?' He sniggered, knowing that what he had just said was nonsense.

'We are interested in a boy called Duffy. We understand you had him in one of your classes.'

'Last year's infamous 4X. Recently bereft of its most sinister alumnus. I refer to the late Johnny Crosbie. What is your interest in Duffy? I would have thought him the least likely boy in town to fall foul of the police.'

'Why do you say that, Mr Flockhart?'

'Because Duffy's a profound moralist.'

'You said he was in this infamous class. He could not have been very clever, surely.'

'He didn't do well in examinations, but that was part of his morality.'

'I don't understand.'

'I used to tease him. I used to ask him when he was going to join the human race. By which I meant accept all its failings: you know, greed, envy, rivalry, belligerence, etc.'

'You are making him out to be a kind of saint.'

'He asked too many questions for a saint.'

'What kind of questions?'

'The kind only a philosopher could answer.'

'Did he ever ask about declaration of war?'

'Yes, he did. How do you know that? He wanted to know why a nation, after it had declared war on another nation, thereafter considered it had a legal right to kill and destroy. He wanted to know what was the basis of that legality. No other pupil, not even in the Sixth Form, has ever asked me such a question.'

'And what did you tell him?'

'What would *you* have told him?'

'This is not a game, Mr Flockhart, it is a serious investigation.'

'Then it must have to do with Crosbie's death. I should think that's the only serious investigation going

in Lightburn at the moment. But what could Duffy
have to do with that? He and Crosbie were worlds apart.
Duffy's a pacifist. He sees the problems of force too
simply, as pacifists do; which is why I can't be one
myself.'

'You think he's simple-minded then?'

'Lots of people think Jesus Christ was simple-minded.
Turn the other cheek, do good to them that treat you
badly. Duffy's simple-minded in that kind of way. People
can be honest, generous, truthful, peaceful, etc. So why
aren't they all the time? Why are they so often dishonest,
mean, mendacious, belligerent? I used to advise him to
restrict his expectations, like the rest of us. People have
gone mad because they expected too much.'

'Did you think Duffy might go mad?'

'It crossed my mind sometimes. If you suffer too many
disappointments it's hard to stay sane, wouldn't you think?
What would be the ultimate disappointment, gentlemen?
The outbreak of nuclear war. In those sad brown eyes I
used to see Armageddon and the Holocaust.' Flockhart
chuckled. He was enjoying himself, showing off to these
dumb, overpaid policemen.

'Did you ever tell him about a famous writer who wrote
that judges should have rolls of toilet paper in front of them
when sentencing people?'

'When sentencing them to death. Yes, I suppose I did.
I often tell my classes that. It was Somerset Maugham.
His own father was a judge. The idea was to make them
remember the common humanity they shared with the
wretches in the dock.'

'Even if those wretches were murderers?'

'Especially if they were murderers. Which of us isn't
capable of murder? When Maugham wrote it there was
still capital punishment.'

Milne spoke for the first time. 'It should never have been
abolished.'

'Nor flogging? Nor transportation for life? Nor the
beating of madmen?' Perhaps because of his headache

and because he dared not smoke in that room Flockhart was beginning to get edgy.

'Do you tell your classes that books tell lies?' asked McLeod.

'I tell them not to believe something just because it's in print. Many books have told lies.'

'Aren't these unwise things to say to pupils not intelligent enough to judge for themselves?'

'If you mean 4X they might not have been what you would call intelligent in that they never passed examinations but they could judge for themselves. They were pretty shrewd at seeing through pretensions, though they did express themselves somewhat crudely. I'm beginning to see what you're after. You think it might have been Duffy that painted the declaration of war on the town hall and tore the pages out of the library books.'

'Who told you about the library books?'

'Mary Purvis. She and I often discuss books. I thought at the time it could have been meant as a symbolical gesture. And then of course there was the excrement on the hymn-books. Who put you on to Duffy?'

'We are not at liberty to tell you that.'

'Do you suspect him of Crosbie's death too? The kids at school have already got a song about that. They assume it was Helen Cooley that bumped him off. They make her out to be a heroine. But if it was murder it wasn't her that did it.'

'Why do you think that?'

'She has too much self-respect.'

'Most people would say she had none at all.'

'They would be wrong. Some of her standards are high. For one thing she would never be treacherous.'

They were interrupted then by Mrs Flockhart charging in with a howling three-year-old in her arms. Without a word she handed the infant to her husband and rushed out again. To his credit Flockhart did not vent his annoyance on the child, though it howled louder than ever and beat at his face with its tiny fists. His smile however was not serene.

As McLeod left the house he had a feeling that he had been given a glimpse of new or different ways of looking at human experience. He might never again be wholly content with the old way.

'That man should be dismissed,' said George.

George's mind was resolutely closed. There were millions like him.

CHAPTER THIRTY-FIVE

Before leaving the house Duffy had written two letters, one to his mother and the other to Detective-Sergeant McLeod. The first he placed on the mantelpiece in the living-room, in a sealed envelope with his mother's name on it; the second he took with him in his pocket, in a stamped addressed envelope, ready to be posted.

Both were very short.

'Dear Mother,
    I am very sorry if I have made you unhappy and ashamed. Things went wrong. Forgive me.
                                    Duffy.'

'Dear Mr McLeod,
    Helen Cooley did not kill Johnny Crosbie. I did. I put the hair-grip in his hand.
                                    Duffy.'

The brown paper parcel which Mrs Munro had looked and sniffed at suspiciously on the landing was not a cake but a plastic can of paraffin. He was going to set himself on fire. It would be his last appeal and his penance.

When he set out, dressed as if for church, he had still to decide where it was to take place. He carried a Bible to mislead Mrs Munro and anyone else who might see him, but it had some other purpose too. His mind was not as clear as he would have liked.

It was a dry cold morning, with little likelihood of rain.

People were queuing as usual on Sunday morning for their newspapers in which they would read with relish accounts of murders worse than his. One or two smiled at him as he passed. They would say afterwards that they had noticed nothing odd.

He stopped at the first post-box he came to, built into the wall. The enamel plate giving the times of collection was bruised with stones being thrown at it. Some people in the district refused to post their letters here, because vandals had been known to drop lighted matches in. This letter to McLeod must reach him, for Cooley's sake. Duffy hesitated therefore wondering whether he should take it to the head post office in the main street. Indecision now might increase until he found himself not able to decide what was the right place or the right time or the right reasons for his self-execution. So he quickly slipped the letter into the box.

He had burnt his boats. There could be no turning back now. Like Cortes, that 'heroic villain' as Mr Flockhart had called him, he must go on, to endure suffering and make his discoveries.

He had considered several places that would be appropriate: the steps of St Stephen's church; in front of the War Memorial; outside the town hall; the site of the building where he had killed Crosbie; in the courtyard of the police station; or at the coup. Surely it ought to be where people would see him. The steps of the church would be best.

In the distance he heard the bells. They fell silent when he came in sight of the church, just as the last stragglers were going in. He would have an hour or so to wait.

He walked among the graves and trees, with withered leaves clining to his shoes. A robin kept him company. He stood beside Mr Porteous's grave. The tombstone was small and plain, with no urns or angels. The inscription, in black not gold letters, said simply: 'Alexander McDonald Porteous, aged 37, beloved husband of Elizabeth and father of Margaret.' Duffy had an impression of a quiet, modest, affectionate man. He had died nine years ago when Margaret was eight. Duffy imagined her at the graveside, mouth firm, eyes dry, suffering inwardly. Nothing or nobody could have comforted her. He imagined himself there too, a child of seven. He had not known then, and he did not know now, whether his own father was alive or dead.

After a while he went and chose his place on the steps, facing the door. He stood there with eyes closed. In the wood a bird or animal screamed.

He imagined the scene in Florence nearly five hundred years ago when Savonarola, who had wanted to make people better than they wanted to be, had been burnt at the stake, having first been strangled as an act of mercy. Duffy felt a tightness at his own throat, smelled smoke, and heard exultant cries. When he opened his eyes he was alone, except for the robin on the step above him. There were no sounds except for the wind in the trees and, inside the church, the singing of a psalm.

Somebody though was beside him, not in body but in spirit. It was Cooley, speaking truthfully as always.

'It's nothing but pride, Duffy. Talk about Porteous being arrogant! What you are thinking of doing would be far more arrogant than anything she has ever done. Who do you think you are, Duffy, if you believe that burning yourself to death would do anybody any good? Jesus Christ? They say He died to save the world, but who's saved, for Christ's sake? Nobody. Give it up, Duffy. It's the worst of your ideas and the others were bad enough.'

'What about Crosbie? What do I do about him?'

She was silent.

'I must do something about him, Cooley.'

'There's nothing you can do. That's your tough luck. Never mind. I'll come and see you in the nut-house, every five years or so.'

She was right. He must not do it. It would be another wrong gesture.

So he went back among the graves to the furthermost corner of the kirkyard where, behind rhododendrons, himself watched by the robin, he watched the church skailing. Down the steps, past the spot where they would have seen him burning, they streamed. They seemed especially happy, as if the service that Sunday, after last Sunday's fiasco, had been uplifting and comforting. Also the sun was coming out and birds were singing: spring would soon be here and winter's wind and rain survived for another year. He saw the Telfer family laughing at some joke of Stephen's. He saw Mrs Porteous, she in her fur coat, and Margaret in her blue one, arm-in-arm, as if they were reconciled again. Chief-Inspector Findlay, his wife, and his grown-up daughter helped Mrs Milne down the steps. Mr Milne must be on duty this morning. Mrs Flockhart was with some teachers from the school. Mr Flockhart must be at home watching their infant. He saw Mr McLachlan of Lightburn Motors who had been friendly towards him last week talking to a friend, about business it must have been, judging from their seriousness: religion was over for the week.

Perhaps their happiness in themselves and in one another was not justified. They had just made promises to God which they would not this week any more than last week try to keep. But justified or not their happiness was as natural and as beautiful to see as this robin now flitting away from him through the trees.

He was shut out.

He would go to the coup and wait. If they came in time he would say nothing. For the rest of his life he would have nothing to say.

Robert Louis Stevenson

Pictures of the Mind

Many highly talented and famous artists have lent striking imaginative interpretation to Robert Louis Stevenson's most powerful writing. This elegant book celebrates the diverse range of art inspired by this much loved author and is the perfect testimony to his ability to entertain.

"a lovely book...glorious illustrations"   *The Herald*
"a wonderful tribute to Stevenson'   *The Independent*
128pp (120 colour plates)   086241 492 X   £14.99 P

The Strange Case of Dr Jekyll and Mr Hyde

Stevenson's chilling study of the conflict between good and evil is an all-time classic, superbly brought to life by Robert Trotter in this best-selling audio version.
"One of the best voices currently recording in Scotland"
Gramophone Magazine

2 Cassettes (2hr) 1 85968 082 8   £7.99

Travels with a Donkey in the Cevennes

In September 1878, Robert Louis Stevenson set out from Le Monastier to tramp through through the wild region of the Cevennes - his only companion was a donkey.
"A beguiling mix of vivacity, warmth and humour" *Good Book Guide*
2 Cassettes (2hr 24min) 1 85968 065 8   £7.99

The Body Snatcher and other stories

The Body Snatcher - By night sinister figures deliver shrouded burdens to Dr Knox's assistants, Fettes and MacFarlane, and although some of the bodies are suspiciously 'fresh', few questions are asked.
Thrawn Janet and *The Tale of Tod Lapraik* - Two terifying tales in Scots
2 cassettes (1 hr 39min)   1 85968 067 4   £7.99

All Canongate titles including those listed above are available direct from Canongate Books, 14 High Street, Edinburgh, Scotland, EH1 1TE. Tel 0131 557 5111
Postage and packing free on all orders within the UK.
Our current catalogue will also be sent on request

Lewis Grassic Gibbon's

A Scots Quair

(ISBN 086241 532 2   £4.99 pbk)

Chris Guthrie, torn between her love of the land and her desire to escape the narrow horizons of a peasant culture, is the thread that links these three works. In them, Gibbon interweaves the personal joys and sorrows of Chris's life with the greater historical and political events of the time.

Sunset Song, the first and most celebrated book of the trilogy, covers the early years of the century, including the First World War. Chris survives, with her son Ewan, but tragedy has struck and her wild spirit subdued. In *Cloud Howe,* as the minister's wife, Chris learns to love again, and we witness the cruel gossip and high comedy of small village life until once again, Chris suffers a terrible loss. *Grey Granite* focuses on her son Ewan and his passionate involvement with justice for the common man.

For Chris, with her intuitive strength, nothing lasts – only the land endures.

'It would be impossible to overestimate Lewis Grassic Gibbon's importance… A Scots Quair is a landmark work; it permeates the Scottish literary consciousness and colours all subsequent writing of its kind.' David Kerr Cameron

A complete listing of our Canongate Classics
is available upon request.

CANONGATE CLASSICS